ROYAL
Bondage

Fever-Hot Dreams

Jaci Burton, Sherri L. King & Samantha Winston

Taming Him

Kimberly Dean, Summer Devon & Michelle M. Pillow

All She Wants

Jaid Black, Dominique Adair & Shiloh Walker

ROYAL
Bondage

SAMANTHA WINSTON
DELILAH DEVLIN
MARIANNE LACROIX

POCKET BOOKS

NEW YORK   LONDON   TORONTO   SYDNEY

Pocket Books
A Division of Simon & Schuster, Inc.
1230 Avenue of the Americas
New York, NY 10020

First Pocket Books trade paperback edition May 2008

POCKET and colophon are registered trademarks of Simon & Schuster, Inc.

For information about special discounts for bulk purchases,
please contact Simon & Schuster Special Sales
at 1-800-456-6798 or business@simonandschuster.com

Designed by Justin Dodd

Manufactured in the United States of America

10 9 8 7 6 5 4 3 2 1

Library of Congress Cataloging-in-Publication Data

Royal bondage / Samantha Winston, Delilah Devlin, Marianne LaCroix.—1st
Pocket Books trade paperback ed.
    p. cm.
1. Erotic stories, American. I. Winston, Samantha. II. Devlin, Delilah.
III. LaCroix, Marianne.
PS648.E7R68 2008
813'.01083538—dc22   2007047627

ISBN-13: 978-1-4165-7722-5
ISBN-10:   1-4165-7722-X

Contents

Llewellyn's Song

SAMANTHA WINSTON

ONE

Llewellyn

GONY UNLIKE ANYTHING HE'D ever felt tore through his body. Everything shook—his hands, his legs, and even his teeth chattered uncontrollably. Darkness crushed him like a physical thing and he tried to push it away, but it pressed down, harder and harder. Confusion followed the shock and pain, and then little bits of memory trickled back. Visions flashed across his mind, bringing with them more terror and pain.

Dragons with dull, iron-gray scales and rusty armor stalking next to hordes of enemy soldiers. The Mouse King, a shapeshifter with a talent for controlling dragons, riding the mightiest dragon, his scepter held aloft. Prince Branagh, in a last, desperate try to stop him, knocking him off the dragon and fighting him in vicious hand-to-hand combat. And he and his brother facing the enraged dragon on their own.

They'd succeeded, killing it when all hope seemed to have fled. But the beast had lashed out one last time, catching his brother across the chest and belly with its razor-sharp claws. Elloran had died in his arms, his pain first washing over Llewellyn then slowly ebbing into cold and darkness.

"No!" An agonized scream echoed in his ears and Llewellyn shot up in his bed, arms outstretched as if to ward off blows. His breathing whistled in his throat as he fought to control his racing heart. Icy sweat trickled down his back and chest. No dragons faced him, no screams assailed his ears, only the silence of the night and his heart pounding in his ears. Slowly he pulled the covers up over his shoulder with hands that still shook from the nightmare.

He wanted to die, for surely death would take away the anguish. He wanted to die, because each day he lived, each minute, every hour, his brother's last minutes came to him as a torture. He rubbed his forehead and a sigh shuddered from him. Elloran had been his twin, and everything he'd felt, Llewellyn had felt, from joy to love . . . to excruciating death. Sometimes he feared to open his one good eye after the nightmare, sure to find his sheets drenched with blood. His other eye was nothing but a memory, and an ache sometimes when the weather turned. One battle had cost him an eye and his twin. Some days are better not lived.

Llewellyn pushed the covers back and sat up. He wouldn't be getting any more sleep that night, and sweat had soaked his bed. Shivering a bit, though not from cold, he got up and went to the window. Outside, starlight glittered off a sprinkle of new snow. Winter settled its mantle upon the land. In the darkness an owl hooted softly and hoofbeats sounded. He lifted his head and peered into the night. Two riders, from the sound of it. His mouth twitched. It must be Sebring and Merlin, come to tell him about their sister's wedding. And they would be wanting something hot to drink and a warm fire. He pulled a tunic over his head and tossed a handful of tinder into the embers.

The horses and riders came out of the darkness, the horses trotting with a light step, the riders wrapped in warm cloaks and nodding with fatigue. They stopped in the pool of light spilling from his window, and Llewellyn stepped outside to greet his friends. "Sebring, Merlin!" He took the horses' reins and nodded toward the house. "You know where the tea is, and the water should be hot. Let me take your mounts."

"Thanks." Sebring yawned, then he threw his arm over his brother's shoulder and said, "Merlin, you owe me a gold piece, I told you Llewellyn would be awake. See, we didn't drag him out of bed."

Merlin looked at Llewellyn and a shadow seemed to pass over his eyes, but he grinned crookedly and said, "Sorry to arrive at such an ungodly hour, but we have some news we thought you should hear."

Llewellyn felt a prickle of disquiet. Merlin's voice had been matter of fact, but he'd caught an undercurrent of tension. But best not to speak out-of-doors, one never knew whose ears could listen in. He tugged on the horses' reins and led them to the stables. He took off their saddles and bridles, rubbing them down with handfuls of dry straw and then putting warm blankets over them before tying them in their stalls.

As he worked, he thought about what might have brought Merlin and Sebring here so soon after their sister's wedding. No doubt the festivities would be shortened, due to the king's death not long ago. But the wedding had been only three days ago, and it took two days to ride to Hivernia from here. Frowning, he closed the stable door and dropped the latch.

Firelight danced on the walls. Merlin and Sebring had lit the lamps so that his house glowed with light. Llewellyn winced. The light showed him to be a deplorable housekeeper. A pile of dirty dishes in the sink, clothes strewn about, cobwebs everywhere.

"Well, it looks like you haven't found a maid yet." Sebring's eyes twinkled as he poured a glass of hot mulled wine and handed it to Llewellyn. "Here, have a drink. We found some wine in your pantry and warmed it up. You didn't think we'd be content with just tea, did you?"

Llewellyn grimaced. "So you got out my good wine and added honey to it." He took a sip. "Heat, honey, spices and dried orange peel. How to ruin perfectly good wine. And as for a maid, I can't think of any woman who would agree to live in the middle of nowhere."

"You should move nearer the village. We're getting to be quite well known there," said Merlin with a wink.

Llewellyn raised his eyebrows. "In that case I imagine they'll be kicking you out any day. Don't worry, you can always stay here, I haven't rented your rooms out yet."

Merlin rubbed his hand over his eyes. Though tired, he still had his cocky grin. "The years we spent here made us appreciate the hustle and bustle of the city, eh, Sebring?"

"There is such a thing as too much quiet," Sebring agreed.

"I took you in and what do I get?" Llewellyn looked at his empty cup and poured himself some more wine. Had he already finished his glass?

"You'd like the village," continued Merlin, eyeing the pitcher of wine with interest. "They have running water in the houses, and you can get fresh eggs and milk every day. There's even a marketplace."

"Sounds dreadful," said Llewellyn, passing the pitcher to Merlin. "Here, finish this. If I drink any more I'll fall asleep."

"We wouldn't want that, would we?" Merlin yawned but poured the last bit of wine into his glass. "You still have the nightmares, don't you?" His voice was suddenly careful, and Llewellyn felt a chill, like a cold breeze at his back.

"Yes."

"We all do." Sebring rubbed his thumb along the top of his glass, not meeting Llewellyn's eyes. He cleared his throat. "So does Branagh. He says he sees him in his dreams, all crooked-like."

The chill deepened. "Branagh? Sees him?"

Sebring stared at his glass, his thumb resting on a tiny chip in the rim. Then he looked up and said quietly, "No one ever saw his body. Branagh fought until they both nearly died, and then you and Elloran killed the dragon king."

A pang as sharp as an ice sliver shot through him, but Llewellyn kept his face still. "He drew most of his power from that dragon. As soon as it died, a foul wind swept over the battlefield and the Mouse King's army turned and fled. We found the Mouse King's armor—empty but so full of blood we thought he'd surely perished . . ." His voice trailed off and he stared at his hands. Scars striped them, scars from sword fights with demons. "We've had so many years of peace." He looked at the two brothers. "Has he come back then?"

"We don't know." Merlin drained his cup and set it down gently. "We came to tell you what we've heard and what we've seen with our own eyes. It started with the ice demon in the cave, the one that nearly killed Prince Branagh. Then, barely a week after Branagh returned to Hivernia, his father died as he rode through a narrow pass. An avalanche, yes, but still . . . it happened in a place made for treachery. Why he passed that way we'll never know. His path lay to the west. Had he gone astray?" Merlin shook his head. "Branagh became king sooner than he'd ever dreamed and Melle had to wait for her wedding. A year of mourning with Hivernia decked in black."

Llewellyn nodded. "All that I know. Tell me what you discovered recently."

"Rumors from the north," said Sebring. He finished his glass of wine and frowned at it. "Demons getting bolder, and then someone said they spotted a dragon. More people spoke up, and it's been hell trying to verify everything. Branagh has run the legs off our horses ordering us around the kingdom. 'Go here, go there, check out that,' you'd think he'd been king all his life." Sebring gave a wry grin. "We've spied out the entire western territory. There are more ice demons than usual, that we've ascertained. But dragons, none."

"What does Branagh want me to do?" Llewellyn picked up the pitcher then remembered there was no more wine. "No, don't say it. I already know."

"You once spoke to Frostbone, years ago. It shouldn't be impossible to see him again." Merlin's voice had gone soft. A breeze would have been louder.

Llewellyn felt the chill again, and this time it settled in his belly. Frostbone, demon king, leader of the ice demons. Not that demons lived by any rules he understood. But they were bound to a king, and years ago they had been slaves to another king, the Mouse King. Branagh had put an end to that and so had he, and not in a small way.

The hole where his eye had been ached and he rubbed the patch he wore over it. Winter came. He would have to set out immediately if he wanted to breach the high pass before the heavy snows fell.

"All right. I'll go north."

"We're going with you." Sebring yawned and cupped his chin in his hands. "After we get a good night's sleep, that is. Have you any clean sheets in this place?"

Merlin sighed. "Now you're asking too much, Sebring. Come on, let's go. I can't stay awake a second longer. Good night, Llewellyn, we'll see you tomorrow."

Llewellyn watched them go, remembering two smaller, younger boys heading up the same stairs together. After the battle, and after they'd lost everything, as he had, he'd taken them in and raised them. Not that they'd needed much raising, being almost grown. He'd taken them in because their sister had been his brother's wife.

He blinked at the fire. How time flew by. It seemed only a week ago he and his brother had whistled at a pretty girl, and she'd turned . . . and smiled at his brother. Melle. He'd forgotten to ask about her wedding. He shook his head. He'd seen her first wedding—to his brother. He'd gotten drunk that night, but only to give his brother some semblance of privacy . . . for their minds and bodies had been linked in a way that enabled them to share things that perhaps they shouldn't have shared, but they couldn't help it.

Elloran had never minded, and Melle had never known, but she'd sensed something, sensed his passion for her, a passion born of Elloran's passion. And so, when Elloran died, she'd fled. To get away from him and to give him a chance to heal. She'd left behind her brothers, Sebring and Merlin. On purpose? Perhaps. At any rate, the boys had helped him more than he'd been able to help them.

A wry smile tugged at his mouth. Melle. Just the thought of her and his body tensed, his cock swelled and his heart . . . well, it had been broken into so many pieces there wasn't anything left of it, but somehow it managed to go on beating and go on hurting. He pushed his hand against the hard ridge of his cock and sighed. There would be no sleep for him. Dawn colored the sky gray and the dishes needed doing. If he left the cottage this way he'd come home to an army of mice. A violent shiver ran down his spine and he swallowed hard. Something was not right in the world and he could feel it, had felt it for a long time, but had been too caught up in his own pain to see it for what it was.

The Mouse King had returned.

LLEWELLYN PACKED HIS BAG in silence and stole out of the cottage. He turned and looked at the peaceful clearing where his cottage and the stables nestled, then he set off toward the north. A forest elf, his feet left no trail and he knew that Sebring and Merlin would not be able to track him. They wouldn't even try. He'd left a note on the table—

I'll go faster by myself, and Frostbone won't tolerate any strangers in his lands. You two will just slow me down and would be in much danger. Go back to Hivernia and tell Branagh I'll see him before winter sets in. If I hurry I'll make it over the pass and back before it's blocked.

Llewellyn

PS—clean the cottage for me, will you? You know where the dishes go.

Two

Tamara

COLD SEEPED INTO HER fingers and toes, but Tamara didn't move. Perched in a thick pine tree, her cloak wrapped around her shoulders, she looked so much like part of the tree that a bird had perched not a hand span from her. Earlier a light snow had fallen and now the sky cleared as evening approached. A red sun hung above the pines and cast its light over the pristine snowfall. To Tamara, it looked as if the world had been dipped in blood.

On the edge of the ravine near the base of a mountain, the Watcher's Tree offered a wide view of the valley below where a swift river cut a deep ravine through jagged black rocks. To her left, behind her, the mountains loomed high, their flanks sloping steeply down to a flat plain on her right. Regularly she scanned the area, starting with the river, then the plain, and finally making sure nothing crept down the mountainside, using the tangled forest as cover. The tribe trusted her keen ears and sharp eyes. She was the watcher. She would not let them down.

When full night fell her watch would end. As long as the sun still cast its rays upon the land, her kind had to stay hidden. The law must be obeyed.

She stifled a yawn and took a few quick, deep breaths. Just because her watch was nearly over didn't mean danger didn't lurk. Some strange magic was afoot, and the tribe had doubled the lookout. Enemies not seen for eons stalked the woods again. The reports had been vague at first. D'ark t'uaths kept to themselves and news trickled in slowly. But when two warriors and a magician vanished over a space of one moon's change, the rumors crystallized into fact. Demons hunted their territory. Ice demons, and others that had no name . . . yet.

The thought sent a shiver down her spine, and she automatically reached for her *glosseer*, feeling it through the fabric of her pocket. The globe felt reassuring. However, her movement dislodged a tiny sprinkle of snow from the pine and she froze, her heart fluttering.

She peered carefully through the branches, searching for a sign of life, some indication she'd been spotted. Nothing moved. No sound disturbed the quiet forest. Muscle by muscle, she relaxed.

A sound behind her made her freeze. Something walked quietly through the woods. It set its feet down as delicately as a deer, but Tamara didn't recognize the pattern. A deer hesitated, advanced, paused. This creature came steadily, nearer and nearer. It never slowed. Holding her breath, she turned her head, careful not to make the slightest noise. The forest behind her stretched its tangled thickets up a steep slope. Nothing disturbed the branches. No birds sang, she realized belatedly. That thought hit her just as a huge shadowy form surged out of the underbrush and leapt straight up her tree.

Tamara bolted from her hiding place, winging out to the edge of the branch and grabbing her *glosseer* from her pocket. She had time to feel the rough bark in one hand, the sharp prick of pine needles and a sticky patch of sap before something caught her foot and yanked her backward with incredible force.

Her *glosseer* fell from her hand and she saw it twinkle then vanish in the snow. The tree branch tore from her hand and she fell, hitting her head hard . . .

NIGHT. COLD. WIND CALLING to her. *Tamara! Tamara!* Feeling came back slowly but everything was eclipsed by the cold. She managed to open one eye, then the other. Her lashes stuck together. Dried blood? Stars spangled the sky. Night. Night? Hadn't it been . . . evening? The sky blurred, then cleared, blurred again, then cleared. Tree branches moved across her vision. She blinked. No, trees didn't move, but she moved, or rather, something carried her.

She tried to understand in what position she lay, but aside from her eyes, staring upward, nothing else responded. Not her arms, or legs, or fingers. Only her eyes, and now she felt her heart pounding, pounding in sheer panic as she became aware that something carried her, but her body felt heavy, strangely numb. Why couldn't she move? Terror pulled whimpers from her throat, but she barely heard them for the pounding of her heart. What carried her, and where did it take her?

Time went mad then as she watched the stars wheel across the sky. Did she sleep? Sometimes she woke in panic, so she must have slept. Waking only terrified her more, for each time she had to remember all over again. Sometimes she awoke to the sound of footsteps, other times she awoke to the vision of her *glosseer* falling into the snow, her hand outstretched to catch it.

Whatever carried her never faltered, never slowed, and paid no heed to her screams or sobs.

She woke up again shivering from cold. The sky had a gray cast to it—dawn came. Had she screamed? She must have, for her throat hurt with each breath. She couldn't remember anymore. She didn't know anything anymore. A faint vision came to her, a golden globe sparkling as it fell. She fell. The sky lurched and suddenly she hit the ground. It didn't hurt. Nothing hurt. Nothing.

The sun peeked over the horizon and cast its light into the cave where she lay. She could see the light arrive, silently, creeping across the cave floor until it touched her fingers. She knew where she was now. A cave. But what had attacked her? She hadn't recognized the shadowy figure that had surged out of the trees. She'd never seen that sort of demon before. A demon yeti? The thought made her pause. Well, at least she thought. Her mind seemed clear, but her body had been broken. She saw blood on her fingertips and try as she might, she could not move them. Even the cold had ceased to bother her. She must be dying. Would the creature wait until she died to eat her, or would it kill her first? A slight rasping sound alerted her. She held her breath until the creature walked into her line of sight, and then she started to scream.

LLEWELLYN HAD STARTED DOWN the worst part of the slope when he heard the scream. Instantly he froze, searching for the origin of the sound. It rose to a pinnacle of sheer terror and pain. It came from below him.

Dropping his gear, he flung his cloak down and seized his knife, bow and quiver. Then he picked his way carefully down the steep cliff, not letting the screams lure him into rash haste. It could very well be a trap. His kind were not welcome in this country, and he knew it.

With one eye, judging distance became tricky, but he managed to descend the cliff and stay under cover. Using the boulders and stunted trees, he edged toward the sound. It grew fainter, as if all strength had been spent. He saw now where it came from. A narrow opening in the rocks that looked like it led to a cavern.

Not good at all. To enter would be like entering a trap. The sun slanted inward, so as soon as he stepped in front of the opening his presence would be known. He glanced at the sky. Another two hours before the sun would move enough to let him slip near. The scream came again.

He sighed, called himself an imbecile, and darted into the narrow passage, his bow held before him, an arrow nocked. He thought he would be ready for anything. He didn't expect to find a behemoth. The creature spun around at his entrance and roared, its gigantic claw raised for attack. No time to think, he let loose the arrow and nocked another, let it loose and grabbed another, all the while backing out of the cave.

He'd need a hundred arrows before he could kill a behemoth. The beast roared and swiped at him, the great, curving claws striking the rocks, sending chips of stone flying. Llewellyn aimed and shot, catching the beast in the eye. It might not blind it completely, but it would hurt it and give him time to think of something. The beast's roar nearly deafened him. The cave echoed with its cry and a huge crack appeared in the wall. A boulder fell, missing him by inches.

Llewellyn raced outside and headed uphill, leaping from boulder to boulder, anxious to put distance between him and the creature. It followed him, bellowing with rage. He turned and loosed yet another arrow. Three lodged in the beast's chest, one in its eye, and the last one he shot hit it squarely in the other eye. Llewellyn sent a silent prayer of thanks to his archery instructor and crouched low while the behemoth lumbered toward him. Then he spotted the cliff. He hesitated, then taking a deep breath, he yelled hoarsely and sprinted to the edge.

Putting himself on the edge of the cliff and shouting had seemed like a good idea at the time. Now, with the behemoth crashing toward him, its fanged mouth open in a snarl, its claws flashing, he had a sudden doubt. And what if the beast could see him clearly? He'd end up a dead elf, that's what.

He tensed, then as the behemoth made one last lunge he leapt sideways, kicking out at the huge shoulder as he went by. The behemoth sailed over the cliff, its roar of fear growing fainter until cut off by a tremendous thud, then silence.

Llewellyn peered over the edge and winced. Not a pretty sight. He glanced back at the cave. What had the behemoth captured? Whatever it was, he hoped it still lived. Behemoths didn't take small bites.

He slithered down the slope, picked up a couple stray arrows, then hesitantly made his way into the cavern. The sun shining at his back lit up the cave. On the floor, in deep shadow, lay a woman.

Noiselessly, he walked to her, his heart heavy. He'd arrived too late. Her neck was bent at an impossible angle, her face turned toward the entrance, her eyes wide and unseeing. Sorrow sent him to his knees, and he put his hand on the ground, touched warm blood. Warm?

His shadow darkened her face and her pupils widened. Alive, but barely! He took her hand and felt for a pulse. Faint and uneven. All right, he was a healer, after all. He reached for his medicine bag tied to his waist, and drew out a branch of balsam. He held it inches from her lips and breathed on it gently and steadily until the branch glowed with a faint light. Her spiritual energy, or chi, still answered, and the balsam would keep it safe. Laying it on her chest, he rested his fingertips lightly on her stomach. He closed his eye and concentrated, feeling his own chi leave his body through his fingertips and enter hers.

His chi shuddered. So much damage had been done. One kidney had been crushed, her back had been broken, her leg shattered and several ribs snapped. Her heart still beat strongly and the bleeding had mostly stopped, partly from loss of blood pressure and partly from shock. He reached deeper into himself and found the energy he would need. Carefully he set it aside, picturing it in a golden ball, captive. Then he took a deep breath and cast his mind out of the cave. No one would answer his song, he had to do this alone.

He needed fire and air, water and earth. The woman's injuries would require days of healing. His strength would have to be parceled out and saved, for each séance would drain him beyond measure. With a deep sigh, he pulled away, leaving his chi in her body to keep her alive until he returned. Rocking back on his heels, he looked at her once again, and suddenly realized she was a d'ark t'uath.

Not that he knew a great deal about them. They considered themselves children of the earth and of the night. Ruled by a queen, they had nothing to do with the other fae. Shunning the day, they roamed at night. Little was known about the d'ark t'uath except that they lived in a matriarchal society, had no contact with others and practiced stone magic. Magic of the earth, magic of the night. He touched her hand and whispered, "Find the strength to call upon the Earth Mother. I will return soon."

First he draped his cloak over her still form. Then he used a spell to light a fire near her, to keep her warm and to offer reassurance if she awoke before he came back. He needed to gather many things and it would take a while in this strange country, where he didn't know the lay of the land or even where to find a spring. He didn't pause to worry though. Laying his bow and arrows at her side, he jogged lightly out of the cave and headed downhill. Water, fire, earth and air. All these things he had to gather before nightfall, and already the sun had turned orange and dipped toward the hills.

TAMARA DREAMT OF SPRING. Warmth touched her face and hands, and the clean scent of balsam soothed her despite the pain that still nearly overwhelmed her. She sensed that she was no longer alone. Something protected her. A golden light, almost like that of a *glosseer*, lay on her chest. Even without opening her eyes she felt its presence. Her chi had gotten stronger too, and now she opened her eyes, unsure what she would see.

Her last vision had nearly driven her mindless with fear. A behemoth had loomed over her, its fangs dripping, its claws outspread, about to plunge into her body. Then all had gone dark again. Quiet surrounded her. The behemoth no longer loomed over her. Instead, the last red rays of sunset cast a warm glow into the cave, showing a bow and quiver of arrows on the floor beside her. She glanced down and saw a cloak lying over her, covering her from neck to foot. The warmth she'd felt came from a small fire, nothing but embers now.

The bow and arrows did not look familiar, neither did the cloak. The cloak smelled of the open air, of long journeys and pine forests. It belonged to a forest elf then. She'd never met one, but she didn't fear them, even if it was a male. Her clan sometimes traded with the forest elves from the northeast. Perhaps she'd gotten lucky and a group of traders had found her. The thought relaxed her and she found herself drifting off to sleep. *No, stay awake. You have to stay awake!* It might be traders, it could be men, or enemies. If a man found her sleeping, according to her clan mothers, their brutishness would assert itself and they would violate her . . . or worse.

Her eyes snapped open and she let her breath out with a hiss. Better stay alert. Using her chi, she examined her wounds. Jaw, shoulder, ribs, kidney, back . . . That gave her pause. Healing backs took a long time and a great deal of chi. She hoped that whoever had saved her had a troop of healers. Her leg also had shattered. Pain came and ebbed in waves, and she spent some time and precious energy trying to control it. But her wounds were too severe.

The best thing to do would be to rest and gather her strength.

She called forth the powers of the earth, thankful that whoever had found her had not moved her from the ground. Slowly she drew energy from the stones, sucking it to her like water from a sponge. The earth magic would help, but she needed more. Her life still hung from a spider's thread. Closing her eyes, she sent a prayer to the Earth Mother asking for strength. She had to get back to her clan and warn them of the danger in the mountains. A behemoth roamed nearby. A shiver made her ill for a second. Despite the fact that her rescuer had chased the behemoth away—it would return. A bow and arrows, as clever as they may be, could never kill a behemoth.

THREE

The Enemy

W HEN SHE NEXT OPENED her eyes, her first thought was to berate herself. She'd fallen asleep despite her determination to stay awake. She shifted, and intense pain hit her. Her mind skittered from the pain and she nearly blacked out again. Then she got hold of herself and managed to look around.

The fire burned high and she'd been moved. Now she lay on a bed of woven willow branches, a finely woven blanket over her body, keeping her warm. Someone had set her leg and she could tell her bones had started to mend by the difference in the pain. No longer a dull and sickening feeling, rather it had gotten sharper and had started to itch. She tried to flex her fingers but still her body refused to obey her. However, she could feel her body now—the nerve endings had started their slow healing. Relief washed over her, and she trembled suddenly. Her teeth chattered.

"I made you some tea."

The voice came from behind her. Low, deep, deeper than any voice she'd ever heard, it raised the fine hairs on the back of her neck. She'd prepared herself to see him, but in her helpless, weakened position, panic seized her. A man! She'd never set eyes on a man. Her clan never allowed men into their territory unless it was in specific places set up for trading and weddings, and they told terrible stories about what happened if a man caught you in his lands, and what men did to women in their countries. Not all men were mindless brutes, her clan mother had told her daughters. Some came to trade, and some came with news of other countries. But best be wary and treat most men like brutish enemies, which was how her clan considered them. And one stood right behind her.

Llewellyn watched as the woman awoke. She grimaced with pain, then looked around, taking in her surroundings. He imagined her fear must be overwhelming, and he didn't want to startle her. When he judged she'd settled down, he spoke and stepped into her line of sight.

Cool gray eyes studied him carefully. There was no sign of fear in her gaze, only a quiet watchfulness. He had never seen a d'ark t'uath, so he didn't know if her kind considered her a beauty, but each time he saw her his breath caught in his throat. Her finely chiseled bones appeared fragile, but she'd survived an attack by a behemoth, and mended quickly. Already her pulse beat strongly and her breath no longer whistled in her throat.

Carefully, he held a straw to her lips so she could drink the infusion he'd prepared. It would give her strength and help her heal. She took a tiny sip and her eyes widened. "Are you the traders' healer?"

He cocked his head. "Traders?"

"Yes, you came with a group of traders, didn't you? We have been expecting some. How fortunate you came to this side of the valley. I thank you for saving me. When your companions return, we can move to the trading post. The behemoth will want its cave back."

Llewellyn had never heard such a mixture of assurance and wariness in a voice. He nudged the straw to her lips. "Drink it all. I am a healer, yes, but I have no companions. I travel alone." For the first time her eyes widened in fear, and he hastened to reassure her. "The behemoth won't come back, it's dead."

Now outright disbelief lit her eyes. How could someone have such expressive eyes? She didn't even need to speak. "Drink," he said. "The behemoth fell off the cliff and now feeds the crows."

She drank, never taking her eyes from him. Afterward, her eyelashes fluttered and she slept, though it seemed she fought even that healing sleep. Murmuring soft prayers of healing, he knelt by her side, keeping watch. They would be there for a while yet. She thought she could be moved, but he knew better. He didn't have the strength to carry her down the mountainside, and he couldn't pull her on a travois—any sudden movement could be fatal. No, he would stay with her until she healed. Hopefully by the full moon she would be able to stand and he could take her to her people. Then he could go on his mission. Already he chafed at the delay.

Bowing his head and touching the stones he'd laid on her chest and stomach, he sang the healing song for the twentieth time that day. His strength left him, fatigue made his head swim, but he managed to finish the chant. Resting his head against the side of the bed, he closed his eyes a minute. The fire warmed the cave, but he had to collect more wood for the evening. Then he'd better find some food. The woman needed lots of food to keep her chi strong. He opened his eyes and found himself staring into the woman's gaze.

"I will soon be able to help you. I have called the earth spirit to my aid and each hour sees me growing stronger."

Llewellyn opened his mouth, intending to tell her he'd chanted himself hoarse and his healing powers, not hers, had helped her. But prudence held his tongue, for he knew nothing of her beliefs. Instead he said, "I go to gather food."

She nodded, and her eyes lit up. "I moved, did you see? I moved! Praise the Earth Mother!" Her smile blinded him, then she grew serious again. "Go, do not worry about me, elf man. But take heed, I am helpless and at your mercy now, but if you dare take liberties with my person, when I recover I will kill you," she said with cold certainty.

He stopped his smile just in time. "You have nothing to fear from me."

"I have nothing to fear from anyone. I am Tamara, watcher for the d'ark t'uath clan. My mothers and sisters will avenge any hurt I suffer that I cannot avenge myself."

"I am Llewellyn Fairnight, and I had better go now before the sun sets." He picked up his bow and quiver.

"Has it been three days already?" Her face paled and she darted a glance out the cave entrance, where the sun's last rays cast red light upon the rocks. "Three days since I stood guard. My clan must think I too disappeared, like the others, and now they mourn me."

"The others?" Llewellyn paused. "What others?"

She looked undecided, then said slowly, "Some of our clan have vanished, and strange things are afoot. The watch has doubled . . ." Her voice trailed off. "Some say there is a new wizard in the mountains, and that he has spell-cast demons to his side. Our clan remembers the last war, when the Mouse King's forces nearly overran our valley. When he was killed we rejoiced, however, it seems new danger has come but from where or what it is, exactly, we haven't yet ascertained."

"My quest takes me to Frostbone, for demons have entered Hivernia."

Her eyes widened. "Frostbone? Hivernia?" Lip curled, she said, "What happens in Hivernia concerns us not. Brutish men rule that land."

Llewellyn looked at the horizon, where the sun was no more than a sliver of scarlet. "I have to go. We will speak of this later."

"I will speak of it if I wish," said the woman, closing her eyes.

He almost told her she'd speak of it whether she wished or not, but something told him that he'd better be circumspect, or risk losing her trust. He left the cave and darted into the cover of the trees. Evening fell, and a fat buck drank at the waterhole he'd found. But the buck would be too big and he hadn't the time to smoke meat. He waited patiently as the sky darkened until a pheasant wandered to the water's edge. Then, with a prayer of thanks to Mistral, he shot the bird.

Roasting on the spit, the pheasant made Llewellyn's mouth water. But most of all, he wanted to sleep. Tamara slept deeply, but she might awaken and need him. He had to stay alert. He'd blocked the cave's entrance with branches from a thorn tree, and, in the unlikely case another behemoth came, he'd piled a heap of dry tinder near the branches that he could set on fire to chase the beast away. Tamara had mentioned ice demons too, but it had to get much colder before they left their northern home. He still had three months before dead of winter. Three months to find Frostbone and find out what pushed the ice demons south and what evil made behemoths leave their mountain refuges far to the northeast.

Tamara watched beneath lowered lashes as the elf man moved around the cave and wove a rack to smoke some fish he'd caught. Didn't he ever sleep? It worried her, for some reason, to think that men didn't sleep. It would give them an unfair advantage over women. Was that how they'd subdued her sex in other lands? Then there was the question of size. He must be almost twice her size. That didn't mean anything except that they surely dominated their women by size and strength, giving them no rest and beating them into submission.

Her heart beat faster, but she didn't move. He thought she slept, and she wanted to examine him more. He moved back into her line of sight. Straight black hair tied back with a leather strip. Skin burned brown by the outdoors. A patch covered one eye, the other eye caught the light and glittered like a dark amethyst. He turned and stared straight at her and for a moment she thought he'd seen she was awake, but he turned back to his task.

His hands moved deftly and the rack soon took shape. Laying it against the wall, he took the fish he'd laid by his side and hung them on the rack. Fascinated despite herself, Tamara watched the first man she'd ever seen up close. The differences fascinated her. His shoulders seemed so broad, and his hands, with their tendons standing out as he worked, looked strong and capable. She shivered, a strange tremor running through her. At that slight movement he looked up, his eye dark with concern.

"Are you feeling better?" He got up with a fluid movement and was at her side in an instant.

Her stomach contracted, but she let none of her fear show through. Her clan mother had said often enough, "Never let them see your fear, otherwise the brutish males will ravish you."

Tamara studied him, but he only looked concerned, not aggressive. You never knew though. "I feel much better. When will you take me to the trading post?"

"Your wounds are too grievous, if you receive another shock you won't survive."

She heard the truth in his words. Her chi, drained by the effort of healing herself as fast as she could force it, would not last. Especially if she were jolted. She had to be patient. "You said you wanted to speak to Frostbone. How is it you know the ice demon king?"

A shadow passed over his face. "I fought in the last war against the Mouse King. Before, I hadn't realized the ice demons even had a king."

She sneered. "You wouldn't, coming from Hivernia. The fae never bother to learn anything about the world to the north, except when it happens to bother them."

"As far as I know, d'ark t'uath are part of the fae kingdom." He spoke quietly but his one eye flashed.

The d'ark t'uath part of the fae kingdom? She shuddered. "You know nothing then. We come from the east, whereas you came from the sea, from the south."

Her words must have surprised him, for his eyebrow shot upward. "That's part of our legends, yes, but we have lost all trace of our ancestors, and have never found them again. Ships sailing south rarely return, and when they do they bear stories of huge sea monsters and tempests, but no land. It's as if we came out of nowhere. How is it that you know of this?"

"Our winters are long, and our legends many and oft told. As for the creatures you call ice demons, they are not true demons, being made of flesh and blood, though their flesh may be icy and their blood a poison ichor. But I forgive your ignorance. In Hivernia, ice demons must be rare. How is it you know of Frostbone?"

"When my brother and I defeated his dragon, we freed the ice demons from the Mouse King's control. Frostbone came to see me."

Surprise rendered her speechless an instant. "Your brother and you defeated the Mouse King's dragon? Rog? You fought Rog?" At her words the skin on his face tightened but he never blinked. "After Rog, I imagine a behemoth seemed child's play." Why did she needle him? He'd saved her, nursed her, and obviously hadn't come all the way from Hivernia to play healer. She drew a deep breath. "I apologize. It's none of my business why you've come seeking Frostbone. I would hear more of the battle you fought with your brother, for our clan speaks of it but as a legend."

For a minute she thought he would not reply, then he bowed his head. "There is little to say. The battlefield was immense, but Rog dominated it, towering over both armies. As my brother and I fought on the west wing, with the archers, we saw the prince's battalion attack the dragon. Suddenly there came a stroke of luck. In the distance, we saw the Mouse King fall from Rog. In the confusion, my brother and I found ourselves facing the beast." He stopped and looked toward the fire. "It was either kill or be killed."

"Is that how you lost your eye?" She wanted him to look at her again. She found his face . . . intriguing.

Instead he stood and moved behind her, and from the sound of it he took his bow and arrows. "I lost my eye and my brother that day. So if you'll excuse me, you'll have to content yourself to your clan's legends. I will speak of it no more." He passed in front of her on the way out of the cave, but didn't turn around. His cloak swirled out as he turned the corner, and then he disappeared.

Disappointment prickled her, and something else. It was almost as if she didn't want him to leave her. The thought gave her pause. No, that couldn't be right. She had better focus on getting well now.

Alone, Tamara lay on her cot and tried to concentrate on healing her bones. She gathered her chi and linked it with the power of the stones surrounding her, taking comfort and force from the earth. The sooner she healed, the sooner she could leave. But the thought of never seeing the tall, one-eyed elf again sent a pang of sorrow through her. Stunned, she let go of her chi. It ebbed back into her body like water into sand but she hardly noticed. How could she feel anything but scorn for the enemy? Instead, she had the strangest, strongest longing to see him again, to hear his low, deep voice, and to feel his hands as they rested on her body.

Another, sharper shudder stabbed her. This time it started in her lower belly and her womb contracted. A low moan escaped her lips. How often had she felt this craving, this need to mate? It affected all the females of her tribe, but mating was reserved for a select few. Her clan mother had warned her about this—that close proximity with a man would sometimes bring this on. But she had to resist—familiarity would lead to disaster. Her clan chose the men needed for mates. The rule had been written and must be obeyed. It was vital she escape. She had to get away from the elf man before something happened they both regretted.

But why? whispered a voice in her head. *Why?* She cast her mind back and tried to pinpoint the exact moment things had changed.

Everything had started during a massage. As Llewellyn slowly rubbed feeling back into her muscles, his hands sliding up and down her thighs and belly, her head had begun to spin. She'd wanted to ask him to stop, but the words stuck in her throat. Instead, she'd closed her eyes and let the sensations wash over her. His hands were so deft and so strong. When her clan sisters had massaged her, it hadn't felt like this—as if each nerve answered his touch with a quiver. Dazed, she'd uttered a soft moan.

"Are you all right?" He'd stopped and leaned over her, his face inches from hers.

She didn't know what came over her. An irresistible urge raised her chin so that her lips touched his, and then . . . he'd pressed his mouth against hers. She looped her arms around his neck and pulled him to her, her hips lifting, an incredible longing in her womb. An ache, as if her whole body was empty and needed filling, had shaken her. Her arms had tightened even more, and he'd responded, his body hardening.

As he pressed the hard ridge of his cock to her belly, a flood of heat washed over her. Her thighs parted and she lifted her hips . . . and a stabbing pain in her back had nearly made her pass out.

He'd pulled back as if stung, and she'd turned her face to the wall, confused and humiliated.

How could she have done that? He was a man! A brutish man, and her clan mother would kill her if she ever found out. She clutched at her covers, shivers racking her body. Sometimes she and her clan sisters had gone to spy on the traders. They'd hidden and seen them from a distance. Looking at men! The law forbade it, and so it had excited them, but when they'd been found out their punishment had lasted for weeks, and she'd hardly even seen anything but vague silhouettes. This broke all the rules of her clan.

So each time he left the cave, she'd do her utmost to speed her healing, before her body betrayed her once more. He'd made it easy, keeping his hands to himself, only lifting her to help her turn over. But each time he touched her, her skin tingled with delight.

He was a healer, she told herself sternly as he washed her. He'd taken care of her when she lay unconscious and he knew her body. But it didn't change the fact that she was awake now, and whenever his fingertips brushed against her skin, or she caught his gaze, she forgot all about the law of her clan.

As she lay there, her mind in turmoil, things began to clarify. Why had she always volunteered for the jobs furthest from her cave? Why did she seem to seek the solitude and uncertainty of scouting, rather than the comfort of the warm caverns and the company of her tribe? Because she was unsatisfied, that's why. The realization was like a spark of light in the darkness. Finally things she'd been afraid to face crystallized into fact. She was not made to spend her life in the caverns. She wanted to go out into the world. It still frightened her, and the idea that she might never see her clan again made her physically ill. But deep in her heart she knew now what she had to do.

She only hoped Llewellyn would forgive her.

FOUR

Forces of Night

*T*HE MOMENT SHE'D BEEN waiting for struck just as Tamara finished healing her back. Llewellyn didn't realize that she'd spurred on the healing process. She'd poured all her energy into it, draining her chi until she felt it fray like a thread about to snap. A couple times she'd nearly broken that thread, feeling her life slipping away and holding on to it by the sheer power of her will. But it had been worth it. Today, while Llewellyn was out hunting, she'd stood up and managed to take a few shaking steps.

She'd stood, bracing herself against the wall, and made her way to the cave entrance. The sun had set, and a hard frost lay on the ground. Wind whipped the tree branches, and she saw dark clouds piling up on the horizon. Winter came on soft feet. Soft, silent and deadly. A chill breeze stirred her hair and she shivered. The fire needed tending and Llewellyn would be back soon. She'd shuffled back to her bed, exhaustion making it hard to breathe. Sweat covered her body and she'd shivered suddenly as cold air struck her. But she'd walked on her own. Fierce determination had always been her biggest asset, her clan mother said. She certainly needed it now.

Lying in her bed, she wrapped the blanket around her and tried to get warm. The fire died but she didn't have the strength to get up and put more wood on it. Cold seeped into her bones, leaching her life energy away. She knew that to sleep was to die, and she struggled against the lethargy that enveloped her but it was a losing fight. Her plan had failed. She had misjudged her strength. In her world that was fatal. She tried once more to stand, to go put some wood on the fire, but it was too late. Her limbs shook uncontrollably and darkness settled over her mind.

LLEWELLYN PULLED HIS CLOAK tighter around his shoulders. The freezing wind whipped it, but he didn't feel the cold. He did feel hunger though. In order to heal, Tamara needed lots of food, and he'd given up his portions so that she could eat. Now his stomach felt as if it melted into his backbone and he clenched his teeth against his hunger pangs. Game was getting scarce though. Winter arrived, and the deer had already left the mountainside, heading for sheltered valleys. They should do the same, as soon as Tamara could move.

He breathed a sigh of relief as he saw a rabbit in his snare. Dinner would be rabbit stew. He hurried back to the cave, not wanting to worry Tamara. He stepped into the cave and glanced at her out of habit. She lay still, her eyes open and unblinking. His heart gave a painful leap. The rabbit fell from his hands as he knelt at her bedside.

"Tamara!" He felt for a pulse, and found it faint. Her body was like ice. Her blanket was damp and freezing.

Cursing, he threw more wood on the fire. Flames licked the dry wood and it crackled as the fire caught, but the air in the cave remained icy. Llewellyn hesitated, then shucked off his clothes and slid onto the bed next to her, pulling his cloak over their bodies. He wrapped his arms around her, drawing her close, curling around her back. As his body warmed her, her heart started to beat strongly and she sighed, cuddling against him.

He tried not to notice her breasts but his hand kept brushing against them. *It's just to keep her warm*, he told himself, and he cupped her breast in his hand, stroking her nipple with his thumb. Her nipple stiffened, and Tamara shifted in the bed, cuddling even closer to him with a little sigh.

As she moved, her buttocks came in close contact with his cock and all the longing he'd tried so hard to repress flamed up. His shaft pulsed, lengthened, and pressed even harder against her buttocks, nestling right between her thighs. Holding himself absolutely still, he tried to think of ice demons, of ice cubes, of icy cold rushing streams.

It did no good. His cock got even harder, and he trembled with the effort of not thrusting into the hollow formed by her inner thighs. He should get out of the bed, pull away, but then her arm slid over his belly as she turned over.

A surge of blood stiffened his cock until it hurt, and he groaned. Seeing her, touching her, being with her day by day was making it impossible for him. He had needs, and one of those needs lay pressed next to him, her satiny skin growing warm under his touch, her soft hair tickling his cheek.

He opened his eye. She looked back at him, a flush on her cheeks. "Thank you for warming me up." It was the first time she'd ever thanked him.

"You're welcome." He shifted, trying to move his cock away. It slid across her belly and touched her pubic hair. Immediately a surge of desire shot through him. He tried to say something and failed, his voice catching in his throat.

Tamara uttered a little sigh and before he knew it, put her arms around his neck and pulled him close. Now her soft breasts crushed against him and his cock pushed between her legs. She didn't pull away. Instead, with a breathless laugh, she said, "I want to see what all the fuss is about." With that, she reached down and took his cock in her hand.

The shock of her cool fingertips on his burning cock made his balls contract and he drew his breath in. Didn't she know she played with fire? She pulled back, her wide eyes staring up at him. "It's so hard," she whispered. Her voice trembled.

Her fingers tightened on his cock, but he managed to gasp, "Let go, I've got to skin the rabbit."

Instead, she turned around again and pressed her buttocks against his cock. "No, I want you." She caught his shaft between her thighs and squeezed tightly, pulling his hand to her breast. His hand didn't protest. He cupped her breast, his fingers curling in delight over her taut nipple.

Tamara thought her whole body would burn to a crisp. Her sex ached with a longing she'd never thought possible. In the clan, she and her sisters had eased their needs with deft caresses. She knew what an orgasm was, and she knew what a man and a woman did together—but according to her clan mother, it would be a brutish, violent experience. Obviously, her clan mother had never been with a wood elf.

Her clan mother had warned her about the mating lust . . . but the warnings had faded into a red mist in the back of her mind, because all she could think of now was screaming, "No, don't stop, whatever you do, don't stop!" She wanted to scream, but only a sigh escaped her lips.

As Llewellyn pinched her nipples, rolling them between his fingers, her head spun. Dizzy, she tried to speak, to tell him how good it felt, and then he reached between her legs and gently slid his finger into her slit.

"Oh yes, please!" There, she'd said it. Or at least, she thought she spoke. Little whimpers seemed to be all she could manage. Oh, by the mother earth! He touched her clit. Touched it, rubbed it, teased it with the tip of his finger.

Wetness surged out of her cunt, and a spasm of sudden need shook her from head to toes. Now the whimper turned into a cry, and she tightened her legs around his cock, thrusting her hips backward. Her cunt was so wet that his fingers slipped and slid into her tender flesh, dragging sensations of tingling and delight.

"Oh Llewellyn!" She teetered on the edge of release. The tingling grew into a burning, and then he pushed a finger into her sheath. One finger, then two . . . and he wiggled them gently back and forth. His thumb still thrummed her clit, and suddenly she couldn't breathe.

Her muscles tensed, her nipples stung, and he eased his fingers deeper. He pushed his thumb against her clit, his calloused skin rough against her hypersensitive nub. As her sheath clenched around his fingers everything went black. Her head spun right off her shoulders and the whole cave bucked and tilted. An orgasm like nothing she'd ever experienced ripped through her and her cunt contracted violently around his searching fingers. She grabbed his hand and pulled it closer, feeling his fingers sliding even deeper, and a scream tore out of her throat as the throbbing in her womb intensified.

He bucked against her, his hand tightening on her breasts, and suddenly his cock began to quiver. He groaned, the sound low and rumbling, growing like a volcano on the brink of eruption.

Nervous shudders racked her body. Was this where he turned brutish and raped her? Had her clan mother been right after all? Still dizzy from her orgasm, weak, she couldn't hope to get away. She tensed, waiting for him to go berserk.

Instead he put his hands flat on her belly and held her to him while his hips thrust against her. His cock, caught between her thighs, slid back and forth, and then wetness spurted from it as he groaned louder and arched his back, his skin shivering like a wild horse's.

Tamara cried out as he did, caught up in his passion. She tightened her thighs and reached down, seeking his cock. Her hand touched wetness, and the tip of his cock, and her thighs, sticky now with his seed. As her fingers brushed against the tip of his cock, he groaned once more and thrust against her hand. She felt his seed spurting against her palm and her body responded with a sharp mini-climax. It was too much. Dizzy, spent, exhausted, she let sleep drop over her like a blanket made of stones.

*   *   *

LLEWELLYN DREW A DEEP, shuddering breath. In his arms, Tamara slept deeply, her breathing light and even, her body warm. Warmth stole around him, wrapping him in its embrace, luring him toward sleep.

His stomach growled and he blinked. Sitting up, he gently extricated himself from Tamara. He slid out of the bed and tucked his cloak tighter around her. She stirred, but didn't waken. Her face, in sleep, lost its arrogance. Her mouth went soft, she looked . . . What was he thinking? She was d'ark t'uath! They had no future together. Her clan forbade relations with males and she would never leave them. There had never been a d'ark t'uath who left her clan. Never.

But he could dream. He seemed good at impossible relationships. Stooping, he picked up the rabbit and then skinned it, putting it on the spit to cook. As he turned the spit, he watched Tamara. Her eyelashes fluttered and she looked at him. A pink flush spread across her cheeks. Her gray eyes, immense in her pale face, sparkled.

"That smells good."

"You're hungry, it's normal."

"I wouldn't know."

"You've never eaten rabbit?"

"I've never had sex with a male before." Her dimples deepened. Dimples? He hadn't noticed before . . . He suddenly realized he'd never seen her smile.

"Technically it wasn't sex." He found himself grinning back at her. Her smile lit up her whole face, and he had the most absurd urge to gather her in his arms and squeeze her tight.

"We made love," she said, her dimples still in place.

"No, you're still a virgin." His words, for some reason, made her pale.

"Are you sure?" She didn't look happy.

"Yes. What would your tribe say if they knew you made love to a man?" The words were out of his mouth before he could call them back, and the smile slid off her face like water from a stone.

In three strides he was at her side. "I won't say anything, I swear by . . . "

"No. Don't swear." Her voice was bloodless and her cheeks had paled. "If they found out, I could be punished. But nothing happened, so don't worry about it."

"I won't betray your trust. Believe me. Now eat. You need your strength. We have to leave as soon as possible. Before anything else happens between us."

Firelight made deep shadows on her face and he couldn't read her thoughts. But it seemed to him that the sparkle had gone out of her eyes and he wondered why. Was it fear that her tribe would banish her? Did she regret what had happened between them? "I'm sorry," he said, handing her a wooden bowl of grilled rabbit.

She picked at it listlessly. He crouched next to her and touched her shoulder. "I want you to eat and regain your strength."

"So you can send me back to my people."

"Isn't that what you want?" He knew he sounded surprised, and he caught a flash of hurt in her eyes.

"I thought so. But now I am not sure. I'm confused and feel as if the winds of winter are shredding what beliefs I held true. My tribe believes males are violent beings, only useful for procreation and best left alone. But you are not like that. I . . . " She broke off and shook her head. "I don't know what I want anymore. Part of me never wants to leave you, and part of me only wants to return to my tribe." Her strength lay in her absolute fearlessness. She faced everything, even her doubts, head on.

Impressed with her honesty, Llewellyn said, "I think it would be best for both of us if you returned to your tribe. I have a mission to go see the ice demon king, for it is possible that the Mouse King is back."

"The Mouse King?" Now Tamara's eyes widened with real shock. "No!"

"I fear it is true. That is the real reason I'm going north. The ice demon king must see me. Years ago Frostbone called me his friend. I hope he will look upon me kindly now and pledge his help when I tell him the news."

"The Mouse King. How can you be sure?"

"Dreams." He grimaced. "I know, that's not very substantial. But Branagh, king of Hivernia, suffers from them, and so do I. All those who fought against him have recurring dreams of the Mouse King. That, and the surge of ice demons in Hivernia, tell me something is very wrong. The Mouse King is a shape-shifter, so he can take the form of an ice demon. I think he's somehow worked his way into their hierarchy."

"If it is so, then you run a terrible risk going into their territory."

"I think not. Frostbone will protect me if he finds out what I say is true. Remember, the ice demons have more to lose than we do. Once, they were slaves to the Mouse King."

"True. Frostbone has a huge debt to you. I hope he will honor it. Demons are strange beasts. One never knows what they are thinking or how they will react. We avoid them at all cost."

"Very wise," said Llewellyn. He nodded toward her bowl. "Eat!"

"I am eating." But she didn't. She took a small morsel and nibbled it. "What do you feel for me?" she asked.

The question took him by surprise. "I like you." Oh, wrong thing to say. Her face darkened. All right, he could be as brave as she was. "Do you want the truth?"

She nodded warily.

"I'm confused. I know you must return to your people, but I want to keep you near me always. I love watching you when you sleep, when you eat, when you laugh and even when you cry. I think you are beautiful and strong. You are stronger than I am. That amazes me."

"Huh. Physically you can tie me in knots." She looked pleased though.

"Perhaps. But mentally you seem to be able to face things I cannot. I don't know if I would have survived being savaged by a behemoth and left in a cave to die. If someone I considered an enemy saved me, I don't know if I would have given my trust. That would have made healing nearly impossible. You trusted me with your life, and that took such strength I can't imagine." He grinned at her. "Eat."

"I'm not hungry." She set the bowl down and looked up at him, her eyes huge. "Or rather, I've got another hunger. One only you can assuage."

He didn't know how she did it. Her eyes seemed to fill with darkness, like swirling clouds, and the darkness was deep, pulling him closer. Before he knew what happened, his body had reacted. He took her bowl from her, setting it down before stripping his leggings off and sliding onto the pallet with her. She opened her arms and legs and he sank into her embrace.

Her skin was hot, her eyes incandescent with desire. When she arched her back, his cock, already stiff, found her sex. He reached down and felt with his fingers. She was ready. Her wetness coated his fingers and he groaned. His cock drove into her passage. It was tight, but she grabbed his hips and pulled him into her. His cock slid into her sheath smoothly and she uttered a little gasp.

"Did I hurt you?"

"No!" She gave a little laugh. "It's just surprising, that's all. It feels . . . heavy inside me." She moved her hips, and his cock lodged into her sex right up to his balls. The feeling nearly drove him mad. He knew that if he started thrusting he'd lose it. He hadn't made love in too long.

"Don't stop," she pleaded.

"I wouldn't dream of it." He buried his face in the crook of her neck, breathing in the musky sweetness of her skin. He closed his eyes, his whole being concentrated in his loins.

"Next time it will be better," he moaned, trying to control himself. He managed to slide in and out a few times, but then Tamara lifted her hips with an amazed cry. It undid him. He shattered into a million spasms of delight, thrusting with all his force into her.

She wrapped her legs around him, her breathing getting gradually slower. Then her arms slid off his shoulders, her legs unwound, and he saw she was sound asleep.

He pried himself off the bed and managed to stagger to the spring and fetch a bucket of water to heat next to the fire. Then he went back to the pallet and collapsed next to her, burrowing into her warmth with a deep sigh.

FIVE

Forces of Day

THE NEXT DAY DAWNED cold and bright. Tamara woke and stretched. She'd done it. There was no going back. She waited for a minute, motionless, afraid to think too far ahead. But there was no sense of impending doom, rather, she felt a strange lightness in her bones, as if invisible chains had been shed. Her body felt both sore and supple. Her back had healed. Her health had returned. And she was so hungry she could eat a behemoth. She poked Llewellyn.

"Husband. Go fetch me something to eat. I'm starving."

He raised his head and his one good eye stared at her with a mixture of emotions she couldn't put name to. Mostly disbelief, she thought.

"Excuse me?"

"What part didn't you understand? I'm hungry!"

He raised his eyebrow. "No, not that part. Why did you call me husband?"

Well, here it was. The moment she'd both feared and hoped for. "Because you are my husband now. In my tribe, a d'ark t'uath is considered married once she loses her virginity. Usually we marry between ourselves, but the tradition is inviolate. We made love. I was a virgin. You are my husband."

There was an awkward silence. His smile seemed to last longer than a smile should. The muscles on his face hardened, but his good eye gave nothing away. "Did you know this when you decided to make love to me?"

"Yes."

"And you made love to me anyway. You made your own decision." He was speaking more to himself than to her, so she didn't answer. He sat still, staring over her shoulder.

She didn't like his silence. She sat up and pushed him. "Out of bed. Food."

With a movement like a quick snake, he turned, pinned her arms over her head and held them there. She'd forgotten how strong males were. "I'm sorry. I don't take orders very well." He lowered his head to her chest and took one of her nipples in his mouth. He sucked it, teasing it with his tongue. The effect was a violent, stabbing sort of ache in her cunt. It grabbed her womb and tightened it. A flood of wetness dampened her inner thighs.

"Are you angry with me?" She had to know.

He paused, but didn't let go of her. "No. But I think you need to learn that some decisions are better made together, not alone."

"I had to do this on my own," she whispered. "I didn't want anyone to influence my choice."

"It doesn't seem that way to me," he said, and taking her nipple in his teeth, he bit down gently but firmly. Pain and pleasure stabbed through her.

She struggled and he let go of her nipple, but he didn't let go of her arms. Instead, he took both her slender wrists in one hand, and holding her immobile, with his other hand began to explore her body. He stroked her neck, her shoulders, her breasts, her belly, and then dipped between her legs and stroked her sex. He inserted one finger between her labia and slid up and down, just brushing her clit and teasing the entrance to her passage so that it gaped wide, wanting to take him in.

"Please," she gasped, arching her back. She needed him to plunge inside her to still that ache!

But he continued to tease her. His fingers were agile and gentle. His touch featherlight and yet masterful. Soon she was weeping with frustration, writhing to escape his grasp. She could see his cock, it was erect.

"Take me," she begged.

"Please?" He paused.

"Please!" she hollered. The cry tore from her throat.

He let go of her hands and parted her legs, then slowly inserted his cock into her body. She watched, fascinated, as his body melted into hers. They became one. He moved, his hips lifting and thrusting and his cock, shiny now with her wetness, slid in and out of her sex. Llewellyn held himself up on his forearms so she could see.

And she watched, more and more turned on, as he penetrated her. She loved watching it pull in and out. But soon her vision blurred and a burning, urgent longing took hold of her.

"Harder," she begged, and he obliged. The wave crested over her, submerged her, and left her panting and drained. Llewellyn uttered a hoarse cry and she felt small spasms deep inside her, and she knew he'd ejaculated. It set off another orgasm, smaller this time, that shook her body. She wanted to slide back into sleep again, but she had to get up.

"Husband, I need to leave the bed." She paused. "Please?"

He chuckled. "Go ahead. I brought in some water and filled a bucket last night. The water should be warm."

Tamara sat up and stretched. Tiny whispers of pain reminded her where her wounds had been, but the healing powers of the Earth Mother and of the wood elf had worked. Her bones had knitted, her organs mended and her skin was once again smooth and flawless. And dirty. She missed the sponge baths Llewellyn gave her. With a grin, she went to the bucket and began to wash, making sure he was watching her.

He pretended not to notice, but he kept his good eye in her direction. She hid a smile and drew the sponge over her neck and chest, swirled it around her breasts, then dipped it between her thighs. She washed the sticky proof of their lovemaking away, all the while keeping an eye on Llewellyn. His cock hardened again. She felt an answering ache in her belly, but her sex was sore. She winced as the water stung. She would have to wait a while before impaling herself again on his wonderful cock. The thought made her dizzy and she took a deep breath.

There were herbs in the water—herbs to clean and to scent. The wood elves smelled like the forest. There was balsam and birch, and some other things she didn't recognize. When she finished, she took another sponge, wet it and went to the bed.

"Bare yourself, husband," she said.

He cocked an eyebrow.

"Go on. I won't hurt you." She knelt and washed him, paying most attention to the parts of him that most fascinated her. How interesting! What a fascinating texture. Soft and hard, smooth and rugged, his scrotum was so soft, and his cock was so hard.

She glanced at him and saw his eye was closed, his fist clenched.

"Let yourself go," she purred, and stroked him some more.

He did. All over her hands. Interesting. The sight sent tremors all through her body. She hadn't known she could have an orgasm just by looking at a man ejaculate. It was exciting.

She washed him off and then stood slowly. She put the sponge back in the bucket. Llewellyn rose on his elbow and looked at her.

"It is the time to dress and talk. There is much to be decided today." Now that she was married, she had a different set of responsibilities. And they started with letting Llewellyn know all about her tribe and their traditions, so he would know just what she'd chosen, and what she'd given up.

He nodded and got out of the bed. She couldn't get enough of his body. So tall, with his straight black hair and muscles that looked to be carved from stone so sharp and hard-edged they were. She could stare at him all day. But she had other things to do now. She pulled her tunic over her head and put on the warm leggings Llewellyn had given her. He dressed too, and put a pot of water on the fire to boil. When their breakfast was ready— a pot of tea and some dried berries and smoked fish—they sat together near the fire.

Llewellyn hadn't said a word, and when they finished eating he put his empty bowl down and looked at her expectantly. "Am I really your husband now? What does that mean for you and your tribe?"

She was glad he didn't sound angry, and she took the time to consider her answers. "Yes, you are my husband now. We have no ceremony to mark a marriage. What seals a marriage is the act of making love and breaking the hymen. Usually a marriage is between two women. Men are only for making babies."

"I wish you'd told me this before," he said softly.

Stung, she replied, "Would that have changed anything?"

He hesitated. "I don't know. I just would have preferred to know beforehand, that's all."

"I'm sorry." She raised her head. "You can divorce me whenever you wish. All it takes is that you say three times, 'I divorce you.' Then you will be free. Since men cannot live in our tribe with us, this is what they do. They proclaim the divorce and then they leave."

"But what about the children?" Llewellyn wanted to know.

Tamara shrugged. "If the child is a girl, she stays with the tribe. If it is a boy, the father makes a pact to come and get him, and raise him in his tribe. Is that what you want?"

"I didn't say that."

"I know. I'm sorry if you feel I've trapped you . . . "

"I didn't say that either." He reached over and grasped her wrist. "I want you. I need you. The moment I saw you I thought you were the most fascinating woman I'd ever seen." He let go and leaned back. "I accept that you chose me as your husband. It's over and done. But I would know more. Continue."

"We—"

"I would like to know one thing," he interrupted, and she saw a twinkle in his eye.

"Yes?"

"What do you use to break your hymens in your tribe?"

She felt a flush warm her cheeks. "What do you think? We have toys made for loving. They resemble your cock—though I admit they are not as fine."

He grinned, and she realized he'd been teasing her. "You are too curious for your own good. My tribe would have taken great joy hanging you by your wrists and coaxing your seed from your cock. That's how the clan mothers mate. The male is tied so he can't become violent." She giggled at his expression.

"It sounds like every male's dream come true." He cleared his throat. "Sorry. I didn't mean to make fun of your traditions. Now, continue. What does being your husband mean for me?"

"We are bound to one another. We are as one. Everything I own is yours, and vice versa. If we divorce everything is divided fairly between us. It means I will accompany you to the north to speak with Frostbone. I have linked my destiny to Hivernia and given up my place in my tribe. I cannot ever go back. Not even to gather my belongings." Her voice faltered, but she took a deep breath and straightened her shoulders. "I'm afraid I didn't bring much to this marriage. But I swear I will try to be a good husband too."

He blinked. "You're my husband too? I thought you were my wife."

"We have no wives in our tribe." She shrugged.

"In my tribe, you are my wife. You will have to get used to it. I'm the husband, you are the wife. Got that?"

Well, she could accept that small thing. After all, what was a word? Her tribe had told her about the inequalities in other tribes' marriages. She hoped hers would prove to be based more upon her idea of a marriage. "We are equal in the eyes of the law in my tribe," she reminded him, "even though I no longer live with them."

"In my tribe too," he answered. "There is no difference between the worth of a man and the worth of a woman."

"That's not what I've heard," she said.

"Long ago, there were laws that created inequalities. But they have been revised. Your tribe should keep up with the times," he said.

She knew he teased again, but she nodded. "We must avoid my territory. I am now a traitor to the d'ark t'uath. If you wish, you may go to the trading post and tell them I am alive. But I must stay out of sight or I will be captured and put to death. That is the law."

He paled. "Tamara . . . "

"I knew what I was doing," she said. It hurt, of course it did. But there had always been a streak of restlessness in her. The world seemed too small, confined to the d'ark t'uath's caves and valleys. Now she belonged to the rest of the world. Part of her still cried in pain, but for the most part she was looking forward to what life had to offer now she was married to a wood elf. "Will your family like me?" she asked.

He took her face in his hands. "They will adore you." His mouth found hers and she melted into his kiss. *Life should always be so sweet*, she thought.

SIX

The Camp

THE TRIP NORTH TOOK them through d'ark t'uath territory. Tamara disguised herself as a man, putting padding in her tunic's shoulders and pulling her hood over her head and her scarf over her face. At the trading post, Llewellyn went to speak to her clan's representatives while Tamara remained hidden in the forest.

The two d'ark t'uath, armed to the teeth, motioned for him to lay his arms down and approach. He did, and they relaxed slightly. "I am Llewellyn, I come in peace," he said.

"I am Fia, and this is Rhyanna." The tallest d'ark t'uath, the one called Fia, approached him and looked him over. "You have nothing to trade. Why have you come here?"

"I come to give you news of Tamara."

Fia uttered a small gasp. "Tamara? She disappeared nearly a fortnight ago. Have you found her? Is she wounded?"

"No. She is safe. She has chosen to leave the tribe. Her message is this: 'I, Tamara, was caught and mauled by a behemoth while on guard duty. I lost my *glosseer* at the foot of the tree. The behemoth took me to his cave and would have killed me, but a wood elf rescued me. He helped heal my wounds, and I decided to marry him. I have cast my lot with the tribe of the wood elves. He is bound on a mission to see Frostbone. It is for the good of all that you let him pass.' That is what I was bade to tell you." Llewellyn stopped and waited.

The two women looked at each other in consternation. "Are you the wood elf Tamara has married?" asked Fia.

"I am."

"And you quest to Frostbone?" This was asked by Rhyanna, in a slightly more acidic tone.

"There is concern that the Mouse King has returned."

Now the silence was tinged with fear. Fia spoke first, her eyes narrowed. "We had not thought of that. What is true is that more demons than before have been sighted, and even your story of a behemoth rings true, for we have seen several far from their mountains. We wondered what kind of trouble would cause them to leave their haunts."

"What do you plan to do? Frostbone does not suffer elves or fairies in his territory. He will kill you on sight."

"I know Frostbone. He will speak to me. The land of Hivernia is preparing for war. The new king, King Branagh, is now raising and training his army. Once again the wood elves will take up their bows and fight alongside the fairies."

"We have heard that the new queen of Hivernia is a wood elf." Rhyanna raised an eyebrow.

"That's right." Llewellyn paused. "I would ask a boon of you. Tamara is no longer part of your tribe. But she must have some belongings that are dear to her. I would ask you to give them to me so that she might have something to remember her tribe by."

"Her tribe is now yours. By the laws of our tribe, she may not take anything with her. She knew this when she decided to marry you." Rhyanna waved dismissively.

"I bid you farewell then," said Llewellyn. He hadn't counted on getting any of Tamara's belongings. He'd tried though. He made his way back through the woods to where Tamara was hiding. She'd been listening in.

"I told you our tribe forbids us to take our belongings with us." She shook her head. "You are a very stubborn elf."

"But a nice one, you have to admit."

"Yes." She tilted her head. "So it's true that an elf is now queen of Hivernia? That must have been a shock to most of the fairies."

"You heard correctly. Melflouise is now queen of Hivernia."

"You sound as if you know her well."

"She was my brother's wife."

A pause. "The one who died."

"Yes." He dug his toe into the snow. He really didn't want to talk about Melle or Elloran with anyone, but he supposed Tamara had a right to know.

"I will wait until you are ready to tell me about them. You don't have to say anything."

He looked up at her, surprised. "So you read minds now?"

She laughed. "I didn't think you sprang to life on the mountainside the day you saved me. You had a life before, and it was an interesting one. You have the scars to show it. But I imagine it must truly hurt to be wounded here." She pointed to her heart. "Perhaps we were meant to find each other. I will help you heal, and you will help to fill the emptiness I've always felt."

"Empty? Why?" They started up the slope. The day was still new, but they had a long way to go before they reached the first outpost camp.

"I have always been dissatisfied with my life. More times than I like to admit I infringed upon my tribe's rules and was punished. My clan mother despaired of me. She tried, but nothing I ever did filled the void inside me."

"Do you miss anyone in your tribe?"

There was a pause while they scaled the last bit of cliff, then it was downhill for a while. She trotted easily. Like all fae, she could walk on top of snow and was light-footed and fleet. They moved well together, he thought.

"I miss my clan mother, and some of my friends I will miss bitterly. It pains me that I will never see my home again. I lived in a large cavern of many galleries in the Winding Brook Valley. It is as beautiful as its name implies. Our caverns are vast and comfortable. I hope your caverns are as nice."

"We don't live in caves."

She missed a step and stumbled. "Where do you live?"

He grinned. "In a house. I hope it's clean when I return. If not, Sebring and Merlin will answer to me."

"Your maids?"

"My brothers-in-law. They are Melle's brothers, and a pair of troublemakers they are, too. You'll see, they can charm the bees from their honey, and all the girls in the village are besotted with them."

"You are a wood elf. How many other tribes are there of your kind?"

"We wood elves form seven tribes. Then there are the elves of the great plains with their magnificent horses, and the marsh elves, shy and reclusive. We've always counted the d'ark t'uath as part of our clan. We refer to you as the dark elves or the stone elves." He held a branch aside for her and then ducked under it. "Then there is the fairy kingdom. Fairies live in great cities, like Hivernia City. They have built castles and roads, seaports and . . . whatever it is fairies build. They love everything colorful and rich. We elves are more simple. We like things that come from nature and we don't try to change them."

"I don't think I'll like Hivernia City. Will we live in the forest in your house?"

"We will have to visit Hivernia City after we see Frostbone. But don't worry. I know Branagh and Melle and they will make you feel welcome. Melle knows what it's like to be an elf living amidst fairy folk. Are you tired? We can rest."

"No. Let's continue until we reach the camp. Then I will lie down and sleep for a thousand years."

Llewellyn looked at her closely. Her skin seemed pale and her eyes darker than usual. Pain drew fine lines around her mouth and nose. "The camp is on the bottom of the next gorge. We will be there in half an hour."

When they got there, Llewellyn was relieved to see that they would be alone. It was a small cave, set in between two mighty boulders. Sometimes traders came to the outpost camps, so everything was ready for travelers. There was a stack of firewood outside, and Llewellyn found a large bucket and went to the stream to fetch water. When he got back, Tamara had already built a fire in the huge stone fireplace.

"That heat feels good," he said, ducking through the deerskin flap that served as a door, pouring the water into a kettle and hanging the kettle on a chain set over the fire.

"I thought wood elves were impervious to cold," she teased.

"We are, but that doesn't mean we don't appreciate a nice fire. What about you?"

"I don't suffer from cold. I'm not as impervious as an ice demon though."

"We will be in Frostbone's territory in three days if we keep up the pace."

"I will try not to slow you down." She looked fragile, wrapped in her cloak, the firelight making deep shadows on her face.

He took her in his arms. "I'm not worried about that." He paused. "I'm still getting used to being married, to tell you the truth. I never thought I'd get married one day."

"Why? Your brother married. Surely you ... " Her voice trailed away as she watched him. "Oh. The queen. You were in love with your brother's wife."

"Yes." It was best to tell the truth.

Her eyes became shuttered. "Are you still in love with her?"

He thought about Melle. It was like probing a sore, but his emotional wounds seemed to have healed. He actually smiled. "No. I'm not. You have to understand," he went on, becoming serious. "My brother was my twin. We shared everything, even our dreams and our emotions. When he fell in love, he dragged me in with him, and when he sang his elf song, I sang too. I couldn't help it."

Tamara slid her arms around him. "I understand. We haven't sung together yet. But someday I hope that we will. Our love is still too new and unexpected."

"You're right." He kissed her cheek, relieved that she didn't expect him to sing. The elf song was something that tore out of your soul. It only happened on certain occasions. He'd heard Melle's song and it had shaken him to the bone. His brother's song had taken his own voice away for a long time. Now, perhaps, he would find his own. Only time would tell. Until then, he was content to learn about Tamara.

She blinked, her face to the flames. "So, what about taking your clothes off?"

"Excuse me?" He nuzzled her neck and she giggled.

"I want to see you naked again."

"Only if you take yours off first."

She slipped out of his arms and threw the cloak off. In the firelight, her body looked golden. He caught his breath. Her long dark hair fell to her hips, and her breasts were heavy and rounded. Her hips flared gently, and her legs were long and slender. But he sensed a hidden strength in her.

She cocked her hip, teasingly, and cupped her breasts with her hands. "They ache for your touch," she whispered.

His cock was already stiff, and when she slid her hands over her breasts, it got so hard he thought he might explode right into his breeches. "Hold on," he gasped, shrugging off his tunic and breeches as fast as he could.

Tamara chuckled. "I have long watched my clan sisters pleasure themselves with their toys. They sometimes use two, one for this entrance, and one for this one." She turned and bent over, her buttocks jutting into the air.

"I have but one toy for you," said Llewellyn, his breath coming fast. By Mistral, she could bring his blood to a boil faster than fire.

"Then show me how you pleasure your women in your tribe. I wonder if it's better to have one living toy attached to a male body, or two toys that one can play with at will?"

Llewellyn narrowed his eyes. Was this a challenge? He'd show her. He grasped her shoulders and spun her around, crushing her to his chest. He lifted her chin for a kiss. "We start like this," he said, and then pressed his mouth to hers.

He kissed her slowly, letting his tongue and teeth explore and tease her mouth. She was a fast learner, and soon he couldn't tell who was breathing harder. His lips felt swollen and hot when they at last drew apart. Her eyes were hooded with desire, her mouth slack.

Then he knelt and ran his tongue down her chest and over her breasts. He sucked on each nipple, giving them equal attention. When they stiffened he lowered his head and traced a path of kisses to her thighs.

She tensed. "No!"

"Yes." He grinned at her. "Open your legs. That's an order."

She hesitated, then parted her legs. Llewellyn put both hands on her thighs and parted her labia with his thumbs, revealing her sex. It was swollen with passion. He leaned forward and found her clit with his tongue. Eagerly he lapped at it until Tamara's legs began to tremble.

"Let me lie down," she begged. "My head is spinning."

"I hope so," he said. Still kneeling, he helped her lie back on the soft cloak and then bent to his pleasurable task again. He licked and nibbled gently on her clit and softly, teasingly, he stroked his fingertips ever so lightly against her slick flesh. Her labia swelled and grew moist, and even her passage opened and contracted.

Tamara writhed upon the cloak, her hands clutching at the edges of it, her knuckles white.

"Let yourself go," he chuckled, sliding one finger, then two, into her passage.

"Oh yes!" she cried, bucking against him. But he wasn't going to let her give in to her passion yet.

"Just relax, stop trying to hurry it." He grinned, and then wriggled his two fingers, making them vibrate like the wings of a hummingbird. Her hips lifted off the floor as her back arched and a flood of hot wetness dampened his hand. He pressed his lips to her sensitive clit, and then sighed in satisfaction when he felt her contractions massaging his fingers.

Panting, Tamara raised herself on her elbows. "Where did you learn to do that?"

He withdrew his fingers and with a wolfish grin said, "You might actually like it in Hivernia. The fairies have many different ways of satisfying their needs, and they are not at all shy about sharing."

Her face turned pink. "You've shared before?"

"I did spend time in Hivernia." He stood and stretched. His cock was still hard, and he stroked it, staring at the woman lying on the floor before him. Her eyelashes fluttered and she smiled.

"It's my turn now." She knelt and put both hands on his groin, rubbing suggestively.

"Only if you're up to it," he said.

"Oh, I think I can manage. I recover quickly." With that, she slid her hot mouth over his cock and began to suck.

Sweet Mistral! By Thaw's spring flowers! Llewellyn had to grab the stone wall to keep upright. Her mouth was sensuous and the sight of her full lips moving up and down his shaft while her fingers seemed to have an urge to explore all his nooks and crannies . . . By Mistral! He sucked in air and held it as one of her fingers found a particularly sensitive cranny and delved deep. Her mouth suctioned lustily. He felt his balls contract to somewhere around his stomach. And then her delving finger delved even deeper, and he lost it.

He thought maybe his head had come off, maybe. At any rate, one thing was sure—his cock was empty. It had exploded into her eager mouth and she'd gulped his seed with an expression of pure delight. It must have echoed the look on his face—he hoped. He had a sneaking suspicion that when he came he probably looked witless, because he certainly felt that way. The only thing that existed was his cock and the lips hugging it.

He sank to his knees and faced her.

"Where did you learn to do that? And don't tell me your clan sisters or whatever you call them have cocks."

She batted her eyelashes. A very womanly thing to do. "I just made it up."

He collapsed onto the cloak and curled up tight. He felt empty, drained and rather confused. She curled up next to him, her arms around his shoulders.

"What's the matter?"

"I was thinking of sharing you, and I wasn't very happy about it," he admitted. "It's not an elvish thing to do. It's a fairy thing. But if we go to Hivernia, you may be tempted to try."

"Let's deal with that when it happens." She tucked her head into the crook of his neck and he felt her breathing even off and deepen.

She slid into sleep as easily and trustingly as a child. He lay awake for a long time. Part of it was hunger. And part of it was wonder that he'd found someone who could fill that aching emptiness he'd felt for so long. But soon the wonder and hunger faded, and he fell into a deep slumber.

SEVEN

Frostbone

T HE NEXT MORNING TAMARA woke and saw she was alone. She didn't worry. Llewellyn would be off hunting. They needed supplies. She washed, donned her clothes and set off to gather some food. The camp was set in a deep valley. At the foot of the camp was a rushing stream. Tamara followed the stream until she found a likely spot, and then she dug for cattail roots, dogtooth violet roots, and even some old dandelion greens and roots. In the winter food was harder to find, but Tamara had grown up in these valleys and she knew where to look.

Her pouch filled, she wandered back to the camp. Her stomach might be empty, but her mind was full. She had chosen Llewellyn without his consent. Perhaps now he accepted that. They were alone together, and she could help him on his quest. But what about when they returned to his homeland? He might not be as enamored with the idea of being married. He had been in love with his brother's wife—he'd admitted as much. She was now queen of Hivernia. They would be expected to spend time there.

None of her clan sisters or mothers had ever, to her knowledge, been to Hivernia. For one thing, the clan was not allowed to stray out of its valleys. And that was another thing bothering her. She'd had time to think her actions through and knew what she'd given up. But now that the act was done and she'd committed herself, she was starting to doubt.

She looked up and saw Llewellyn's tall silhouette near the entrance of the cave. Her heart gave a funny flutter then. His straight black hair was plaited and he'd affixed a blue feather to the braid. His eye patch covered the deep hole where his eye had been, but his other eye was deep amethyst, sometimes cold, sometimes burning. He turned and saw her, and a tremor seemed to run through him. He flashed her a wide, white grin. Something deep inside her unknotted and she smiled back.

"I've got some roots for us."

"Splendid. I managed to snare a rabbit and brought down a pheasant. If you want, there is some meat on the spit. We should leave soon. I want to make it to Frostbone's territory before the real snows start."

They ate and then set the camp up for the next travelers. Taking their meager belongings, they set out once again. Tamara felt better each day. She was still not perfectly healed, but each hour that passed gained her new strength. She was glad, for she knew she would need it to face the ice demon king.

Three days passed before they reached the outskirts of Frostbone's land. It was marked by standing stones. Huge menhirs, some thrice as tall as a man, stood in ragged lines. Tamara paused before stepping through.

Llewellyn put his hand on the stones and spoke clearly. "Frostbone, it is I, Llewellyn Fairnight. I have come to speak of matters that concern us both."

"Can he hear you?" Tamara turned and watched, disquiet prickling up and down her back.

"He said to use the stones to call him. I think we best wait here."

Tamara looked around. They stood on a windy plateau. The stones stretched as far as the eye could see in both directions, and in both directions there were no trees, no shelter from the biting wind. "Even I, a stone elf, as you call me, can feel the bitter cold of this place. I hope we will find shelter soon."

"Don't count on it," said Llewellyn. He wrapped his cloak twice around himself for warmth and nodded to Tamara to do the same. "Conserve your body heat and strength. The ice demons need cold to survive. I think we may find out what it feels like to freeze before this interview is over."

They huddled together. Night fell, and the stars blazed above them. Tamara started to feel the chill seeping into her bones. It made her remember lying on the floor of the cave when the behemoth had found her. She was about to say that to Llewellyn when a sparkle caught her eye. She stiffened.

"Yes, I saw it too," he breathed in her ear. "Don't move, but be ready to run if I say."

She tensed, waiting. The sparkle grew brighter and drew nearer. As it did, she caught her breath in wonder. She'd seen ice demons before—who living in the far north hadn't? But she hadn't seen their sleighs, or the white-furred creatures that pulled them. Larger than deer, with long, silky white fur and silver antlers, the creatures were harnessed to a crystal sleigh driven by an ice demon. It motioned to the sleigh.

Llewellyn helped Tamara into the sleigh, then drew a fur cover over her knees. Tamara was too bemused to speak, but Llewellyn said, "Thank you for coming to get us. This is quite comfortable."

"Hang on tightly," said the ice demon. Its voice sounded like snow crunching beneath boots.

Tamara barely had time to grasp the sides of the sleigh before the demon shook the reins and the white deer fled into the night. They ran so fast that Tamara's eyes watered and the tears froze on her cheeks. She cuddled closer to Llewellyn, and he put his arms around her. The night sky wheeled above them as the sleigh whispered across the snow. Sometimes they crossed lakes or rivers. The ice was black and the deers' hooves hissed like ice skates. The journey seemed endless, or perhaps it was just the deep silence. Everything was frozen solid, even the air seemed to cut like sharp, cold quartz. Tamara's cheeks felt numb and her fingers and toes tingled with frost.

"We've arrived."

Llewellyn's voice roused her from slumber. She opened her eyes, blinking, and then sat up and stared. They were in front of a magnificent palace made of sparkling ice.

Starlight ran up and down the towers, and lamps cast pools of light that lit the palace from within. The demon waited until Llewellyn and Tamara had climbed out, then he drove off, the sleigh whooshing in the snow.

Tamara took Llewellyn's hand, squeezing it tightly. Together they walked over an ice bridge and under a clear arch to enter the brightly lit palace. The door was ice, the floor was packed snow, and the sconces on the walls were ice crystals that held stones that burned with a cold fire and glowed blue, white or yellow. Everything shimmered and sparkled. It was breathtakingly beautiful.

Their footsteps echoed in the wide hallway. There were ice demons everywhere. They stood in a line and there was only one way to go between them. Tamara felt her hand crushing Llewellyn's but he made no protest. Her heart hammered in her chest. The ice demons didn't move. They could have been carved out of ice except for the strange blue fire that danced within them. And then they arrived in the throne room.

Silver-frosted tinsel hung in garlands from the ceiling and there was a huge white tree in the center of the room. Ice crystals glittered and shone upon it. On the throne sat the biggest demon of all, Frostbone. He too looked as if he were carved from a block of ice. The blue fire that lit him was paler than most—almost white. His eyes were like two blue flames. He stood as they entered and said, "Welcome to Winterhaven. I have been waiting for you, Llewellyn Fairnight."

Llewellyn stopped at the foot of Frostbone's throne and bowed. "I'm honored to be here. I've heard of your palace and its beauty, but mere words cannot describe it. I feel most privileged."

"And this is your mate? Be welcome."

Tamara had to agree with Llewellyn. The beauty of the place was simply astounding. She gave a bow too, and said, "Thank you for your hospitality." Her voice didn't waver a bit.

Frostbone said, "It is the least I can do. Llewellyn Fairnight and his brother freed us from the Mouse King."

"Don't forget Branagh," said Llewellyn.

"I have not." Frostbone clapped his hands. It sounded like bells ringing. "Bring refreshments for our guests. Come sit down. We have much to discuss and little time."

"So you too have heard," said Llewellyn softly.

"Many of my people have been lured away by the tempting promises of a wandering ice demon. He promised more land, better hunting and riches for all. It seemed too convenient to be true. The ones who left were young and foolish. They have been stirring trouble on the borders and so I send my troops or go myself to apprehend them. But this new demon is too clever for me. By the time I arrive he has faded away. And I hear his army grows stronger. Many rocs have joined him. But the worst news is that he has somehow joined forces with the behemoth king. That's why so many of their kind have fled. The old, the sick and the weak are being pushed out of their lands."

"The one I killed looked old," said Llewellyn, nodding. "So the Mouse King has somehow found a way to return."

"Yes, and despite my warnings many of the younger ice demons have decided to join him. He wears not the same face, nor rides a dragon. This time, I think his strength lies in the behemoth king, for how else could he get so powerful in so short a time? He must wear the disguise of an ice demon though, and somehow fooled the rocs into joining his side. That was a heavy blow. The rocs guard the passage through the mountains to the north, and if our people cannot use it anymore, we will be hampered in our summer migration."

"I will return to Hivernia with this news. It grieves me to see your kingdom under such a threat. Be assured that Branagh will send his army here, and we will combat at your side."

"Your offer is generous. I hope it will be timely. As you can see, it is winter solstice soon, the most important of our traditional fêtes. I will use this as a chance to gather my troops together. We will be waiting for Branagh's army."

An ice demon came bearing a silver tray with drinks. Tamara took one and winced. The cup was freezing cold. The drink was icy, but delicious. She found herself enjoying the sweet wintergreen and spice flavor.

"Come, I will show you to your room," said Frostbone when they had finished their drinks. "Tomorrow, at first light, the sleigh will take you back to the standing stones. I wish your visit could have been longer, but I have much to do before winter solstice. If the war is not over by spring thaws, we will surely lose everything."

"I know that," Llewellyn didn't touch him, but he raised his hand and held it with his palm facing Frostbone's chest. "We will make haste."

Frostbone nodded and held his hand out too, nearly, but not quite touching Llewellyn. Then he left them.

Their room was made of ice. Windows with ice panes looked out over the endless tundra. The moon had risen, casting everything in a silvery glow. Tamara sank down on the bed. It was hard, being made of carved ice, but it was covered with a pile of deep furs. "I thought that demons were unable to speak our language."

Llewellyn nodded. "Most cannot. Frostbone was under the Mouse King's spell for a long time. They are immortal, or nearly so, unless someone cuts their heads off. I don't know much about their way of life. In the summer they retreat to deep caves of eternal ice. Here, in this land, they can live for most of the year. But Thaw finds it eventually, even if it is for a short time. If the Mouse King is not defeated, he may take over this land and enslave the ice demons once more. Frostbone is afraid of that."

"I would be too," said Tamara. She couldn't suppress a shudder of fear. The last time the Mouse King had enslaved Rog, a mighty dragon, and had used his power. Now, if Frostbone spoke the truth, he had the behemoth king's might. If only she hadn't left her tribe! She had to be able to convince them to send a troop of warriors. She hugged her knees to her chest. She could still do that. It would be at great risk though. The penalty for coming back into the tribe after leaving it for a male was death. But when the clan chief mother heard her tale, she would surely waive her punishment and agree to help Hivernia and the ice demons defeat the Mouse King! And then, after that, she had to find a way to give Llewellyn back his elf song, and at the same time discover her own. Only true love would unlock the notes of that song. It was too early to tell, but she found herself wishing with all her heart that Llewellyn was the key.

She stared out the ice-paned window at the night sky, where mysterious borealis shimmered red and green. Her world suddenly seemed to teeter on the edge of a knife, and she wasn't sure which way it would fall.

LLEWELLYN COULD TELL TAMARA'S mind was in turmoil. He thought he could guess at some of it, for they shared the same fears and doubts. But he wondered how much of it was due to regret at

leaving her home. A d'ark t'uath had never left her clan to marry—
at least in his time.

After he undressed, he sat next to her and ran his hands over
her back, massaging gently.

She sighed and leaned back into his embrace. He lifted her
tunic off and then slid under the covers with her. Together they
soon had the furs toasty warm. And the touch of her skin was
enough to arouse him. He slid his cock between her legs, slowly
pushing it in and out, practically purring as the satin skin of her
inner thighs stroked him.

She kept her back to him and pressed her buttocks closer,
opening her legs to catch his cock with them. "Got you," she giggled, and squeezed tightly.

He reached over her shoulders and captured one of her
breasts in his hand. "Got you too," he said. He loved the feel of
her breast—heavy and firm, her nipple hardened to a little pebble
when he pinched it. He pinched it gently, rolling it between his
thumb and forefinger. Then she reached down between her legs
and grabbed his cock.

That made him groan aloud. Her fingers closed around it and
then she started a slow but steady pumping, coaxing him to move
his hips. Her own hips pressed backward and she spread her legs
so he felt the wickedly wet heat of her sex.

But she didn't let him press his advances. Letting go of him,
she twisted around so that she faced him. Without a word, she
looped her arms around his neck and kissed him. He let her mouth
explore his. She urged his lips apart with her tongue and then ran
it over his front teeth, then dipped it in his mouth. She tasted
of spice and wintermint. He opened his mouth wider, deepen-

ing their kiss. His breath came quickly as the image of her lush lips closing over his cock came to mind. He crushed her to him, wanting to melt into her kiss, her arms, her embrace, so that he couldn't tell where he left off and she began.

"Wait." She broke off. Her face pensive, she leaned up on one elbow.

"What is it?" His mouth felt swollen, his eyelids heavy. His cock throbbed with each of his heartbeats. He wanted to thrust it into her, to hear her cry out . . .

"I wanted to say that I love you." She said it quickly, then, to his surprise, blushed.

He let the words sink in. They felt right, falling into a place he'd kept free. A place that hadn't been filled until now. A smile tugged at his mouth. "I love you too, Tamara. I'm glad you chose me as your husband."

Sheer relief flashed in her eyes and they filled with tears.

"No, don't cry, my love." He took her face in his hands and drew her down for another kiss. He loved losing himself in her kisses.

She rolled him over on his back and straddled him. Her thighs spread on each side of his waist, she offered him a clear view of her sex. That was nice. But even better when she lifted her hips, balanced above him for a minute, then, ever so slowly sank down onto his cock.

He watched, his throat going suddenly dry, as she eased herself down. Reaching the bottom, she thrust her hips forward, grinding her pelvis against his and sending shocks of pleasure through his cock as he felt it hit the mouth of her womb.

He uttered a loud groan as she slowly lifted herself upward

again. The cold air hit his cock, wet with her juices, and made the heat of her body even more sizzling. He could hardly breathe anymore. His heart was going to burst out of his chest. He reached toward her, but she grabbed his wrists and held them pinned over his head, her breasts brushing against his chin. He lowered his head and sucked at one of her nipples with his mouth. It was taut, and when he suckled it Tamara ground her hips even more firmly against his, wedging his cock even deeper inside her.

Shivers of delight ran down his spine. Then Tamara leaned over and pressed her lips to his. At the same time, she increased the tempo of her strokes, her hips lifting and falling faster and faster. His cock was burning. His tongue reached and parried hers. His cock head hit her womb with each long, hard plunge into her. Coherent thought fled, all sensation gathered in his belly and started to grow. Soon all that mattered was his cock driving to her womb, and each second, each minute seemed to lengthen and then become perfectly crystalline, hardening in his loins. Pain merged with pleasure until his muscles clenched, and then a flutter began in his chest. Suddenly he felt her cunt pulsate wildly as a blinding orgasm ripped through him and a golden note left his throat as he began to sing. A higher, silvery note joined his as Tamara threw her head back and sang. Music burst from her throat in a symphony of emotion.

Elf song! The sound wrapped around them and bound them together. Each long spasm as he ejaculated echoed in a note rising from his throat. Part of his chi left his body in the song, part of his heart. A soft golden glow seemed to envelop them as their chi met and melded together. Ripples of music washed over them, wrapping around their bodies in a visible cloak of music.

Afterward, the very walls seemed to vibrate and echo with their music. Tamara raised her head from off his shoulder and looked at him, her eyes dancing. "I hope the demons don't mind noisy visitors," she said.

Llewellyn pulled her down on top of him then rolled over, throwing his leg over her hip and pinning her against his chest. "I don't care. I'm too tired to care, for one." He blinked and laughed softly. "I didn't expect that."

"I did." She would always surprise him. She kissed his lips softly. "I hoped, at any rate. I hoped with all my heart."

Her eyelashes fluttered closed as she spoke, and to his amusement her last words ended in a soft snore. He kissed the tip of her nose and made sure the covers were securely wrapped around them before closing his own eyes and drifting to that place dreams haunt.

EIGHT

Hivernia

THE JOURNEY BACK TO Hivernia was uneventful. Llewellyn would not let Tamara speak to her own tribe. He went to deliver the message himself, but didn't wait for a reply. They were in a hurry to reach Hivernia before the snows blocked the passes completely. They were already late.

Tamara fretted as they climbed the slopes, but her worries were unfounded. Bald Pass, the northernmost pass in Hivernia, was snowed in but still open. There were troops of elves there, and every day they cleared the passes by order of King Branagh, the elves told them as they stopped in a small hut and had some lunch.

Tamara was still shy around so many different men. The ice demons hadn't counted, but the first glimpse she got of a group of men elves together made her cling to Llewellyn's arm in panic.

"They won't hurt you," he said, trying to pry her grip loose and get her moving again.

She hung back, but when he started to go on without her she bounded to his side. It took a few minutes for her to get up the nerve to say hello, and when they didn't shout or go crazy, as her clan mothers had warned her they could, she relaxed. Maybe her clan had been exaggerating. As the night deepened and they sat around the fire chatting, she decided that yes, there had been a lot of exaggerating, and if she ever got the chance to go back to her tribe she would set things right once and for all.

The rest of the route was easier. It was mostly downhill, and the routes and passes were all open. And then one morning they awoke to the sound of hoofbeats. Tamara still couldn't stop her reflex of hiding in Llewellyn's strong arms whenever strangers approached, and she was grateful for the fur cloak that covered her head and face—a royal gift from the king of the ice demons, Frostbone. Each had received a fur-lined woolen cloak. Llewellyn's was black and dark green on the outside with black fur, and hers was blue and silver with pale gray fur.

Llewellyn raised his arm in greeting, and his voice rang with joy. "Merlin! Sebring!"

The two men were wood elves, with russet hair cut short around their well-shaped heads and bright green eyes. They flung themselves off their steeds and ran to Llewellyn, one taking him in his arms and hugging him before stepping back and giving him a shake. "Why did you leave without us!" they cried.

"Merlin, this is Tamara. My wife."

Tamara had the satisfaction of actually seeing someone's jaw drop.

Merlin bowed over her hand. "Pleased to meet you, Tamara Fairnight. My name is Merlin, and this is my twin brother, Sebring."

Sebring bowed as well, and kissed her hand.

"Pleased to meet you," said Tamara, bemused by their courtly manners. *They must be from King Branagh's court,* she thought, and their next words confirmed this.

"We came as soon as we heard you'd been spotted. Branagh wants you at the court now. Yesterday. As fast as the horses can carry us." Merlin laughed.

"We didn't know you were married, or we would have cleaned your house."

Tamara suddenly remembered where she'd heard their names. "You're the queen's brothers," she said, suddenly shy again.

"Yes." Sebring gave her a blinding grin. "She will be so glad to see you, Tamara. You have no idea."

The thought that the queen would be glad to see her made her spirits lift.

"Here, take our horses. We'll ride double on the one we brought for you," said Merlin.

"I've never ridden." Tamara balked when the horse was led up.

"Well, that makes things easier. You ride with me. We'll take the fresh horse," said Llewellyn. He boosted her up and then swung on behind her. She rather liked the closeness. The charm evaporated after about an hour, when her buttocks screamed that under no circumstances would they take any more jolting. Her legs burned. Her stomach churned. But she clenched her teeth and said nothing until they stopped for the night. They had covered an amazing distance on horseback, she realized.

She also realized that she was incapable of moving without screaming in pain.

Llewellyn took one look at her and then carefully carried her to the fire, where he used his healing skills once again. This time for blisters, bruises and strained muscles.

Merlin and Sebring helped sing the healing songs, and Tamara let her chi open and absorb their powers. The next morning she dreaded getting back on the horse, but Llewellyn said, "We're almost there. By lunchtime we will be at the city gates. Hold on. I know this hurts, but you'll get used to it, I promise."

"I will never sit on another horse as long as I live," she swore.

"Never say never," said Llewellyn, and she knew he was right. If they rode to war, they would have to move swiftly. The thought was sobering. She was even more cowed when the city came into sight. It rose overhead, bigger than anything she'd ever seen. It dwarfed even the mountain it had been built upon, as row after row of houses and finally the castle rose into the air.

They had come out of the forest and onto the plain. The city was built on a small mountain right in the middle of the plain, giving it height and protection. A river wound lazily around the base of the city, and Tamara could see bridges arching over the river and even some fishing boats sailing along it.

There was a great wall encircling the city. They rode to the nearest gate, a huge wooden affair that lifted like a drawbridge. Now it was down, and the horses trotted over it, making far too much noise for Tamara's liking.

The whole city was too noisy. She cringed at the sight, and Llewellyn wrapped his arms around her tightly and crooned soothingly into her ear.

"Don't be frightened. We'll soon be at the palace and I'll find us a quiet room where we can rest."

"I'm not frightened, I'm never frightened," she replied haughtily, but she had a hard time pretending she wasn't quaking with fear. The streets were paved with smooth stone, there were trees lining them, and though it was winter, some of the trees still bore leaves. Fairy magic, she decided.

There were fairies bustling about, and she was interested to see that they didn't look too different from elves. They were finer boned and smaller than elves. Tamara thought the men were not as handsome as Llewellyn. They had lighter hair, mostly blond or light brown, and their skin was much fairer too. They dressed in all the colors of the rainbow, and the women had very low-cut bodices.

The fairy women were exquisite, very petite, with intricate hairdos and makeup and clothes that bespoke many hours in front of a mirror. The children were smaller than elf children, and Tamara was amazed to see how beautifully they were dressed. Like little adults she thought, watching a little girl and her mother strolling down the street. They even had pets on leashes—something an elf would never own. Even the elves' horses didn't wear bridles. Elves didn't own animals, so when Llewellyn asked her what surprised her the most, she replied, "The dogs on the leashes."

There were shops galore, and that finally caught her attention. The displays of bright silks and gauzy dresses, gold and silver, and even the bakery and fruit and vegetable shops tempted her, as they had trays of wares set out right on the street. Red and yellow apples, oranges, kumquats, pears, grapes of all colors, huge melons and berries that glittered like jewels. And the rich scents coming from the bakery! Cinnamon, cardamom, garlic, honey, lemon, orange blossom and ginger all mixed with the warm smell of fresh bread. Tamara's mouth watered painfully.

"Can I have one of those?" she asked, leaning over and pointing at a hot cross bun. Her stomach rumbled. Llewellyn tossed the baker a coin and gave the bun to her. She bit into it and sighed with delight. "I think I'm going to like it here," she said.

He hugged her, and Sebring, who'd overheard, said, "Just wait until you have dinner at the palace. Melle used to work in the kitchen, and she still oversees the menus. I don't know why Branagh isn't obese."

"Because Melle makes him work it off in bed," retorted Merlin.

Tamara choked on her bun and Llewellyn guffawed. "If the king hears you you'll be thrown into the dungeons for disrespect."

"Here we are," said Tamara, looking up at the main gate of the palace. Two guards waved them through. She was nervous again, and worried that she had sugar all over her mouth and bun in her teeth. She wanted to make a good impression.

"You look beautiful," said Llewellyn, reading her mind. Or maybe it was the fact he'd caught her wiping her mouth on the hem of his cloak.

Grooms came to take their horses—elf grooms, who knew horses—and Tamara followed Llewellyn into the palace, Sebring and Merlin at her heels.

King Branagh was standing in front of his throne, waiting for them. Tamara thought he was very ordinary looking. He had hair the color of dark honey that looked as if no comb could tame it, clear eyes the color of caramel—she was still hungry, she realized—and a crooked smile. His back was slightly crooked too, she saw, and he walked with a limp. His hand,

when he reached out to shake Llewellyn's, was scarred. He'd
been in many battles. Here was a man whose looks were deceiv-
ing, Tamara decided.

Next to him was a wood elf—Queen Melflouise. She was as
tall as her husband and had the most tranquil expression Tamara
had ever seen. Her eyes were green and cool, and as inviting as
the depths of the forest on a sunny day. Tamara felt at ease with
her right away. She didn't dress like a fairy. She kept her simple
elf garb, but on her it looked regal. Her dark red hair was cut
short, and Tamara remembered hearing she'd been part of the elf
militia—an archer, if she wasn't mistaken. Short hair meant she'd
fought. She kept it short, or had she cut it in anticipation of battle? Tamara felt a prickle of disquiet. Their visit was not a social
one. She could feel the tension in the air.

Then she heard the words, "This is my wife, Tamara," and
Llewellyn stepped back and left her standing alone in front of the
king and queen of Hivernia.

Tamara dropped into a low curtsy, mindful of her manners.

"It's wonderful to meet you," said the queen. She gave Tamara
a beautiful smile. "I hope you'll enjoy your room. I put you in a
quiet part of the castle. I remember how hard it was for me to
adapt to life at court."

"I can't believe Llewellyn finally got married," said Branagh,
who patted Llewellyn on the shoulder and to Tamara's surprise,
came up to her and gave her a bone-crushing hug. "I owe your
husband my life," said Branagh, taking Tamara by the arm and
leading her to a table set with a tea service. "I fought an ice demon
and was pierced by an ice shard. Lucky for me, Llewellyn, Merlin
and Sebring were in the area."

Tamara soon forgot her shyness as they had tea. The queen insisted she call her Melle, and the first time she'd called the king "Your Majesty," he looked blank and then gave a wry laugh. "I still can't get used to being called that. Please, call me Branagh. I can't bear it when my friends use my title."

"You didn't think you'd have to use it so soon," said Melle with a sad smile.

"True." Branagh put his teacup down and wiped his mouth with the back of his hand. Catching Melle's look, he sighed and picked up a napkin. "I was a soldier all my life. And then a recluse and a ranger," he explained to Tamara sotto voce.

"Not exactly Mr. Manners, I'm afraid," laughed Merlin. "But now that you've mentioned being a soldier, perhaps we can speak of what brings us all together."

Branagh nodded, his eyes suddenly flashing, and Tamara caught a glimpse of what made him king. "I have gathered my troops and they are waiting at my aunt's keep, near the border. My cousins have their troops as well and are on the move. It's the first time we've fought a winter battle, so most of the planning has involved supplies and fodder for the horses. That's why we've taken so long."

Llewellyn gave them the news from Frostbone, and a deep silence settled over the table.

Then Branagh shook himself and said, "That's bad news. Behemoths are almost as bad as dragons. That said, at least they don't fly or spit fire." His fingers drummed on the table. "Llewellyn, I want you to stay with the healers. I fear there will be great need for your talents. Tamara, are you a healer?"

She shook her head. "No, I'm a scout. If you need me, I know all the routes through our land north of Bald Pass. I can find passages for your mounted troops."

"All right. I accept your services. You will be promoted to captain, and I will assign a group of scouts and messengers to you." Branagh stood. "I have much to do before dawn breaks tomorrow. I would like to have the troops and supplies ready to move by the next full moon."

"Five days?" Melle sounded faint.

"Yes. Your archer troops are ready. The mounted archers, under Sebring, are ready. Now I have a scout. If Tamara leaves tomorrow with her team, they can guide us to Frostbone's territory faster than I'd hoped."

Tomorrow! Tamara felt her heart sink. She and Llewellyn were to be separated! She looked at Melle's white face and realized that most of the couples living in Hivernia were about to be split asunder by the war. Some would never see their spouse again. The d'ark t'uath had taught her the importance of duty and responsibility. She would not let Hivernia down.

Llewellyn's hand found hers beneath the table and they held tightly to each other. One more night together. And then, who knew when they would meet again? She did not worry for herself—a scout wasn't in the midst of fighting. And Llewellyn would be in the healing tents. They would get through this, and then start their life together.

"I was hoping to go home and do some cleaning," said Llewellyn, giving Sebring and Merlin a dirty look.

Branagh gave a short laugh, then shook his head. "I'm sorry about your honeymoon," he said. "If it's any comfort to you, Melle has given orders for dinner to be taken to your quarters. Why don't you take Tamara to your rooms? I'm sure you would like some time alone together before daybreak."

LLEWELLYN WAS GLAD TO get away. The look on Tamara's face when she'd realized she had to leave the next morning had pained him. He'd said nothing though. She knew her own worth, and Branagh's army was in desperate need of scouts who knew the lay of the land north of Bald Pass. Tamara was a godsend, and he could not begrudge her to his friend and king.

The room—or rooms, rather, as it was an apartment—were as Melle promised—quiet. Set apart in the old part of the castle, they were not in the fashionable wing. The apartment had a small vestibule where they hung their cloaks, a bedroom with a fire already laid, and a bathroom with a copper tub and hot and cold running water.

Llewellyn thought Tamara would appreciate that, but when he mentioned that she snapped at him, saying that the d'ark t'uath had hot and cold running water, thermal spring fed, and who did she think they were, barbarians?

"I'm sorry. I don't know much about your people," he told her. After a minute, when she didn't reply, he added, "You're not going to like my house much. I have to go fetch my water from a well and heat it in the chimney. I suppose I'm the barbarian."

She kept her back to him, fiddling with the taps, running first the hot water and then the cold. Her back spoke volumes to him. It said, "I'm tired. I'm not happy. I'm not a barbarian. I'm pissed at you."

"I'm sorry," he said.

She turned around and he saw he'd probably misread her. Again. Her face was pale and traces of tears marred her cheeks. "I'm not angry with you. I'm just a little overwhelmed, that's all." She bit her lip then blurted out, "We have hot and cold running water but our bathtubs are made of rock and they're not half as luxurious as this."

"Well, that's a relief," said Llewellyn, gathering her in his arms. "I was really afraid you'd hate our house."

She looked up at him. "You said our house. That's the first time you've called it that."

"It sounds right, doesn't it?" He had the absurd urge to laugh. It did sound right. His arms tightened around her, and she tipped her head up for a kiss. How could he resist? Somehow, in the middle of the kiss, they overbalanced and fell into the tub.

The water wasn't hot enough. Sputtering, Llewellyn pulled Tamara out and then, because she was laughing too hard to be of any help, he took her clothes off for her. He took his own off too. It was better when they were both nude, he decided. He pressed his body to hers. Her skin was so smooth and warm, and when they rubbed together he swore he could feel sparks. Her breasts brushed up and down his chest, and her nipples hardened. He closed his eyes, better to enjoy the sensation of her naked body against his. Their thighs pressed together and his cock, now hard, speared her in the stomach. She reached down and captured it in her hands, kneading and rubbing until his knees started to tremble. And then he caught sight of the mirror.

The full-length mirror showed two elves, one in a definite state of excitement, standing on a pile of wet clothes.

"Let's go to the bedroom," Tamara suggested. She glanced in

the mirror and raised her eyebrows. "The possibilities are endless, I agree."

"If you get down on your hands and knees and turn this way, I think the view will be . . . "

"Interesting. I've always wanted to see how I looked from the back and in the throes of an orgasm," Tamara said. Somehow Llewellyn didn't think she meant it.

"You don't have to look." He was wondering how he could get her on her hands and knees before he came all over her. His cock was so stiff he was afraid to touch it lest, like a popper-seed pod, it would explode. When he was young he'd liked playing with those seed pods. The gentlest touch made the pod burst apart and tiny seeds shoot forth.

Now he knew what that seed pod felt like.

Tamara knelt very slowly and gave a saucy wiggle with her buttocks. She put her chin on her shoulder to look over her back at the mirror and her eyebrows went even higher. "I didn't know I was so sexy from this angle," she purred.

Llewellyn wanted to move, but he didn't dare until he'd gotten better control of himself. Then Tamara spread her legs.

"Look, I'm all wet," she said in a hoarse whisper.

She was. Her sex glistened. His cock gave a twinge. Llewellyn took a deep breath. Getting down on his knees behind her, he was careful not to look in the mirror. When he slid his cock into her passage, he couldn't resist a glance to the side. A tall elf with an eye patch and rather unkempt, long black hair arched over a curvaceous elf with long dark hair and delightful breasts. As he watched, his hands crept up her sides and latched on to her breasts.

"Oh, go gently!" she said. Then, when he thrust his cock into her, "Go harder!"

He loved watching his cock slide in and out of her tight sheath. Things got more and more slippery and exciting. Her nipples brushing against his palms became hard little pebbles. Her back arched and she reached between her legs and touched his balls.

"Gently," he gasped. Her fingers massaged his balls in time to his thrusts, and in the mirror he saw that she was touching her own clit, rubbing her thumb against it.

He held off thrusting so he could watch that for a while. But his buttocks contracted of their own accord, sending his cock plunging back into her sex. Tamara let go of his balls and grabbed at her clit, arched her back even more, and a stream of music left her throat.

He joined her a second later, elf song bursting from his throat just as a jet of hot seed shot into Tamara's womb. He held on to her waist, his hips thrusting madly, their elf song rising in urgent harmony, then falling into a gentle duet.

And he caught sight of his face. Yes, men looked half dazed, half dim-witted when they came. He was glad to see Tamara had her eyes closed.

The bed was softer than he was used to, and so the night passed slowly. He didn't dare move though, for fear of waking Tamara. She'd been so exhausted she'd barely touched her dinner, and she would need her strength and rest. Somewhere in the wee hours she woke and clung to him and they made love again. This time softly and gently, like the smallest of waves breaking upon a calm shore. Their song was just a whisper in the night.

And then it was morning, and the trumpets sounded. Tamara and Llewellyn said their goodbyes in private. Neither knew when they would meet again, but no tears were shed. Now was the time for action and determination.

In the courtyard, Tamara's team of scouts and messengers was gathered. Llewellyn was glad to see that Merlin was part of her troop. Branagh and Melle were there to bid them farewell. They would be following with the bulk of the army within the week, if all went well and the weather held. The sky was gray and heavy with snow. But that would not stop them. After crossing Bald Pass, they would send news.

Tamara twisted around once on her horse to wave goodbye. Then she rode off and didn't look back. Llewellyn stood on the battlements until she was lost from sight. As her troop vanished, the first snowflakes began to fall.

Melle came to him and touched him lightly on the shoulder. "She is a remarkable woman."

Llewellyn nodded. He didn't need to tell Melle that he missed Tamara already. That seeing her ride away was like losing part of himself. She knew. In less than a week Melle would be leaving Branagh to join the archers, while Branagh would be at the head of his army, leading them all to battle.

The air grew colder as he stood there, and he realized the wind had turned and was out of the north. Everything, it seemed, was conspiring against them.

"I'm going to the supply captain to check that everything is set for the hospital tents."

"I'll see you for dinner tonight," said Melle. She pulled her cloak tighter around her shoulders. She too had noticed the change in wind. Her eyes, as they scanned the sky, were dark with concern.

Llewellyn made his way through the city. The people were subdued. They knew war was upon them. Their sons and husbands had armed themselves and prepared to leave. Winter solstice was near, the festive season. But not this year. This year the mistletoe and holly would go ungathered. Tinsel and lights would stay packed in their boxes. The solstice gifts would be practical and dangerous things this year—cloaks, bows and arrows, boots, swords, knives and love knots made of hair.

Until the Mouse King was defeated once and for all, war would once again haunt Hivernia. Llewellyn quickened his pace. The faster it was over, the faster he would be with Tamara. He sent a silent prayer to whatever gods might be listening, then, taking a deep breath, he knocked on the door to the supply room.

For him, for Hivernia, the second war against the Mouse King was about to begin.

NINE

The Scout

AMARA DIDN'T LOOK BACK. If she had, her heart would have broken. Instead, she gazed ahead between her horse's pricked ears and studied the landscape. The rising sun broke through the heavy cloud cover and sent shafts of pale apricot light through the gray air. But the light was cold, and flakes of snow began to drift through the air.

Merlin, on her left, was silent as well. Behind them, the troop he'd assembled rode without speaking. There were no words that would soften the day, or make the bleakness brighter. Everyone was alone with their thoughts. The only sounds were the steady clopping of the horses' hooves, and in the city, the ringing sound of the forges as the smiths hammered out swords and shields. The ringing would go on day and night now.

They left the city by the north gate and headed straight across winter-bare fields. And still Tamara didn't look back. Instead, she began to plot the easiest way to her tribe's valley, and then onward, ever north.

The plain seemed endless, but all too soon the forest was ahead and Tamara realized the sun was directly overhead. They had been riding for hours. She was glad they'd given her a calm, steady horse. Her riding skills were still rudimentary, and her legs and buttocks were starting to ache dreadfully. She sighed. Her horse was not tired, but she was, and hunger pinched her stomach. She was just about to call a halt when Merlin reined in his horse. They had barely entered the forest, and the plain behind them was just visible through the trees.

"Are we stopping to eat?" asked one of the troop members. Gavin, Tamara thought his name was. There were five of them and she had just met them that morning.

"No, someone is coming over the plains." Merlin got off his horse and drew his sword. "I don't know if it is friend or foe but our mission is secret, so we'd best hide. Go deeper into the forest and take the first path to the right. You'll find a grove of holly. Stay there and wait for me."

Tamara started to say something along the lines of "I don't take orders from a male," but she bit her tongue and nodded. Merlin and she were both leaders of this troop. He had taken charge this time.

"Come," she said to the men, and they galloped down the path.

The holly grove was dense, and the dark green thorny leaves made good cover. Red berries glowed brightly in the trees, making the scene look festive. Tamara knew holly was prized for many things, being hard and smooth grained. At another moment, she would be searching for branches to cut for arrows. But her heart wasn't in it. She fiddled with her horse's reins and wondered why

Merlin was taking so long. Surely he could turn away whatever meddlesome person had followed them. The group of men obviously thought along the same lines, because they started to wonder aloud what could be keeping Merlin.

Hoofbeats alerted her to someone approaching. She held her hand up for silence and the men behind her quieted. Merlin cantered into view, his expression unfathomable.

"What is it?" she said, then caught sight of two other riders, not far behind him. Her throat closed up. "Llewellyn," she managed to say.

"I SUPPOSE BRANAGH LET you go," said Merlin. They had made camp and were sitting around a small fire, grilling their meat on a skewer. This would be their only warm meal for the day. At night it would be too risky to light a fire.

"No. He wanted me to stay." Llewellyn looked bleakly at the fire, then smiled at Tamara. "I told him I'd be there for the first battle, that I'm not much use until the wounded start arriving. He finally agreed. It took Melle's intervention to convince him to let me go, however. Otherwise I wouldn't be here at all."

"What about you, Sebring? What's your excuse? Aren't you supposed to be with the archers?" Merlin didn't sound angry with his twin. Instead, Tamara heard relief in his voice.

"Well, you're supposed to be with the archers too, don't forget. Just because you're off on a vacation trip north . . . " Sebring's words trailed off and he gave a little cough. "I wanted to go with you at least part of the way to see for myself what was happening. My men are highly trained, we don't need to shoot arrows at targets. Actually, I told them all to go home, say their goodbyes and get ready for battle. Some of them hadn't been home in months."

"That was a wise move," said Llewellyn. "But some may not come back, you know."

"I know. It's a chance I had to take." Sebring shrugged. "I have a feeling my men will be waiting for me though. All of them."

Tamara's hand crept out and found Llewellyn's. "I'm glad you came," she said. It was incredible how light her heart felt now that he was here beside her. The war and all its possible horrors receded. Alone, she was just half a person now. But with Llewellyn she was complete.

"We're in this together, all of us," she said, and the men looked at her and nodded.

They ate lunch and were on their way before the hour had gone. The whole afternoon and evening would be spent riding, and then the night would be spent camped in the dark, hidden in some cold corner of the great woods. But she would have Llewellyn beside her, his cloak over her shoulders, his arms around her body, keeping her warm. Her cheeks grew hot at the thought and Llewellyn, riding beside her, gave a soft chuckle.

"I can read your thoughts," he said in a whisper.

"Then you know how much I love you," she said.

"I know how much I'm glad I came along." His horse jostled against hers, his knee brushing her leg. "I'm coming with you when you go to see your tribe. I'll speak to your clan mother myself. She'll listen to me because Branagh has given me a scroll for her. It will tell her the truth of what's going on. After we're done I'll take you with me to the healing tents and we'll stay together for the battle. All right?"

Llewellyn's presence might save her from the punishment of leaving the tribe. Her clan mothers were not stupid. Such a great threat meant they had to join forces with Hivernia. Tamara thought of her kinswomen, who would certainly be fighting alongside Branagh's troops. But she knew Llewellyn would be mad with worry if she fought in the battle. "All right," she said. And at those words, she knew her fate was sealed. They would stay together. It was meant to be. As the sun dipped below the trees and the forest grew dark she knew she'd made the right decision. She and Llewellyn would be together for all time.

Arctic Dragon

DELILAH DEVLIN

ONE

A BLANKET OF FRESH POWDER muffled his footsteps. For a moment, the bitter cold wind died down. The stillness invited him deeper into the clearing. Something in the air alerted him, an intuition that was part of his true nature told him to wait.

Wind had blown snow against large tree trunks, forming deep banks where the tall green sentinels stood close together. Everywhere pure, pristine white dusted the tops of branches, cloaking them in rich, thick wonder. Precious sunlight peeked from behind a dark gray cloud and refracted like a billion tiny prisms on frozen crystals that gilded the uppermost layer of the snow.

His breaths seemed loud, intrusive and he concentrated on being quiet so that he didn't disturb—not that anyone would hear him this deep in the wilderness.

Rather, all was hushed, expectant. Quiet like he preferred now. Content at last with his own company.

The first few months had been the worst. The silence had nearly driven him nuts. Now, he barely noticed. Sounds other than voices, the hum of electricity or the roar of a passing engine were replaced with softer, more predictable ones—the rustle of pine needles as a breeze swept through outstretched branches, the resonant creaking when snow weighed the branches down. The rustle of animals as they scratched in the snow for food.

The voices inside his head had also faded. The strident ones that had called him a freak and the startled screams—well, they couldn't reach him here.

If he missed the company of a woman—so be it. Other parts of his existence flourished in the solitude. *Almost* filling the aching void. The decision he'd made had been the right one. He'd spend the rest of his life—however long—alone.

Do no harm.

He lived by that rule now. At least in regard to people.

For now, he had a stew pot to fill, and he'd tracked a lone deer through the forest to this spot. A soft snort, and he found the doe digging with her hooves to uncover whatever she could still forage beneath the snow.

Drake tugged off his mittens and raised his rifle, setting the stock snug against his shoulder. He had the doe in his sights and slowly pulled back on the trigger, when an unexpected tinkling sound, like bells carried on the wind, drew his attention. His gaze strayed for only a moment. As his attention returned to his quarry, a sudden icy wind swept up snow, obscuring his view.

The shadow of the deer still in his scope, he pulled the trigger, jerking the barrel upward at the last moment when he realized he wasn't looking at a doe at all—but a woman on a bay-colored horse!

The shot went wild, but the horse gave a high-pitched whinny and reared, dumping the woman to the ground before bolting.

Drake threw down his rifle, swearing silently as he clomped on unwieldy snowshoes toward the figure lying like a spill of red paint against a white canvas. Her fur-lined scarlet cloak fanned around her slender body. He knelt in its folds to reach for the woman who had yet to open her eyes.

He ran his hands over her body, checking for broken limbs, cursing himself for a horndog for noting generous curves beneath her dark gold gown. But it had been a long time since soft curves had yielded beneath his palms. Not much in the way of padded layers of clothing protected her from his inspection, just the soft fabric. What in hell was she doing wearing a costume in the wilderness in winter, even one made of heavy velvet?

Finally, she stirred, moaning softly.

He sat back on his haunches, noticing at last the luster of her mink brown hair and brows and the thick lashes that fanned the rims of her delicate eyelids. They fluttered then lifted, revealing gold flecked brown eyes.

Struck by her beauty, he stared. Her eyes were wide set and large; her nose elegant and straight. The shape of her face was slightly triangular with a small chin that took no attention away from the sweet curves of her soft, plump mouth.

"Who are you?" she asked, with a voice as light and sweet as the bells he thought he'd heard before.

He shook his head to clear away his lustful thoughts. "The idiot who nearly shot you," he said, his own voice thick and rusty from disuse. He cleared his throat. "Can you move? Are you hurt?"

"I'm fine, I think."

"What the hell were you doing out here?"

She gave him a distracted frown. "Riding." Then rising on her elbows, she glanced around her, blinking. "My horse, Windancer . . . "

"He bolted when I fired."

Her confused stare returned to him. "He's gone?" Her eyes widened until the white surrounded the brown iris. "We must find him."

No "I must find him." She'd included him, without even wondering if it was wise.

Snow had begun to fall again—thick, fat flakes that swirled in the rising wind, a blast of arctic chill. Knowing it was the wrong thing to do, but seeing no other choice, he said, "I'll look for him after the snowfall ends. We need to get you inside."

Oh hell. He'd have to take her to his place. Something he'd sworn he'd never do. She might not be any safer there. He'd lived alone too long. With her lush beauty, she was too much of a temptation.

Her mouth opened, but then closed, her lips forming a thin line. "I have to find my horse. I can't stay here," she said, casting a wild glance around them.

"In a few minutes, we won't see more than a few feet in front of us. A storm's coming in."

"You don't understand—"

Although, it was the last thing he should do, he held out his hand. "Come. We'll talk later. *After* I get you out of the cold."

LARIKKE STARED IN DISMAY. She couldn't go home with him. *They'd be alone.* Her, alone with a human? Unthinkable! Humans were so short-lived and violent. *Think of the scandal it would cause!*

"We'll both freeze if we don't get out of this weather," he said slowly, as though speaking to a child—one not so very bright.

Only she knew she wouldn't. Freeze, that is. This is what she got for her stubborn bid for freedom. Stranded in a wild land— *with a man.* Her mage would no doubt cluck like a hen when she recounted the tale of how she'd ridden the wind and landed on her backside in a snowbank before a human as handsome as any damnable frost faerie.

She'd only wanted to put Thure firmly in his place. Remind him who was in charge of her destiny—that she had a will of her own.

And maybe to inspire him to anger and to let go of the firm hold he kept over himself whenever they were together. She wanted to see the powerful male beneath his princely trappings.

Rather like the prime specimen before her.

Oh, why couldn't this human have been as hairy as a polar bear? Or as ugly as a walrus? Oh no! His eyes were a crystalline blue. His hair was silvery blond and fell well past his broad shoulders. Clean-shaven, his jaw was sharp-edged and strong. His brows, although drawn together in a fierce frown, were full and nicely shaped but hooded piercing eyes. Despite the layers of clothing he wore, she could tell his frame was tall and thickly muscled.

The few humans she'd met long ago, thickheaded and thick-bodied warriors stopping on their journey to Valhalla, didn't compare. A crude, ungifted species, they'd never aroused much interest. But this one, with his rumbling voice and burly frame, nearly stole her breath away.

Perhaps she was simply addled by her spill. Or maybe she was just feeling the familiar, deepening need for something different from her prescribed future—something wicked and deplorably *wrong*. She cleared her throat. "I must insist we find my horse."

He rolled his eyes and tugged her to her feet. Then before she could brush away the snow clinging to her mantle and give him the setdown he deserved for daring to handle her so familiarly, he bent and swept her over his shoulder.

Larikke's mouth gaped. Now, this was a view of the world she'd never seen. Upside down, suspended on the shoulder of a barbarian, several long moments passed before she could gather the breath to do more than sputter in feigned outrage—for his rough handling of her person was . . . intriguing. "What do you think you're doing?" she gasped.

"What you haven't the sense to do yourself," he grumbled, as he trudged through the snow.

Blood rushed to her head and *temporarily* northern parts, filling her with a breathless expectancy—something the prince of the frost Faeries had never managed to do with his polite wooing. Larikke gave a huff, but didn't bother to struggle against his firm hold.

Instead, she brought her fingers to her mouth and issued a piercing whistle. The expected whinny never came. Could Windancer truly have deserted her? Was he even now making his way back to the palace without her? Gudvin would have his guts for garters!

Well, there was only one thing to do. Since she was truly at his mercy, she might as well play nice. Pressing her hand against his lower back, she arched up. "I accept your hospitality, sir. You may put me down now."

"We're already there," he said, his voice deliciously gruff. He set her on her feet next to what looked like a snub-nosed metal sled.

"It looks as though you've lost your horses too," she sniffed.

His startled gaze landed on her.

She shrugged. "You really should have let me wait for my horse. He'd have no trouble pulling your little sled."

Proving his barbarian pedigree, he grunted. "Climb on." He pointed to a leather saddle atop the odd conveyance.

Only to humor him, Larikke gathered her clothing and clumsily straddled the sled then tugged her skirts to straighten them around her. When she glanced up, he shook his head.

"What?"

"Scoot back."

When she hesitated, he swung his leg wide, climbing over the sled, just behind its steering handles, then he pressed backward, nearly sitting in her lap. Larikke slid as far back as the seat would allow, but still found her front plastered to his back—and her thighs snug alongside his.

Before she could voice an objection to his proximity, the conveyance roared to life, jerking forward, and then skimming over the snow fast as a seal in water. Hastily, she grasped for something to hold on to, her hands sliding around his waist to grip him hard.

She pressed her cheek against his shoulder and squeezed shut her eyes as they sped past trees that blurred the faster they went. Just when she was beginning to enjoy the heat of his body pressed close to hers and the vibrating rumble between her legs, the sled hurtled over a crest and left the ground, only to land with a thud on the far side before speeding away again.

The idiot would kill them both! Her immortality seemed a mite more finite by the second. "Will you please slow down?" she shouted above the roar of the invisible horses.

"Already there," he said, this time sounding suspiciously smug.

"You said that before," she muttered.

The sled slowed, and then drew to a smooth halt.

Larikke peeked around his shoulder to find they'd stopped in front of a rough log cabin. "I was wrong. Not a human. A troll," she muttered.

"What did you say?"

"Never mind. I assume this is our destination?"

He climbed off the sled and looked at her expectantly.

She stared, wondering when he'd offer her a hand. When he didn't appear to take the hint, she decided to outwait his bad manners and gathered her skirts, willing strength into her trembling legs.

"For fucksake." The blond barbarian bore down on her, his hands outstretched.

Larikke squealed when he gripped her waist and lifted her from her seat. He deposited her next to the sled and raised one eyebrow. His message was clear. He'd carry her again if she refused to move along.

Gathering her considerable pride, Larikke gave the invisible horses a wide berth and headed toward the house, now only a looming shadow behind the whirling white snow.

She realized with a start that the pale sunlight waned. The day had been short, but not surprisingly so, given how close to Northland they were. Would anyone at home even notice she was missing?

Nearer the door, she saw the outline of figures lining a pathway in the snow. Sentries? Around a hovel? Only when she drew nearer she realized they were encased in ice, their skin, hair and clothing translucent. *Frozen solid!*

Was he a powerful mage? She darted a glance over her shoulder and found him alarmingly close. Would he enslave her thusly if she didn't do as he bid? Thinking she may have been captured by a very *gifted* creature indeed, she was surprised she wasn't more afraid.

Then again, he'd thought only of her safety. Her comfort. He'd brought her out of the cold to rescue her after all. Not that she really needed rescuing. Only he didn't know that, did he? He had no clue as to her identity. If he knew, what would he do? Ransom her to the frost faeries? She shivered at the thought.

Thure would expect a large reward in return—rule over her kingdom. Her flight into the arctic wind had been to escape his attentions in the first place.

The barbarian mage reached around her, thumbed the latch on the crude wooden door and swung it open. Dark as a cave inside except for the red embers of a smoldering fire in a hearth, the cabin smelled pleasantly of wood smoke and a strong pine scent she couldn't place. She waited patiently while he shut the door behind them, dropping a board into a brace to lock them inside.

"I'll get the fire going. Make yourself comfortable," he said, roughly, not looking her way.

She strode farther inside, surprised to find the room larger than she had originally thought. As he lit lanterns on the table and above the mantel, she took stock of her surroundings. Thick braided wool rugs in a riot of vibrant colors covered the floor. Deep-cushioned leather couches flanked the fireplace. Dark cupboards, shining from a fresh application of beeswax, reflected the warming glow of the fire. A cozy room despite the cabin's rustic exterior.

However, what drew her fascinated gaze were the paintings gracing the crude log walls. In colors deep and vivid, they depicted nude women, lying atop disheveled beds and green meadows on coverlets of crimson, royal blue and yellows as vivid as the rare roses her winged suitor brought her during the midnight sun. The colors were alive, sensual, the whirling textures of the paint itself drawing her to touch, but the poses of the women disturbed her.

Legs splayed wide, palms cupping generous breasts, fingers sliding into glistening sexes. Her body stirred at the images as she imagined them tempting the barbarian with their naked flesh. Arousal rose swift and urgent inside her.

Had she landed in the lair of a mage who used sex magicks? The thought should have horrified her, but she'd seen proof of his powers in the sentries guarding the door. How else could she explain her response to the pictures and to him? She should have been horrified—or at the very least deeply embarrassed.

A footfall behind her made her stiffen.

"Let me take your cloak," he said, his voice gruff.

"Will you enslave me in ice?" she asked, glancing warily over her shoulder.

His eyebrows drew together in a frown, and his gaze swept over her. "Enslave you?" he asked, tilting his head.

"Like the poor creatures guarding your door."

"Damn." Suddenly, he gripped her shoulder to turn her toward him. Then he reached for the frog closures at the top of her cloak and plucked them open. He slid the cloak off her shoulders to let it fall to the floor.

She found herself being pulled toward the fire, but his hands didn't stop their wicked work. "Stop that!" she said, swatting at his dexterous fingers as they made quick work of the buttons at the neck and along the side of her gown.

"I won't harm you," he said, between tight lips. "You're suffering from hypothermia. Your dress is wet. I need to get you out of it."

"Hypothermia?" What was he saying? "Is that a curse?"

"It will be if we don't get you out of those clothes and warm," he said, his voice steady, but roughening.

Had he already used his magick? She was certainly growing warmer by the moment. Allowing him to finish stripping away her gown, she stood in front of him with the fire warming her backside.

His intent expression didn't fill her with alarm. Instead, a glowing warmth from within left her breathless. What did he see when the soft undertunic slid to the floor? How did she compare with the women mounted on his wall?

He knelt and skimmed down her thin stockings, making a disapproving noise. "These won't keep you very warm." He pushed them to her feet and removed them along with her slippers, then slowly stood.

Finally nude, she shivered in anticipation of what he'd do next.

His gaze slid quickly over her, his cheeks reddening—but he turned and swept up a throw from one of the couches and drew it over her shoulders. "I guess you're fine. Your skin's warm enough."

Her skin prickled and she shrugged off the throw, letting it sift to the floor. "It itches."

"It's wool," he said, his jaw tightening. "It'll keep you warm until your clothing dries."

She wrinkled her nose. "It itches."

One eyebrow rose. "You'd rather be naked?"

She drew a pillow from the sofa and sat on it before the fire, wrapping her arms around her knees, pretending his presence didn't trip her heartbeat.

He sighed. "I'll take that as a yes." His feet shifted on the floor beside her.

She stretched her legs, lifting her toes toward the fire and studied the way the firelight limned her legs, all the while aware of his gaze sweeping their length like a heated caress. Did she dare give in to temptation? Shouldn't she fight his seductive allure?

He drew a ragged breath.

She glanced up and found his dark gaze roaming her body, landing on her legs, sliding upward to her hips. She tossed back her hair and let him stare at her bared breasts.

"Would you mind if I sketched you?" he asked softly.

Her glance darted toward the paintings. Is this how he seduced the women? First, he captured their souls on canvas? She remembered his roughness as he'd forced her over his shoulder, his strength when he'd lifted her from the sled. He'd brooked no argument from her. Would he be the same way when he came over her in lust?

Thure's lovemaking had been gentle. He'd treated her respectfully, even when he thrust inside her, begging her first for the

privilege. Somehow, she knew this barbarian wouldn't be as def-
erential toward her rank. The thought of just how ungentlemanly
he would be had her breasts tightening and a heated glaze seeping from her pussy.

"I won't mind," she whispered, holding his hot gaze.

He turned away, striding stiffly toward a cabinet in the corner and drew out a thick sheaf of paper and black sticks. Setting
them on one of the leather couches, he unbuttoned his jacket and
shrugged out of it, then rolled up the sleeves of his red shirt.

Larikke forced her stare back to the fire and tried to relax as
he scratched the paper with the black sticks. She'd never watched
a man create a painting—only seen the finished products which
the faerie folk traded for in the faraway land. Her gaze lifted to
one of the paintings, this one of a woman with her head thrown
back, her teeth buried in her lower lip. She looked pained, but
Larikke recognized the source as passion.

Thure was skilled and had brought her a gentle release a time
or two, but she'd often yearned for something a little wilder. She
wanted to be swept outside herself, frightened by the power of
her desire.

Perhaps this interlude was her chance to taste true freedom
from the expectations placed upon her. Soon, Gudvin would
know she'd not returned from her ride. He'd mount a rescue,
scouring her usual trails. When those proved futile, he'd search
his golden orb to locate her.

She couldn't stay here. But she might use the time spent here
to learn her true nature—and explore the passion that even now
rose up to cause her breaths to catch and her nipples to swell.

The scratching paused. "Would you touch yourself?"

Larikke blinked. If she did something so decadent, could she tempt him to show her his barbarian side? "Like her?" she asked, tilting her chin toward the painting.

He shook his head. "Do what pleases you."

She dipped her head, embarrassed she didn't really know what that might be. "I'm not sure . . ."

"Start with your breasts, then."

TWO

*D*RAKE HELD HIS BREATH as she tossed back her dark hair and fitted her palms to her breasts, lifting them and squeezing. His fingers tightened around the charcoal he held, and it snapped.

He couldn't believe she'd agreed to model. One moment she'd been as haughty as a princess, defiantly naked, then her avid gaze had sought his paintings and he'd sensed a softening. Awareness crackled in the air between them, so palpable his body hardened, his cock swelling uncomfortably inside his pants.

Her round little ass was perched on his pillow, her toes pointing toward the fire. He could imagine the heat warming her feet and the inside of her thighs—and knew how that heat would feel wrapped around his waist as he drove inside her.

But he'd promised her he wouldn't hurt her.

So he picked up another charcoal stick and concentrated on capturing the soft curve of her chin as she stared down at her breasts, the graceful indent of her trim waist, the fullness of her hips and thighs.

Her fingers splayed on her breasts and pink nipples peeked from between them, making his mouth go dry.

"Pluck your nipples," he heard himself say in a gruff voice.

Her teeth nibbled her bottom lip, but she complied with his request, twirling the tips of her breasts between her thumbs and forefingers, and then releasing them. Apparently not satisfied with the result, she tugged her erect little nipples, stretching them, and then stared again as their color deepened from pink to a lush berry. Her gaze swung over to him. "What else?"

He swallowed to wet his dry mouth and looked down at his notepad, realizing he hadn't added a line since she started playing with her nipples. "Angle yourself toward me. Let me see between your legs." Why had he asked that? It was pure torture looking at her ripe curves. Would she really let him look at her pussy?

She rose on her knees and placed her hands in front of her on the braided rug as she rearranged her legs. Her round breasts swayed then shimmied as she seated herself again, this time her legs pointed toward him—just three feet away.

Her eyelids fell to half-mast and her hands cupped her breasts, hiding them. Then she slowly parted her legs, bending her knees to tilt up her hips, just enough to let him stare at the part of her he craved most.

Moisture glinted on her cunt, the opening framed so beautifully by dainty pink inner lips.

"Lean back. Rest on your elbows," he rasped, flipping to the next sheet of his pad.

She lay back, her breasts flattening with the change of position. She seemed to intuit exactly what he wanted to ask next when she tilted her pussy higher.

He drew her sex—just the soft curve of her inner thigh and the lush little lips, using bold lines to trace the sweet curves and light little strokes to capture the whirls of her dark pubic hair.

When he tore his gaze from her cunt, he caught her staring at him, her eyes glossy and wide, her nostrils flared as though scenting him for arousal.

The pad hid his rampant erection, so he took a deep breath and narrowed his gaze in warning. "I won't fuck you, you know."

"Why not?" she asked, her tone curious rather than insulted.

"Less complicated." True, but not the whole truth.

"You don't want to fuck me?"

He snorted, and continued to fill in her parted thighs and the deep shadow that hid her back entrance.

"So, you would like to fuck me," she murmured. "I wonder why you won't."

"Less co—"

"Complicated. I know." She fell silent.

"You could use your fingers," he murmured. "I'd like to watch that."

"Why not use yours?"

He held up the charcoal.

"I see." She drew a deep breath and shifted to rest on one hand. Her head tilted and a slight smile curved the corners of her lips. "Perhaps you would like to guide me? Tell me how to proceed?"

The little witch was teasing him? With her legs open and her pussy oozing honey, she already had him so hard he could barely think past the throb building between his legs. Knowing he shouldn't sink any deeper into lust—for her own good—he bit out, "Comb through your curls."

With the hand she'd freed, she smoothed her fingers over her lower belly, then threaded them into her short dark curls, tugging and combing over her mons, then lower to finger the hairs edging her outer lips.

"Dip a finger inside your pussy."

Her breath gasped, but her index finger slid into her cunt and stilled.

She hadn't shied away from the coarse words. Her cheeks were pink, but her lips parted. She was aroused. "Pretend your fingers are a cock and fuck them in and out."

She didn't shy away from this request either. Her fingers trembled and swirled around her opening, then sank inside, disappearing into her fragrant, juicy cunt. Her eyes closed as her fingers slid in and out. She strained to reach deeper, sinking her fingers to the top of her palm, then out—this time the action was accompanied by moist succulent sounds from the juices she stirred.

Drake's cock poked at the pad on his lap, and he gave up trying to hide his erection. With a sinking feeling in his stomach, he realized he couldn't resist her invitation. He'd been lying to himself when he thought he could look, but not touch.

He couldn't touch without burying himself inside her either. He placed his papers beside him and knelt in front of her.

Her eyelids still at half-mast and her mouth pouting, she spread her legs wider. "Touch me," she pleaded.

He held her gaze. "We do this my way."

She nodded quickly. "Anything you want. Just please come inside me."

He wanted nothing more than to lean over her, press her to the floor and cover her with his whole body. He wanted to kiss her plump lips and lose himself in her warmth and sweet woman scent. But that path led to dangers she could never imagine.

Instead, he reached for one soft, pink foot and brought it to his mouth.

Her eyes widened, curiosity burning in her gaze. When he sucked her big toe into his mouth she gasped, releasing a nervous laugh.

He let go of her toe with an audible pop. "Ticklish?"

"No. Surprised," she replied, her voice thin and high.

Feeling challenged, he licked the sole of her foot with the point of his tongue.

This time she jerked. "Yes!"

"I thought so."

"Don't torture me."

"Never my intent," he lied. He cupped her heel, clasping her toes with his other hand and licked his way along the top of her foot, turning it to follow the inside of her ankle.

The arch of her leg as it pointed outward drew apart her thighs, opening her cunt. The dark pink flesh beckoned him closer and he trailed his tongue up her thigh, stopping to suckle the tender flesh of her thigh as she wriggled and sighed.

Closer now to her center, he trailed a hand up her other thigh as he continued to lay soft, wet kisses until his hands and his mouth met the plump outer lips. The fresh scent of her tempted him, but he didn't dare use his mouth there, so he suckled her lips and slipped a finger into her moist channel, gliding inward, twisting, raking his knuckle on her inner wall.

"Please, more!" she said, resting a heel on the back of his shoulder.

"Let me pleasure you," he whispered, thumbing her swelling clit.

"Anything, please!" she groaned. She reached down and gripped his hair, trying to pull his face closer to the juncture of her thighs, but he turned his head and nipped her wrist.

"My way," he warned, his voice thickening. When she let him go, he used one hand to spread her lips wide and thrust three fingers into her.

Her thighs quivered and fell wider apart, her head rolled on the rug back and forth as her breath quickened. The soft, creamy undersides of her breasts trembled as the nipples peaked toward the ceiling above them.

He thrust deep, twisting to tunnel into her, searching for the little spot of nerves deep inside her vagina, finding it when she cried out and stiffened.

Pulling out he curled his thumb into his palm and curved all his fingers and slowly inserted his hand into her, not stopping when she whimpered or when she moaned she couldn't take any more.

Drake didn't believe her because she lifted her hips to pump up and down, helping him screw inside, circling, stretching around him until he found her G-spot again and scraped his knuckles there again and again.

Her scream was thin, reedy, and died softly as she sobbed, spasming around him, clasping him tight with her inner muscles, and he knew he had to be inside her, had to feel her convulse like that around his cock.

He dragged his hand out, and squeezed her hips. "Turn around and get on your knees," he said, his voice harsh with the arousal that burgeoned at the front of his pants. He was painfully hard and full.

She rolled over and braced herself on her hands. Her body quivered as she widened her knees and let her belly sink enough to lift her buttocks, offering herself to him.

Then he remembered and groaned. "I don't have any protection."

"I won't harm you," she said, her words choppy and breathless. "I promise. My pussy hasn't any teeth."

A laugh at her wit caught him unawares. He tried again. "I don't want to impregnate you."

"Oh. Well, you can't. So, don't worry."

Although he knew better, he couldn't resist. He'd been too long without a woman, and this one was a fantasy come to life. Maybe that was it. He'd been alone so long, he'd finally lost his mind.

Quickly, he removed his shirt, pulled off the long-sleeved undershirt beneath it and tossed them to the side.

Next, he toed off his boots, unbuckled his pants and shucked the rest of his clothing, all the while aware of her curious, heated stare as she peered over her shoulder. Her gaze rested on his cock as he crawled back to her and her lips parted around a wheezing gasp.

"Change your mind?" he asked.

She shook her head. "Surprised, again," she said, the sound strangling in her throat. Then she turned to stare straight ahead.

He ran his hands from her shoulders, smoothing over her back, cupping the curves of her full hips, finally caressing the soft mounds of her ass. This he could kiss.

He leaned over her and glided wet kisses over her bottom, smiling when she squirmed and jerked. She tried to tempt him lower with her wriggling, but he held her firmly in his grip and swept his lips over her generous curves.

Her skin was scented with a perfume he found hard to describe. Fresh, with hints of glacial ice and a tincture of coniferous tree. She smelled like a sunny arctic day. He found he preferred it to the floral scents of the many women he remembered.

As her arousal grew, another scent arose—a light musk, as unusual as her perfume. He trailed a finger down the crevice between her buttocks, stopping only a moment to tease her little asshole, then lower to take the glaze from her pussy lips. He brought his finger to his mouth and tasted, then tasted the rest of his fingers, eating her arousal.

He realized his mistake as her flavor exploded on his tongue. Again, a wintry blend of pine nuts and glacial ice, and a musk so refreshing he couldn't resist burying his mouth against her cunt. He'd be quick, coat his tongue with her taste and move away.

Only she sighed and her shoulders dipped until her breasts met the carpet. Her ass tilted higher, giving him maximum access to her pussy. He stroked his tongue inside, closing his eyes at the rush of arousal that sped through him, hardening him unbelievably more. He lapped and dipped, stroking, tasting—all the while tightening his grip since she was trembling again and her knees might go at any moment.

When he felt a trembling deep in his own belly, he jerked back his head and drew deep breaths, seeking calm, seeking to slow his heart and hold back his breath from her.

He wanted more, but he couldn't risk taking her with his mouth. Not full on.

"Why did you stop?" she said, a note of complaint in her breathy voice.

"I wanted to slow down," he said, telling her only part of the truth.

"Well, I don't want it slow."

He slipped his hands between her legs and smoothed them up her inner thighs. "Do you always get what you want from men?"

"Of course," she said, squirming.

He had no doubts she told the truth. Her hair was a cloud of deep, glossy brown against creamy shoulders. Her skin was a pale, unblemished cream all over her body. Her woman's parts were a deep pink that flushed to a darker raspberry when aroused. What man wouldn't be inspired to watch her colors deepen?

His fingers slid higher, cupping her outer lips. He thumbed the hood covering her clitoris, finding her little knot nicely erect. He risked a quick stroke of his tongue there, curving over it, washing it with the flat of his tongue, until he groaned and pulled back again.

To stave off her next complaint, he pushed a finger inside her cunt, all the way past the last knuckle, savoring the way her inner muscles clasped him, urging him deeper. She was well stretched, ready to accept every inch of his length and girth.

Her knees widened—her invitation clear. She was his for the taking, however he pleased.

So many things would please him, but he settled on a hard fucking—it had been too damn long, and his body was rigid. His balls cramped. He thrust three fingers into her, stretching her more, drawing down a fresh wash of moisture to coat her channel, and then he was finished preparing her. Done with trying to be a gentleman. He had to have her.

He pulled out his hand and ran his wet fingers over her bottom, then clasped the firm globes with both his palms and squeezed hard—as much of a warning as he could manage.

"Oh please," she moaned and dropped her forehead to the floor.

He straightened, coming up behind her, nudging her knees farther apart, opening her fully to him. His hands swept her thighs and over her ass, then slid between her legs to open her sex.

His cock bumped against her entrance before finding her center, and then he thrust forward, a harsh, deep thrust that forced the breath from her in a gasp. Her cunt closed around him—wet, hot, clasping. He couldn't hold back the rush of elation another second longer. "Fuck, yeah!"

With a deep groan, he pulled out and hammered back inside, sliding into her snug channel, tunneling forward, then pulling back and pushing forward again. His hips flexed as he powered deep, harder, faster, until the muscles of his ass burned and his breaths quickened.

Both stayed silent except for their harsh breaths. They pounded against each other—her buttocks quivering as she slammed against him, his cock lengthening, thickening, filling her swelling flesh until they felt locked together.

His balls tightened, and he tried to hold off his release, wanted to bring her with him, but his control slipped and a rush of thick, hot fluid jetted from his cock. However, he kept up the movements as his release crested then waned, not wanting to rob her of her second release.

The woman writhing beneath him whimpered and moaned, then suddenly flung back her head and cried out, her whole body stiffening.

When her cunt convulsed around his shaft, he groaned in satisfaction. His eagerness hadn't stolen her reward—and she felt as incredible squeezing tightly around him as he'd imagined. He wrapped an arm around her waist and held her up as he continued to slide in and out, more gently now, milking her excitement until she drooped limply, her breaths shaking her shoulders as she dragged in deep gulps of air. Her cunt relaxed and he slid easily from inside her, already missing her heat.

Already wondering when he could have her again.

He took her to the floor, fitting her back to his belly, caressing her soft, rounded belly and breasts as their heartbeats slowed.

He risked a kiss, pressing his lips against her bare shoulder.

The back of her head snuggled against his shoulder, and she let loose a deep sigh. "Will you finish the picture?" she asked, a smile in her voice.

Glad he'd pleased her and that she wanted more, he replied, "Will you pose for me again?"

"How do you want me this time?"

"On your back with your eyes closed. Your legs wide open."

"Give me a few moments to recover. And I'll need to clean up."

"Please don't."

"I'm . . . messy."

"That's what I want to capture. To remember how wet you are. How swollen."

Her laughter was soft, sexy—embarrassed. "You made me this way."

"Exactly."

"I'm feeling aroused again."

"I take a little longer." He kissed the small spot behind her earlobe.

"Then this will work?"

"Work?" Not sure he understood, but hoping.

"You can 'capture' me on paper. Then when I can't stand it a second longer, you will take me, yes?"

His hold on her breast tightened. "Is this what you want?"

"As long as the storm holds out. Yes."

His chest expanded. This beautiful woman wanted more of him. Wasn't frightened by his roughness. He wouldn't dwell on their parting. For now, she was his. So long as he kept the monster inside him at bay. So long as the storm swirled around them.

LARIKKE WAS ACCUSTOMED TO having people everywhere, constantly underfoot seeing to her needs, but she'd always felt isolated by their constant fawning and deference—kept apart by her rank. Even the prince who wooed her kept her on a pedestal.

With this barbarian mage, she'd never felt more like a real woman. Any woman.

Not a queen.

She raised her arm above her head and laid it on the pillow beneath her, knowing he watched how the shape of her breast changed and captured it with his black sticks.

His gaze rested there a moment, and then dropped again to

his paper. A frown drew his thick brows together, making him look like one of the fierce warring men who'd stopped along the way on their journey to their paradise deep in the heavens.

This man lived alone. Why? Where were the many women whose faces and luscious bodies graced his walls?

"What is your name?" Funny, she hadn't thought to ask him sooner.

His gaze rose to hers and a slight smile curved one corner of his lips. "Just realize we haven't traded introductions?"

Her own lips curved, and her glance slid shyly away. Her legs were spread wide, her sex fully exposed, but she hadn't felt embarrassed until she remembered how little she really knew about him. What a brazen woman she was! "Your name?" She repeated her request. She wanted to know, so that she'd have a name to put with the memory she'd keep.

"Drake. Yours?" he asked softly.

"Larikke."

"Larikke," he repeated slowly, seeming to savor the sound. "That's an unusual name."

She shrugged. "I never thought about it."

"How are you feeling?" he asked, his glance dropping to her breast again and sliding lower. "Are you cold?"

"Never."

"Never?" One pale eyebrow rose.

"I've always lived in a cold region," she demurred, keeping her response vague. Northland wasn't known to those of this realm after all.

"Do you have someone waiting for you?"

"Do you mean a lover?" she said, her tone teasing.

"Or a husband?" His voice held an edge of tension. "Just asking. Since we never got around to introductions and life stories."

"Do you think I'd be here, like this, if I had a husband waiting for me?"

His enigmatic gaze seemed to gather heat. His jaw sharpened.

All this talk of husbands aroused him. Was he jealous at the thought?

She decided to prick at him. "I have a suitor."

"A suitor?"

"Someone who wishes to wed me."

His glance fell to the paper. The hand holding the stick stilled over the pad. "Do you love him?" he asked, his tone deceptively even.

"No." *And I never will.*

"Do you sleep with him?"

Larikke nearly smiled. That he asked the question meant he cared. "Do I fuck him is what you mean."

"Yes," he ground out. "Do you fuck him?"

"Sometimes. He's very, very gentle. Very respectful."

His breaths deepened, raising his bare chest. "Is that how you like it?"

She waited a long moment, teasing him. "You know what I like," she finally drawled.

His chest expanded. "Does he know he doesn't fully satisfy you?"

"How can he? I never knew I wanted something . . . rougher. Until you."

He swallowed, and the muscle along his jaw flexed. "I've finished with this sketch."

Feigning innocence, she asked, "How do you want me now?"

THREE

HIS EYES BURNED OVER her skin, like a tanner etching leather. "Stretched across my bed," he rasped.

Larikke's own breaths deepened. Imagining it already. In his bed. Under him. His lips suckling her breasts, kissing her mouth.

She wanted so badly to taste his kiss.

Cupping a breast, she lifted it. "Where is this bed?"

"Behind you," he said, tilting his chin toward the couch. "I don't pull it out often, when it's just me." He placed the papers on a table and stood.

Not understanding, but curious, she accepted his hand and let him pull her to her feet. He grabbed one end of the couch and lifted it, angling it in front of the fire. Then he tossed the seat cushions to the floor and tugged the bottom of the seat, unfolding a mattress.

Smiling, she clapped her hands. "How wonderful!"

His head tilted and a quizzical expression crossed his face. "Never seen a sofa bed before?"

She shook her head.

"Never seen a sofa bed. Or a snowmobile," his deep voice rumbled. He pulled back the corner of the sheet covering the thin mattress. "Now the question is whether you want the fire warming your toes or your head."

"My toes, I think." Without an invitation she climbed into the center of the mattress and flopped back, spreading wide her arms. "This feels heavenly."

"You act as though you've never slept in a bed."

"Don't be silly. I've never slept in a bed *with you*."

His expression looked mollified—his eyebrows arching as though he never had any doubt of his superiority. "I need you on your knees."

Disappointment knifed through her. "Can't you come over me . . . like this?"

He hesitated. "I can't kiss you."

She didn't ask why, fearing he'd change his mind completely about taking her. "Can you take my breasts in your mouth?"

His head jerked down. A yes, she supposed.

What was it about his mouth? Was his breath rotten? A more terrible thought occurred. Was hers? She clamped her lips closed.

Standing at the end of the bed, firelight shone brightly around his body, making his shape seem sinister and dark. He was so large, his muscles so well defined, he frightened her. Thrilled her to her core. She brought her hands between her legs and drew moisture from her labia, then held up her fingers to him. "Please. Your mouth. Here, at least."

"Jesus!" Drake sank onto the mattress one knee at a time, between her legs, his mouth open as he sucked her fingers greed-

ily into his mouth. His eyes closed as his tongue and lips dragged along her fingers, sweeping away the evidence of her lust.

When he'd finished, he raised his head and gave her a glance that looked as primal and ferocious as any bear closing in on the last salmon in a stream.

She stroked wet fingers across the tight bud of a nipple and circled them on her clitoris. "Your mouth. Here?"

"Fuck yeah!" His back curved as he bent over her mound. He stared at her sex, sliding thick fingers between her lips. Then he glanced up, his lips curving with devilment. "My ass is getting hot."

She giggled and lifted her knees to invite him to her core. "Let's make your couch-bed burn."

He gave a deep rumbling growl and his large, rough palms slipped beneath her buttocks to raise her mound to his mouth. His tongue stroked her, licking up the fluids soaking her lips.

Once again, she strained against his tongue, urging him deeper, dying a little with each quick stroke, quivering each time he lingered to savor and suckle. When a hand reached up to curve around her breast, she pushed into it, telling him without words, he could be a little rough.

A shiver rocked his frame, and he drew back, closing his eyes and dragging deep breaths into his lungs. "Christ, not now," he muttered, withdrawing his hand from her breast.

"What is it? Are you ill?" she asked, missing the warmth that had cupped her.

He gave a sharp shake of his head. "Give me a minute," he bit out. He leaned down and rested his forehead on her belly.

Larikke threaded her fingers through his thick hair and rubbed his scalp as the shudders deepened, then faded away.

When he lifted his head, his gaze was haunted. "We shouldn't be here," he said, his voice roughened with emotion, his eyes filling with regret.

Unaccountably, tears flooded her own, and she tugged his hair. "Tell me what's wrong."

"I can't."

"Do you not want to be with me?"

His hands tightened on her ass, and his head slumped against her again.

His pain was a palpable thing that settled like a weight inside her chest. "I feel how much you want this. I do too." Not understanding his hesitation or why he seemed so distressed, she offered, "We'll do this however you want—however you can."

"You deserve more," he said hoarsely. "Much more than I can give you."

"I want you more than I've ever wanted anything." She spoke the truth. More than her kingdom, more than the faerie prince—she wanted this man. "Come over me."

He shuddered again then crawled up her body, lying over her like a warm, heavy blanket. Never had she felt so overwhelmed. When he drove his cock inside her, she'd never felt so consumed—or connected.

With her hands sliding over his back, she sighed and gave his chest, neck and chin all the kisses he denied her.

LARIKKE'S KISSES BURNED DRAKE'S skin as he thrust into her. With his knees braced, he stroked hard, lifting her bottom from the bed, shoving her up the mattress with each thrust until she held up a hand to push against the sofa back, holding herself in place to take him.

Sweet, so sweet! Her breaths gusted, warming his throat and chest as her lips traced his shoulder and upward, glancing along his jaw.

If he angled his head down just a fraction, she could reach his lips. What he wouldn't give to taste her, mate his tongue with hers. But he couldn't risk it, couldn't harm her. He'd promised himself, promised her. Instead, he fucked her hard, giving her everything he could, powering into her with a harsh precision that built friction and burned her inner walls.

When her orgasm gathered strength, she wrapped her warm thighs around his hips and snuggled closer, pressing upward to smash her soft breasts against his chest—breasts he had yet to take inside his mouth. The sharp little points of her nipples scraped his chest, taunting him, reminding him of everything he couldn't have.

Her palm reached up and cupped his cheek, and he couldn't resist turning into it and kissing her palm, sucking her slender fingers again into his mouth, drawing on them until the shuddering started, and he had to draw back.

"No," she groaned, holding him tighter, lifting her face to glide her lips along his chin.

Just a taste. God, he'd give his life for just a taste. He tipped down his head and rubbed his lips over hers, breathing in her sweet breath, dragging his lips over her cheeks, her chin, then circling his head to deepen the caress—lip to lip.

* * *

LARIKKE NEARLY CRIED HER triumph as his lips sucked on her lower lip, and his tongue glazed the curve of her smile. When a chill breath caressed her lip, she didn't think anything of it, and simply angled her head to open her lips fully beneath his and seal their mouths together.

Frigid air filled her mouth, traveled down her throat, freezing her vocal cords until she couldn't murmur, could only drink in kisses cold as snowflakes and arctic wind.

Abruptly, he dragged his mouth away and rolled away, sitting at the edge of the bed, cradling his head in his hands.

She leaned over and stroked his shoulder, waiting for her voice to thaw to tell him she was all right. Was this his secret? Was this what kept him from gracing her with his kisses?

"I'll get you something warm to drink," he said, his voice thick and scratchy.

She wanted to ask him not to draw away from her, to tell him she was all right, but she couldn't, so she lay back and pulled the sheet over her body, staring at the fire that stirred and hissed as it ripped through a log.

In minutes, he returned with a mug in his hands. He handed it to her, careful not to touch her fingers when she reached for it.

Hurt by his withdrawal, her voice still numb, she watched as he roamed the room like a caged bear, his expression dark. The hot tea soon thawed her throat, but the tightness of his shoulders and face told her he wasn't ready to talk.

So, she'd wait to reassure him when he was ready. In the meantime, the hot tea and the crackling of the fire lulled her. She fought the weight of her eyelids for only a few minutes before surrendering to sleep.

Drake relaxed fractionally when her eyes closed. He couldn't bear to meet her gaze. Didn't want to see the horror grow in her dark amber eyes. Instead, he wanted to hold a picture in his mind of her lying beneath him, taking his strokes, her lips parting around her moans.

Because he couldn't trust himself not to join her on the bed and take her one more time, he gathered his tools—his chisels, brushes and the electric drill—and strode to the wooden door, lifting the latch, opening the door and entering the wilderness naked.

While the shape of her breast was still imprinted on his mind and in his palm, he wanted to sculpt her. Ice and snow bit at the bottoms of his feet, and snowflakes melted on his skin. But he didn't really notice. He strode to the center of the clearing in front of his cabin and set his tools on the ground beside his feet.

He drew in a deep breath, catching the lingering scent on his skin—*Larikke's*—and let it fill his mouth and nose. His body hardened, his cock rising again between his legs. He braced apart his feet and clenched his fists at his side, grinding his teeth together to prevent the roar waiting to explode.

Then the change took him, bones crackling as they elongated, stretching his neck and face, muscle thickening his legs, arms and torso. One moment he was a man, standing naked in a clearing. The next he lost himself to the flurry of sleet and snow that swept around him, consuming him whole.

LARIKKE'S BREATH CAUGHT AND held as she stared through the narrow crack beneath the shutter of the window. When she'd heard the creak of the door as he escaped, she'd rushed to see what he could possibly be doing outside, naked to the elements. What she witnessed filled her with a trembling awe.

The cyclone of snow and ice that swept around Drake's form whirled around and around him faster, building in strength until it drew snow from the ground and dried pine needles from the trees surrounding the clearing, hiding Drake from her worried gaze.

Then as suddenly as the storm had formed, the whirlwind burst apart casting shards of crystallized ice in every direction, pinging against the outer walls of the cabin. In the center of the explosion where Drake had stood was a being she'd only heard about in the fairy tales Gudvin had told her as a child and the wild, frightening stories of the frost faeries.

An ice dragon.

Drake wasn't just his name.

Afraid he'd disappear altogether, she quickly gathered a blanket around her shoulders and ran for the door, flinging it open and rushing into the snow, not stopping until she stood in front of him.

Flakes fell between them as they stared into each other's eyes.

Did he still know her? Had she been rash to run out and greet this mythical creature? They were known for their ferocity and cunning. Although most of his breed breathed fire, a few more rare species of dragon breathed ice. If he chose, he could freeze her like the sentries near the door.

Sensing he was just as curious about her response to him, she stood on tiptoes and slowly lifted her hand toward his chest. Her fingers trembled, but she spread them to caress his hide.

Cloudy breaths gusted from his flared snout, but otherwise he remained motionless as she examined him.

His skin was soft and composed of tiny iridescent scales that gleamed purple, blue and green, depending on how the pale light struck each one. His body was thick and upright. He stood on two legs with feet that spread wide. Toes with long talons curved into the snow. When she reached high to smooth her hands along his powerful arms, they flexed, but remained along his side, his paws fisting tightly.

His neck was long and arched into a strong, broad head with a rigid fan of dark gray spikes from short to long spanning the sides of his snout and ending at the top of his head. But his almond-shaped eyes were the same blue as purest ice from an ancient glacier.

Slowly circling him, she noted more spikes stood on the back of his neck, swelling to hillocks between his shoulder blades and forming only a raised ridge down the rest of his back until it joined his long, arrow-tipped tail.

Most wondrous were the wings held close to his back—snowy white where they followed the bone along the arch of the wings. In between the bones, the skin was soft, pearlescent gray. The texture itself appeared velvety, and she couldn't resist reaching out to feel it. At her touch, his wings swept out as though he were trying to intimidate her.

She ducked beneath one wing and came around to stand in front of him. "I'm not frightened of you, you know," she lied, "but I would like to know why you're out here. Did you intend to show me this part of you?"

He lumbered forward, giving her a fright, but stepped past

her. His large frame bent over a snowbank and scraped up clumps of snow with his talons, forming a tall mound. Then he stood upright, jerked back his head and threw it forward, his mouth opening wide. His breath seemed to blow a stream of ice that covered the snow and instantly formed it into a solid block.

Ambling around the block, he blew at it from every angle, adding layer upon layer of ice until he'd formed a very large block about her height. When he finished, he looked back over his shoulder, his pale blue eyes holding her gaze for a long moment.

Just when she was tempted to break his stare and approach him once again, his wings spread out with a snap, lifted and then fanned down. He left the ground, soaring quickly above the edge of the tall trees until he was out of sight.

Larikke followed the wondrous sight until he'd disappeared. Why had he left? Would he come back? Or had she overstayed her welcome? She shivered and wrapped the blanket more tightly around her shoulders, at last feeling the cold seep through the soles of her feet—and into her heart.

Drake had secrets he likely wasn't happy sharing.

She stepped toward the block of ice, and her toe stubbed something hidden in the snow. She knelt to examine it, finding chisels and brushes and a piece of equipment she didn't recognize. At that moment, it struck her that he had the ability to sculpt the ice. Maybe the gift to create life with his hands.

Perhaps he had been the very creature who had created her.

FOUR

RAKE HESITATED ON THE other side of the door. When he opened the latch, he breathed a sigh of relief.

She hadn't locked him out.

He shivered, cold at last seeping into his bones. He'd shown her something he'd never shared with a woman. Not that he'd planned to. He simply hadn't been able to control the urge to transform and to hell with whether or not she spied on him. Rather, he'd hoped she would remain asleep while he formed his block of ice and began the careful paring away to find the beautiful form beneath the surface—hers.

Inside the cabin, the fire had died down. Only glowing embers remained in the grate, but the room felt snug. He stoked the fire, quietly adding a new log, then walked toward the bed, finding Larikke there, curled on her side. He was weary. Transforming always sucked the energy right out of him. He quietly crawled beneath the sheets, careful not to touch her, not to waken her. He wasn't ready to see whether she would recoil with revulsion or fear from him or accept him. Either would test his tightly held emotions.

So he kept his distance, resting on his side to stare at her while she slept, storing more memories, until he could no longer fight his exhaustion and slept, remembering at the last moment that her expression as she'd stood in front of the dragon had held only wonderment.

THE CRACKLE OF A log shifting in the grate woke her. The room was shrouded in near darkness, but she could make out the shape of Drake lying beside her—his human shape. Firelight gleamed on the curve of his muscled shoulder, his narrow waist and the flare of his thick thigh.

He lay on his side, an arm tucked beneath his head, facing her, as though he'd fallen asleep watching her. The thought warmed her. But then she grew a bit irritated he hadn't wakened her, hadn't sought to at least touch her to reassure her all was well between them, despite what she had done. Spying on him wasn't something she was proud of, but she couldn't help herself. Everything about him fascinated her, like a puzzle to be deciphered.

She went back to the thoughts that had filled her mind when she'd returned to the cabin too excited to sleep. She'd lain thinking about her ice dragon and the enormity of what she'd discovered.

Here was a worthy mate! In the faraway land. Who'd have thought a dragon could survive the human's passion for domination of their environment? Had he remained hidden away to save himself? Or had he always been alone? Something had kept him apart from Northland where he would have been revered. Instead, he hid here in a wilderness. She needed to know why, needed to know if there was something—some *good* reason—why he felt he couldn't be a part of a community.

Foremost in her mind was her sense of duty. She had to marry. She knew whomever she chose would rule with her, and she couldn't risk the future of Northland to someone unwilling to defend it. The frost faeries had already promised, whether or not she married the prince, to be their allies. They brought with them an alliance with a remote clan of dragons—something her council had been quick to point out as an advantage she didn't dare overlook.

Would Drake be willing to come with her, to at least explore the possibility of becoming a part of Northland—and maybe her ally, her lover, *her husband?*

She could envision ruling with him at her side. The strength in his burly body, the fearsome will blazing in his expression and the way he had held himself from her to protect her—all these things told her he was the one. A fearsome ruler for her kingdom and the master of her body.

That he was a dragon would be enough to hold her court in thrall. Dragons had been thought long expunged from Earth during the time of the human knights. His existence here was a miracle.

His loving a revelation.

For now, she had enough of dreams of kingdom building. She wanted to taste him, to feel his hardness surrounding her, penetrating her.

Larikke wondered whether he could be tempted beyond his iron control again. The few times she'd taken the initiative with Thure, his body had hardened beneath her fingertips. He'd

become demanding of her in contravention to his usual deference. He'd lost his control, his hands tightening on her tender
flesh, his cock powering into her. And those had been the few
times she'd truly enjoyed their time together.

Could she stoke a fire in Drake that would overcome his reluc-
tance to kiss her? Her sensual wiles were relatively undeveloped.
If she couldn't seduce him, could she convince him to follow her
home?

Should she just say it? "Drake, would you like to fly on the arctic wind with me to Northland and be my consort?" Was he even
aware of her realm? If not, he might think her crazed.

Why should he even consider it? It wasn't as though they knew
each other well—as though he loved her already. She'd been a
trial to him from the start.

But he did desire her. His body's response and his inability to
hold back his chilled breath told her that. Could that be enough
to convince him to come with her? To at least give their fledgling
relationship a chance to grow, their bonds to deepen?

She'd sensed the loneliness inside him. It echoed her own.

However, if she couldn't lure him to Northland then she'd
carry a memory with her—one to warm her during the endless
winter nights to come.

She snuggled closer to his broad chest, scraping her nipples
in the light furring that stretched across his broad chest. Her
nipples tingled, tightened, persuading her to sweep her hands
across his chest and fondle his small flat nipples before gliding
downward.

She counted his ribs and traced the hard ridges of his abdomen, moving downward still, until her fingertips met the crinkly

curls surrounding his groin. She combed through them, letting them wrap around her fingertips, and tugged gently to test their strength and the depth of his slumber, not wanting to wake him just yet.

His breaths remained deep and even; his eyelids didn't flutter.

Encouraged, she grasped his penis in her hands, marveling at how soft it was when not filled with blood. However, she wanted him engorged and ready *now*, so she scooted down the bed, determined to coax him into hardness again. The warmth of his skin and the scent of his masculine musk had her eager to take him, her pussy moistening already.

Opening her jaws wide, she gobbled all of his soft cock into her mouth, swirling her tongue around the curled appendage while she cupped and squeezed his balls. Slowly, she used her lips to pull him, trying slowly to bring his cock back to turgid life. She twisted her head, tugging this way and that, pulling off him as he filled and lengthened and then returning to swallow him whole.

The first indication he'd wakened were his strong fingers sliding through her hair.

She glanced up, but it was too dark with his face hidden in shadows to gauge his expression. So she came off him. "Do you mind?"

"You're kidding me, right?"

"I don't want to take advantage," she murmured, smiling in the darkness at the roughness of his tone.

"Now you're just being a tease." His palm cupped the back of her head and pulled her back down to his cock.

Happy to accommodate, she sucked the end of his stiffening cock, paying special attention to the groove beneath the soft cap, using her lips to suction and kiss, tonguing the slit at the center of its broad head.

Drake drove his hips forward, pulsing deeper into her mouth, and she loosened her jaws to take his length down her throat. She reveled in the wild trembling of his hips as he thrust inside her mouth. Her breasts tightened, and she pressed them into his thighs as she stroked forward and back to meet his thrusts, sucking harder, breathing through her nose as he thickened so she wouldn't have to stop for a gasp.

He filled her mouth, well past comfort. She suckled and bobbed until her mouth ached, then followed the suggestion of the hand tightening in her hair to release him and crawl up to slide her body flush with his.

"You like living dangerously?" he rasped.

Larikke breathed deeply and playfully walked her fingers along the top of his shoulder. "Have I incited the beast to come out and play?"

"It's no joke, Lari. I could hurt you."

She shivered, liking the way he'd shortened her name. Lovers gave nicknames to each other. "I'm not like the women you've known."

"You're worse—you're slender. Fragile."

"I'm not human any more than you are, Drake."

"Then what are you?"

Duty-bound to protect her throne, she bit back the words she wanted to say. "I can take you," she said quietly. "I promise."

"God, if I believed that . . ."

She cupped his face between her palms and kissed the edge of his jaw, then pulled down his head. With their lips a breath apart, she leaned in and rubbed her mouth softly against his. "Love me fully, Drake."

"I could," he said, his voice harsh and his body straining against her. "It'd be so damn easy."

"Then take me."

"Damn me to hell!" His mouth slammed against hers, and he rolled with her, pressing her deep into the mattress.

Larikke wriggled beneath him, desperately parting her legs, nudging her pussy against his rock-hard cock until he found her entrance and thrust inside. She gasped into his mouth then sucked in a deep breath of icy comfort and found the contrast between the heat of churning hips and chill lips intoxicating.

His tongue stroked hers, tangling, lapping. His lips rubbed, nibbled and sucked. His kiss fired a passion so hot she strained and bucked beneath him, rocking upward to take him deeper.

Drake's body shuddered and he drew back his head, shaking it, trying to slow the tempo of his thrusts.

Larikke wrapped her legs tightly around him and ground against him, not willing to lose the sensations building in her core, tightening her womb. Ripples fluttered along the walls of her vagina until rapture burst over her in an icy wave of ecstasy.

"Christ, no!" Drake's head flung back and his whole body stiffened as a stream of steamy cum burst from his cock, flooding her channel.

Just when her ragged breaths began to deepen and slow, Drake tried again to draw away. A deepening shudder racked his body, and Larikke released him, sliding her legs to the bed.

Drake wrenched away, crawled to the edge of the mattress and fell to the floor. Larikke reached for him, but her hand stopped just above his shoulder as a wind swept down the flue of the fireplace, scattering ashes and embers in a blast of burning, frosted air.

His gaze met hers, his brows drawn close, his expression fierce. Then he was obscured by the flying ash.

Larikke's throat closed tight at the pain she'd seen lurking in his eyes. Then she shut her eyes, knowing what came next. The burst as he shifted pelted her with soot. As the ash settled around her, she grabbed up a pillow and looked frantically around for the last of the dying embers, but they'd all extinguished.

When she met the dragon's gazè, he lowered his head to the mattress. She swallowed a sob and stroked his face beneath one row of gray spikes. "See?" she cooed, her voice trembling, but strong. "I'm still here. Unharmed. I don't fear you, but I think we will need a very large bed and a shield for the fireplace."

He snorted and rubbed his snout along her thigh. He breathed out a deep sigh and his whole body relaxed. In an instant, his form glimmered, softened, and then suddenly melted into Drake, the man. His face in the dim light was relaxed, his expression one of surrender. "I could have breathed ice into your lungs," he said, a jagged note in the low timbre of his voice.

"Then you'd have to warm me afterward to thaw me, but you won't kill me."

"I might have shifted when I was inside you and crushed you."

"I'm stronger than you realize."

"You're so damn stubborn. Why?" he asked, looking up to lock his glance with hers.

Her answer mattered to them both. She sensed victory within

her grasp, but felt no elation—only a calm assurance that their meeting hadn't been an accident. "Because we were meant for each other," she said, stroking his soft, pale hair.

He glanced away and rested his forehead against her thigh. "When you said before, that you aren't human . . . "

"That's not a lie. I wasn't born. I was sculpted from ice. Magick breathed life into me."

Drake's head jerked up. Suspicion narrowed his eyes. "I sold one of my ice sculptures once . . . the figure of a child . . . "

Then he hadn't been the one to create her life. He had shaped her form. Gudvin had much to explain. "Your sculpture was given to my parents. They longed for a child of their own but mother never conceived. They were older when I was created. I never knew how the life inside me was conceived. I don't think they wanted to know."

His lips twisted in a wry smile. "Feels a little like incest."

"Because you made me?" She gave a soft laugh. "I have only one question. All your works of art are of women. Grown women. Why did you sculpt a child?"

He shrugged and his gaze slid away.

He'd been lonely. Maybe yearned for a family. She knew it as surely as the snow would fall again in Northland. But not any longer. She wouldn't allow it. "Come into bed."

Without hesitating, he climbed onto the bed and settled beside her.

She flapped the coverlet to shed some of the soot, but only succeeded in filling the air with it again. She coughed and her eyes watered.

A low rumbling laugh shook the bed beside her. Strong arms

enfolded her and warm lips pressed against hers. His sweet kiss filled her with the chill of winter. He tasted like home.

AT THE SOUND OF an animal's soft snort, Drake raised his head from Larikke's ripe breast and shook away the snow that clung to his hair and cheeks.

When he glanced up, he swore and rolled to the side, flipping up the edge of the blanket to cover Larikke.

That morning, she'd been irresistible, standing in the doorway with sunlight streaming behind her. When she'd run naked into the daylight, he'd grabbed up a blanket and followed her laughter outside.

Shivering deliciously from the cold, they'd made naked snow angels in the bank beside his newest project, and then she'd coaxed him into further insanity kissing him breathless. Making love with her here had seemed natural by that point.

He'd laid down the blanket on a soft pile of snow and reclined on it, lifting his hand to beckon her.

Her face held a look of wicked delight, as though he'd given her a gift she never expected. "Here, in the snow?"

"Why not? I'll keep you warm, but you better be quick."

Her palm slid along his and he tugged her down, arranging her knees on either side of his hips, letting her rest her open pussy along the hard ridge of his cock. "Ever ridden a dragon before?" he growled.

"You know I haven't," she said, her cheeks coloring a pretty shade of embarrassed.

"It's easy, just slide onto the saddle."

"It's more like a thick pommel," she said, giggling. "Perhaps I should be gripping it instead."

"So you expect a wild ride?"

"I'm counting on it." She flipped her hair over her shoulder and rose on her knees, reaching between her legs to lift his cock and center it at her entrance. "My breasts are becoming chilled," she said, giving him a sly smile.

He grinned and cupped her breasts in his palms. "Wouldn't want anything to freeze."

She sank on him, taking him slowly inside her, circling to work her way down his length until at last she sat flush against his groin. "I don't think I can move," she whispered, "I'm so filled with you." Her gaze when it locked with his was glassy with tears.

Drake tenderly caressed her breasts, rubbing his thumbs over the velvety areolas, flicking the tight little nipples with his fingernails. Then he lifted one hand and thrust his fingers into her hair. "Sure you can," he said, pulling her down for a kiss.

A moan gusted between her lips the moment his mouth closed over hers and she did indeed move up and down in tiny, little grinding dips that drove him crazy. Over and over, she lifted and sank, her fingertips biting into his shoulders as she ate his lips, until she tore away and sat up, bouncing with more energy, her eyes squeezed shut.

She'd never been more beautiful, her hair flouncing around her shoulders, her cheeks reddening, her breasts jiggling with her forceful thrusts.

He gripped her hips hard, helping her move faster, digging his heels into their soft snowy bed to lift his buttocks off the blanket and meet her downward thrusts.

Her cunt clasped him tight, her channel rippling all along his shaft in wave after wave of delicious, heated caresses. "I'm coming," she gasped, then she flung back her head, her mouth opening as a cry tore from her throat. Her up and down movements halted and she sat suspended for a moment, anchored on his cock, rocking slowly back and forth while the ripples quivering inside her body slowed.

Drake waited until she opened her eyes and breathed again. "Are you okay?" he asked, fighting the tension in his body as he forced his hands to remain gentle on her hips.

Her lips trembled, but she nodded.

"Cold?"

"No."

"Good." He rolled her to her back, coming over her and pulled out partway from her tight pussy and slammed back inside.

Larikke keened, caught on another wave of release, and wrapped her legs tightly around his waist as he hammered inside her, thrusting hard, relentlessly, again and again. He didn't slow down until her back arched and her head dug into the blanket—only then did he give himself permission to let the orgasm that had held his balls in a vise gush through his cock to spill liquid fire into her womb.

Afterward, they'd held each other close as the snow started to fall again, sharing their bodies' heat, sprinkling leisurely kisses on each other's lips, cheeks and shoulders until arousal slowly built again and he'd moved down to take her breast into his mouth.

NOW, A COLUMN OF men in navy uniforms filled the clearing, fanning out to encircle them. One led a horse. Not hers, for it was soft, silvery gray.

Only he wasn't sure it was a horse at all now that he could make out the fact it had large, feathered wings that quivered at its sides.

The soldiers also weren't men. They had pale blue skin and long black hair—and wings that appeared delicate as a butterfly's wings, but with sharp-edged scallops that glistened as though they were lightly furred in shades of violet, gray, black and silver.

The creature holding the reins stepped forward, his posture stiff, his expression shuttered. His gaze remained raised above them, staring hard into the distance.

He looked pissed.

Drake straightened, heedless of his nudity.

Larikke cleared her throat beside him. "Drake?"

"Stay covered," he bit out, not sure what was happening.

"When I said I wasn't human—I should have mentioned a few more pertinent facts."

"Larikke?" he gritted out, not caring he betrayed a hint of irritation. He didn't like surprises.

"Meet my suitor, Thure."

"No longer, it appears," Thure said, a quiet fury lacing his low voice.

Larikke stepped beside Drake, the blanket wrapped around her body. "We never made promises, Thure."

"My mistake, Majesty."

Majesty? Drake aimed a glare at Larikke, noting the pink coloring her cheeks.

"Another pertinent fact you left out?" he muttered.

"I would have gotten around to it," she said, her lips pouting.

Damn, he wanted to kiss her again. To hell with the blue man watching.

"Gudvin sent us to escort you home," Thure said.

"I don't need—"

"Your command will not be heeded." His gaze bore into Drake. "For your safety, you understand."

Larikke stiffened. "I see." She turned to Drake. "I had hoped for more time."

Drake noted the strain tightening her lips and the way her fingers clutched the edge of her blanket. Her knuckles whitened.

Did she fear Thure? Would he hurt her for her betrayal? "I can make them leave us," he said softly.

Her eyes filled, but she blinked the moisture away. "I should return."

Drake felt as though heavy stones weighed down his shoulders. He tightened his jaw and nodded, unwilling to let anyone know how much her leaving meant. He'd been alone before. He'd known from the start she didn't belong with him.

A soft touch landed on his curled fist, and he dropped his gaze to stare at her trembling hand.

"Come with me," she whispered, turning to face him fully.

The heaviness in his chest lightened fractionally. She didn't want to say goodbye any more than he did. "I don't know you. You lied to me."

"I didn't tell you things about me," she said, her voice breaking. *"But you know me."*

He'd thought he was starting to. But now there wasn't any time left to learn more. "You'd better go." He turned toward the cabin, wanting to shut the door against the sight of her leaving.

She grabbed his arm. "Drake."

When she laid her cheek against his arm, he felt moisture slide down his skin. Her tears. Drake closed his eyes and drew a deep breath.

"I know why you sculpted a child. You were lonely. So was I."

Damn. All those years ago, he'd dreamed of having a family. When it became clear his nature made him a menace to women, he'd given up.

Anger drained away from him. Taking its place was another emotion that warmed his soul. Larikke was the one person who could take all of him. She'd said they were meant for each other. Her words had echoed in his heart.

"We leave now," Thure gritted out.

"We leave when I'm dressed," Larikke said softly but with a hint of steel. Her brown gaze sought Drake's and held.

"What is he, anyway?" Drake murmured.

"A frost faerie."

A smile tugged his lips. "Figures."

An answering grin stretched her lips.

When he enfolded her small hand in his, he squeezed it. "They may have to wait awhile."

Thure cleared his throat. He wasn't giving up. "I brought only one horse."

Larikke lifted one dark brow. "He won't be needing a horse."

In that instant, Drake didn't care he hadn't a clue where they were headed. As long as she wanted him, and if she learned to love him, he'd be more than satisfied.

Further, the only creature she'd be riding when she left would be an ice dragon, because he sure as hell wasn't letting her anywhere near the angry blue faerie.

But he'd tell her that later, after he let her dress.

FIVE

ARIKKE GROANED INTO DRAKE'S shoulder, trying to muffle the sound as he slowly lifted her, dragging her off his cock. When just the tip of sex remained buried in her pussy, she reared back and tightened her legs around his flanks. "Drake, *pleeeaase!*"

His smile wasn't reassuring. The white of his teeth flashed briefly between lips drawn back in a feral grin. The look in his eyes warned he wasn't going to give her exactly what she wanted. His gaze calculating, he dipped his hips and swirled, teasing her, killing her by inches.

Her fingernails bit into his skin as she panted, "You know . . . he's just outside the door . . . waiting. *Hurry!*"

"Maybe I want him to know exactly why he's waiting," he growled.

Then she understood his goal. He was going to make her scream. How . . . primitive! How deliciously male! But she was a queen and couldn't have her sexual appetites bandied about. Never mind Thure and his men had found her moaning beneath Drake with his lips sucking at her breast!

They'd think she was insatiable. Never mind she thought she might be well along the way to being at least lustful. They'd only made it across the threshold before he'd ripped the blanket from her and pounced, lifting her off the floor to settle her cunt over his rampant erection. That it hadn't waned despite the danger he'd faced was proof of his mettle.

Metal she'd gladly have lunging deep into her core.

Men! If Drake didn't end this torture soon, she'd have to take matters into her own hands. Unfortunately, wedged against the wall, Drake bracing her up with his hips and cock put her reach beyond any sensitive manly parts.

Drake circled his hips again, wetting his cock in the fluids gathering at her entrance. "Are you sure?"

"Of course I am," she said, frustration making her sound as strident as a harpy. "He's right outside the door."

His expression darkened. "No. About me coming with you."

She canted her head, realizing he needed something. Reassuring? The thought that this proud, strong creature felt unsure nearly undid her. Damn, but did they have to have this conversation now? Her cunt pulsed around his cock. "Do you think I'll change my mind?" she gasped.

His lips twisted, just as his cock did, thrusting a little deeper this time. "Smurf-boy's not very happy about us."

Although she didn't understand the term, his tone held a wealth of derision. "Thure had expectations." She squeezed him with her inner muscles, gratified when his breath gusted.

"Did he have a right to them?" he asked, his voice growing harsh and tight as his hands gripped her bottom and started a shallow rocking motion that nearly drove her mad.

Larikke rubbed her nipples on his chest then smoothed her palms upward to curve over his hard shoulders, petting him, trying to soothe away his tension. Trying to encourage him to thrust a little deeper. "I told you," she moaned. "I made him no promises. Exchanged no vows. I'm free to be with whomever I choose."

"Why me?" A ragged note in his voice tore at her heart. The doubts worn naked on his face were painful to see.

She understood exactly what he needed. While he couldn't expect an avowal of love this soon in their relationship, he did need to know he was more than just a passing fancy.

Still, his lack of trust annoyed her. Wasn't she getting splinters in her backside while her escorts cooled their heels outside their door? "Do you think I'm doing this to somehow thwart him?" At the tightening in his jaw, she added sharply, "Well, I'm not." *I'm doing this because I want you—and because you're exactly what my kingdom needs.*

"Are you doing it because you don't have any better choices? Seems you were already scraping the bottom of the barrel." Drake forced her down his cock while his hips flexed upward.

Had jealousy prompted him to retaliate? "Thure's a fine knight," she cooed. "And extremely handsome. Any woman would be proud to have him as a husband."

"If you're into faeries," he snarled, bringing her up and down his cock faster.

Larikke tightened her legs and forced a breathless reply, "Faeries are noble creatures and powerful."

"He has flippin' butterfly wings!" he said, pressing her hard against the wall, grinding his cock into her.

"His wings aren't as insubstantial as that." She widened her eyes, pretending surprise. "You're jealous!"

"I'm not worried about any blue-skinned—"

Tension curled around her womb. She was almost there. "Of course you are!" she crowed. "Or you wouldn't make me wait for my orgasm," she shouted.

His snort of laughter brought her down with a thud.

"He's right outside the door isn't he?" she whispered.

"Heard the porch creak."

"You—you—" she sputtered in outrage. He'd been playing with her!

"Want me to stop?" he whispered, his lips hovering just above hers.

"Stop and I'll consign you to the dungeon."

"Where you can have your wicked way with me?"

"Repeatedly," she bit out.

"That's my girl."

She liked the sound of that. Liked even better the savage thrusts he gave her, hammering faster, angling his hips to sharpen each stroke.

When passion finally swept over her, she did indeed shout—a sound cut short by his lips slamming down on hers.

FINALLY DRESSED IN HER soot-stained gown and cloak, she swept out the door with her chin held high, not glancing once to the right where Thure stood beneath the eaves in grim silence.

"What of my horse, Wind—" she started to say, but instead squealed when strong arms jerked her off her feet.

She fought Thure's embrace as he stalked toward his men, twisting to look over his shoulder to shout a warning to Drake.

Too late. Drake lay in a heap on his porch, two of Thure's men flanking his body.

"Thure, what are you doing?"

"Taking matters in hand."

"By whose authority?"

"Mine—as your future husband."

"This is an outrage!" she said, fighting him in earnest now, wriggling wildly to escape his embrace.

Thure tightened his hands, forcing her arms close to her sides.

"Let me go! Drake might be injured."

Magnus, Thure's Captain-at-arms, drew up beside them, slapping a short log against his palm. "He's going to have a headache all right," he said, satisfaction in his voice.

"I swear if you've hurt him . . ."

"You know we are enjoined to cause no harm to humans," Thure said, his voice deadly calm. "I wouldn't break that rule."

"He's not hu—" She cut off the denial. At the moment, she didn't trust Thure due to the icy rage that froze his mobile features.

She didn't know why she didn't tell him about Drake's ability. Part of her feared what Thure might do in anger. Another part felt it only fair that Drake should have the right to decide for himself whether he would seek her out. Did he even know Northland existed?

She had to find a way to get back to him, to ask him. And to be fair, she knew she needed to tell him he wasn't alone—that he had dragon family, although the knowledge might come between them.

Thure thrust her into the saddle of the horse and climbed on behind her. She glanced back at the cabin and at Drake's still form draped over the steps of his porch. This might be the last time she ever saw him. She gave silent thanks. The memory of his loving would be a treasure for all time.

Thure kicked the side of the horse and its wings unfolded.

"I can ride by myself," she gritted out, elbowing Thure's ribs as he pressed closer to her.

His wings folded over his shoulders, gracefully enclosing her in a cocoon of warmth. "I wouldn't want you getting lost again."

"I wasn't lost . . . exactly."

"I will forgive you."

"Forgive me?" she scoffed, anger boiling inside her now. "For what?"

"For playing with a human."

She trembled with outrage that he would mention it, that he would consider it his business.

Thure leaned down, his intent clear.

For the first time, she turned her face away, grimacing as his lips slid along her cheek.

"So you will not misunderstand me," he said, his words coming sharp and bitten like frigid gusts of air, "once we are wed, the only person you will ever lie with will be me."

Larikke's chest tightened. Her stomach felt hollow. If Thure was her fate, her life would be bleak, disappointment a constant companion. Not because he would be unkind, but because he simply wasn't the one.

The horse cleared the tops of the trees, and Thure's men swept in beside them, flanking them. Together, they rose up, seeking the wind and finding it in a chill blast that licked forward and back then slung them toward home.

DRAKE WOKE TO THE faint tinkling of bells and rolled onto his back, grimacing in pain. He found himself staring up at the eaves of his porch and for a moment he wondered what the hell he'd done. Had he had an accident?

Then he remembered . . . Larikke, the blue men . . . and getting clobbered as he came out the door when he'd heard her squeal.

The bells sounded closer.

He winced, and rolled to his side to find Larikke's horse approaching the porch, staring at him. Without the obstruction of swirling snow, he could see that this creature also had wings and an intricate leather harness with tiny bells sewn to the straps.

Larikke was gone. Taken by faeries to who knew where.

Should he follow? Was he a fool to think she really wanted him?

The horse continued to stare solemnly, and Drake sensed there was more intelligence in that steady gaze than he should expect. "Can you find your way home?" he asked, reaching up to pull at the harness and stand on unsteady legs.

The horse whinnied almost as if to say, "Of course."

Drake glanced back inside the open cabin door at the things he had gathered around him to keep him company in the life of solitude he'd chosen. Then not bothering to close the door to keep out the elements and the animals, he swung up into the horse's saddle and dropped the reins. "It's all up to you, buddy.

We've got us a woman to rescue and a faerie who needs his face rearranged."

LARIKKE AND THURE TOUCHED down in front of the palace in the late afternoon. One glance at the guard set next to the door as she swept inside had her stomach dropping to her toes. He wasn't wearing her livery. He was one of Thure's men. In fact, everywhere her gaze landed she found more of his uniformed men. "What have you done?" she asked, unease prickling the back of her neck.

"Just seeing to the security of the palace."

His lazy drawl irked. "Was there a threat?"

"It's not your concern anymore."

Larikke looked into his stony face. His jaw firmed, a muscle flexing along its sharp curve above the stiff collar of his uniform. This was a Thure she barely recognized. Certainly not the polite suitor who'd plied her with gifts of flowers.

Why hadn't he displayed this streak of dominance when they'd been together? She might have found him more interesting. But she'd already given her heart to Drake, and at the moment, the frost faerie frightened her. She straightened her shoulders. "I would like to change," she said in her haughtiest voice.

"Yes, please do. Bathe while you're at it. I want his scent off you."

Larikke flushed, livid. He dared command her? "I take it the council is in agreement with your actions?" she asked quietly, holding herself stiffly, fighting the urge to scratch and claw at him.

His answer was a curt nod, and then he turned on his heels and walked away. *He'd dismissed her! And in front of his men!*

Heat filled her face; anger trembled in her body. "Gudvin!" she shouted into the hall, knowing her voice would carry throughout the palace. She stomped up the curved staircase and swept toward her chambers, gratified to find her own staff waiting to serve her and Gudvin wringing his hands.

"I couldn't dissuade the council," her mentor began as soon as he saw her, his wrinkled face creased with worry. "They said you've an obligation to marry, and the prince brings great wealth and power. They think you're a foolish girl—that you've played with his affections."

"Played with his affections?" she screeched. "Is that what he told them?"

"Thure himself said very little to the council—other than to admit you'd been intimate."

"That's nobody's business!" she hissed.

"N-not that they're displeased, but they do feel you've obligated yourself to marry him."

"I won't marry him!" Another thought crossed her mind. "Where is my guard?"

"All seeing to other tasks—at *his* command."

Frozen in shock, she willed her mind to focus. Then she waved her hands toward her staff, waiting for them to quietly back out of the room, leaving her and Gudvin alone. "I've met someone else," she whispered.

"What?" his voice squeaked. "Where have you been?"

"I was on Earth." She narrowed her gaze at him. "And tell me you didn't know that."

Gudvin flushed. "I didn't tell a soul," he whispered. "I promise."

"Were you watching us in your golden ball?"

"Of course. I mean, I had to know that you were safe." He straightened, drawing his long robes around him. "I did not intrude."

Satisfied Gudvin hadn't spied on their intimate acts, she relaxed. "What else did you see?"

Gudvin's gaze slid away. "That Windancer remembered the way."

Larikke drew back. "Ah . . . I wondered about that. So it was you. You bought the statue from Drake."

"Was that the man's name? He'd made the most perfect little girl."

Larikke reached for his hands and clasped them firmly. "Why didn't you tell me that you were the one who gave me life?" she asked softly.

The mage gave a sad little smile. "I didn't want your parents to know. After all, you were a gift to them, and I didn't want to come between you."

"Well, it explains why you're so dear to me."

His eyes misted. "Larikke, do you know you are the embodiment of your Drake's desires?"

She stood still for a moment, suspecting there was more. "Do you know what he is?"

"A dragon?" His eyebrows rose and a mischievous twinkle filled his gaze. "Of course!"

Her lips curved in a smile at his gnomish expression. "We should tell the council. They would stop the marriage if they knew."

"Knew what exactly? Does he love you?"

Larikke hesitated, that word had never been shared between them. "He wants me."

"Do you only want him too, child?"

She wrinkled her nose. "You make me sound so spoiled."

"And you aren't?"

She took no offense. She was what she was. "Well, I do take some things for granted." She remembered Drake's rough little cabin. "But I've discovered I can be quite happy living with less."

"As long as you have this man? Your Drake?"

She nodded, a calm acceptance settling over her to blot out the remnants of anxiety and anger Thure had caused.

"Then we must find a way to bust you out."

"Bust me out?"

"Just a phrase I learned somewhere."

SIX

RAKE HELD ON TO the horse, sinking his hands into its thick mane as they flew higher into the clouds. The powerful flaps of the horse's wings beat in time with his heart. His legs clung to the heaving sides of the horse, urging him wordlessly onward.

Then a wind gusted by them, fast and frigid. It licked his left side, then his right, wagging lazily until it caught them and flung them forward like pebbles in a slingshot. Windancer changed the angle of his wings and slowed their beating, gliding now on the wind. They flew so fast Drake couldn't drag air into his lungs. The clouds thickened, closing in, muffling the sounds around him. The flapping of the horse's wings was dulled; his breaths grew jagged and loud to his own ears.

When snow whipped his face like thousands of small, sharp crystals, Drake bent low over Windancer's neck. His face stung, and he closed his eyes tight, trusting in the horse's instincts, trusting the fact Larikke had survived this journey.

And just as suddenly, the clouds cleared and the world slowed.

Windancer braked his wings against the wind, and they plum-
meted from the sky. Drake found himself looking down over a
landscape more beautiful than any fantasy he could have conceived.

They flew above a white-capped sea as they approached land.
A large glacier hugged the edge of land, its tall sides shooting
hundreds of feet into the air. Sheets of ice cleaved away to drop
like giant ice cubes into the deep blue water below.

Beyond the glacier, mountains rose—dark lavender capped
with pristine white peaks. Thick dark forest hugged the lower
elevations like a wide skirt.

Windancer swept through a mountain pass and into a valley
that stretched out like a long cape of twinkling lights. There was
a town below and beyond it a palace unlike anything he'd ever
seen in any book. As they drew closer, passing a crenellated stone
wall with round towers at each end, he noted the outer walls of
the palace itself were made of clear, carved ice blocks that caught
the waning sunlight and seemed to glow from within. Several tall
stone spires jutted above the building, giving the palace a fairy-
tale appearance.

Windancer landed inside a bailey, setting down on a cobble-
stone courtyard that had been swept free of ice and snow. The
horse quivered with excitement and snorted, flapping his wings
to brush off snow and waited patiently while Drake climbed off,
holding tight to his harness while letting his legs grow accustomed to standing on land once again.

Their arrival didn't escape notice. Damned blue faeries poured
into the courtyard, but Drake wasn't afraid—not when he could
see them coming.

"Returning her majesty's horse?" A dryly amused voice rose above the muttering of the men gathering around him.

"Something like that," Drake murmured. Now that he was here, he felt a bit unsure whether or not he'd made the right choice. All this opulence . . . he really didn't have that much to offer Larikke. Whereas the blue man looked at home on the upper step of the keep.

"Well, he's back safe. My thanks." Thure nodded, and then gave him a hard-eyed glare. "Now you can go home. I'll send an escort to make sure you don't get lost." He lifted a hand and waved at a couple of the men closest to him—one of whom Drake recognized as the man who'd clobbered him with the log as he'd stepped outside the door of his cabin.

As the faerie drew near and reached for Windancer's reins, Drake narrowed his eyes, waiting until he was close enough . . .

Drake drew a deep breath and forced the change, something he'd never truly practiced, but he found that anger worked just as well as lust. The familiar wind built, whipping the blue man's hair. His eyes widened, but Drake stood straight, focusing on the fact he needed to remember he couldn't kill him.

Larikke clutched Gudvin's cloak as they neared the postern gate, but a ruckus near the front of the castle drew her attention. She grimaced, irritated her escape would be discovered sooner rather than later. Lifting her chin, she reminded herself this was her home. Curiosity had to be fed first! "I have to take a peek," she whispered to Gudvin. "I have to see what's happening."

As they rounded the corner of the building, she saw Thure's men, thickly bunched together, their attention riveted on something in front of them. Their shouts were loud and lively, sprinkled with coarse suggestions.

Thinking two of the faerie force had entered a fight, she was about to turn around to make a hasty escape, when she caught a glimpse of the arch of a large white wing above the heads of the faeries, then a long, proud neck rose, and Drake's dragon face found her above the crowd.

It was just a momentary glance, but it sucked the wind from her lungs, and suddenly, she was pounding at the backs of the men forming a circle around him, forcing her way through until she stood inside the inner ring, watching two faeries trying to take on a dragon.

The battle seemed very one-sided. Never mind the faeries had the advantage of speed, lifting off the ground, circling to find an opening, then swooping in to strike at the dragon's head and flanks with long wooden cudgels. Magnus, the blowhard, looked wonderfully mussed and irritated. His usually cocky expression wiped clean when Drake's barbed tail swept him sideways in the air, and then barreled him into the spectators.

A glance around her assured her the crowd wasn't likely to converge and spoil an evenly matched fight. Just as many shouted wagers favoring Drake as the faeries; all groaned aloud when Magnus took another glancing blow that tumbled him head over heels into the side of the castle wall.

Larikke winced. "Serves you right, you bastard!" she muttered, then turned back, not wanting to miss a moment of the battle. If things turned ugly, she wanted to be there.

At last, one of the crowd stepped into the ring while Drake was occupied trading blows with the one left in front of him. Drake turned just as the faerie raised a pike and flicked his tail, knocking him off his feet.

Larikke was appalled. When another stepped in to strike his shoulder with a pole, she found herself balling up her fists and shouting, "Drake, give him a whack!"

"I wasn't expecting this."

Larikke turned to find Thure standing at her side. "You hardly thought I was going to stay put just because you said so!"

He snorted. "I'm talking about the dragon. I brought you a pact. You brought one as a mate." His expression contained equal parts irritation and resignation. "I believe I'm trumped."

She couldn't help but grin. "You know he's going to kick their butts."

"Likely mine too."

Relieved he didn't seem to be suffering emotions any stronger than irritation, she turned back to the battle which was winding down. Drake had frozen a wing of one of the fighters, trapping him on the ground and keeping him vulnerable to the snaking of his long tail.

Magnus wasn't faring any better as he dodged sharp shards of ice that Drake blew at him. He managed a few whacks to Drake's flanks and one good thump to the side of his head until Drake appeared to lose his patience and roared, letting loose enough ice to catch Magnus directly in the face and chest, tossing him on his back where he lay immobile.

Drake's form melted, and he stood naked in the center of the circle, his chest heaving. "Damn, I didn't mean to do that."

Larikke understood and walked up beside him. "You didn't really hurt him."

Drake's frown deepened as he stared at the frozen look of surprise on Magnus's face.

"Well, you probably left him with a few good bruises, but he's not going to die. I told you, we're a hardy breed up here. You should trust me."

As faeries lifted Magnus and carried him away, Drake's gaze strayed toward the keep. "Where exactly am I?"

Larikke wanted nothing more than to fling her arms around him and hug him with all her might. But the wariness he wore in his tight jaw and rigid posture, held her back. "This is Northland. My realm."

His eyes narrowed at something beyond her shoulder. "What about him?"

Larikke looked back at Thure whose arms were folded over his chest, his face an equally implacable mask. "Thure and I have a pact. That hasn't changed, has it?"

Thure gave a sharp nod of agreement.

"You mentioned before that you needed Thure and his blue men . . ."

Thure's gaze narrowed.

A grim smile curled up one side of Drake's mouth. "For some sort of military alliance. Are you in danger?"

"We live under the constant threat of invasion. Although Northland may seem a frozen wasteland to you, it's actually quite rich. Our mines are coveted."

"What do you mine?"

"Raw crystals." His eyebrows shot up, and she knew he didn't understand. "This is a magical realm. Not one tied to the rules of science as yours is. We believe in magic. Our crystals are precious. Many would try to steal control of our mines."

"What's changed that you thought you needed him?"

"The mages have heard stirrings—seen dark portents." She shrugged. "We don't have anything firm yet."

"But you trust him?" he said, lifting his chin at Thure whose hand slipped to the pommel of the sword strapped at his side.

Larikke gave them both a quelling glare. "There are dark forces all around us. Frost faeries have even been adversaries at times, but we've worked out a mutually beneficial alliance. Their protection for our magicks. Plus they've brought us another group who can help protect us."

"I haven't met anyone of your realm yet. Besides the mines, what makes you so special? And why aren't you able to protect yourselves?"

Thure's lips curved in mild derision. As with most of those who surrounded Northland, they held contempt for the softness of the inhabitants of Northland.

"Our knowledge is what makes us powerful. Our mages have kept us impregnable up to a point. We now find that we need physical protection as well."

"From whom? I'm still not getting it. Who are the possibles?"

"Trolls, valkeries . . . dragons."

Drake's gaze landed on her and rested there for a very long moment. "Like me?" he asked, his voice tightening.

She nodded slowly. "Some are like you. They breathe ice. Some breathe fire. Some storms."

"When were you going to tell me there is more of my kind?"

"I wasn't certain you wanted to come, and I didn't know for sure how much you knew about us. About Northland. In fact, the alliance Thure is bringing us is with a group of dragons who have been particularly insistent on taking control of Northland."

"And you would trust bringing another dragon in your midst?"

"Thure wouldn't, I'm sure. But I trust you." She stepped closer, raising her face to let him see everything she felt for him. "When I was vulnerable you rescued me and protected me. I believe that's part of your nature."

Drake stiffened. "And if I find a kinship with these dragons who wish an alliance?"

"Then I will have to find reasons to help you cement that kinship," she said softly. "I don't want to keep you from family. Here in Northland, we've kept ourselves apart. Some think we believe ourselves superior to the rest of the creatures around us, but we've come to understand we all have certain skills and strengths. I believe we should use them for the benefit of all."

A smoldering flame lit his gaze as he stared. "Where do you fit in with all of this? What special powers do you have? Are you a mage? Why are you queen? You weren't born to it."

"It's true I wasn't born at all, and my parents were only minimally gifted mages. The council of mages divined that I was the one who should rule when I was very small, and I've been raised and trained for just this. We don't question their wisdom, but I'm thinking that maybe I was raised and trained and readied . . . for you."

Drake's gaze drifted toward the palace then back over sky that grew darker and bleaker by the moment. "I never had a place in my world, and I'm not certain I belong here."

Her heart sank. Maybe she wasn't enough to hold him here.

His hand lifted and he cupped her cheek with one large, roughened palm. "I may not belong, but I know I won't ever let you go."

Larikke felt a smile stretch her lips while tears pricked her eyes. "Then stay with me. Let me be your home. We'll belong to each other."

DRAKE STRETCHED LAZILY ON top of the velvet coverlet and glanced around the room. "I have to admit I was relieved there isn't any ice inside your palace. I like a little warmth in a room."

Larikke snuggled closer to his chest. "Mmmm . . . we like our comforts. While the cold doesn't penetrate us as easily as a human, I like my toes toasty," she said as she scraped hers on his calves. "I think Thure's relieved things turned out this way."

"Oh? You never mentioned it."

"He said he didn't think he could have remained polite for very much longer. He knew that as soon as he showed his true nature, he'd have a fight on his hands. The last thing he wants is a woman who's going to buck his command."

"You mean, he thinks you're too strong-willed?"

She wrinkled her nose. "He thinks I'm spoiled," she said, her tone disgruntled.

He grinned. "And you aren't?" He looked around at the food piled high on a tray next to the bed, at the rich linens that curtained the bed and the furnishings that filled the bedroom—all comforts fit for a queen.

"I am what they made me," she pouted.

"Well, you may be spoiled, but I don't think you're self-centered. You understand those around you very well. You saw through me."

"See?" she said, rising on an elbow to smile down at him. "I may be just a snow maiden, but I have my talents." She swept a hand down his abdomen, finding his cock and giving it a playful squeeze. "I have you."

"And you'll have me again," he growled, rolling her to her back.

She shoved her hair from her eyes. Their gazes locked.

He couldn't believe how lovely she was or that she was his. "Mine," he said, his voice rough.

"All yours . . . " she agreed, clasping his hand and moving it over her breast, "to do with as you please."

Golden candlelight reflected on her creamy skin and shone in the luster of her dark hair. Drake couldn't wait to retrieve his paints. He'd capture her just like this, with her eyelids dipping in sultry invitation, her lush lips parting as she waited for his kiss, her cheeks rosy from arousal.

Arousal he'd stoked to a fever pitch.

Leaning down, he sucked her lower lip between his teeth and bit gently.

Larikke murmured, her sweet breath gusting into his mouth. Her body undulated, her belly rubbing his hard cock.

Then he stroked his tongue inside, holding back his breath, tasting her, savoring the flavors of wine and roast meat . . . and her.

Her fingers gripped his hair and pulled him closer, attempting to deepen the kiss, but he didn't want to numb her mouth or her wicked tongue.

To distract her from her intent, he nudged a knee between her legs. She parted them eagerly, and as he nestled between her thighs, he gave her another kiss, sweeping his tongue inside briefly to take one last taste, then he moved down to nip her chin, lick her neck, and slide his lips along her collarbone.

Her breath gasped and her belly rolled again, urging him lower. He palmed a trembling breast and took her nipple, wetting it, lapping at the stem as it swelled.

He lingered there, suckling softly, teasing her with the edge of his teeth, and then suctioning harder until her knees drew up, her feet tucking next to his thighs. And only then did he move lower . . . leaving a wet trail of kisses from her breasts, past her soft belly . . . and as he gazed down at the center of her femininity, he wondered whether a dragon and a snow maiden could make a child.

A question for Gudvin.

But for now, he leaned down and breathed a tiny flicker of icy air at her hooded clitoris, feeling blessed, for once, rather then cursed by his dragon nature as she sucked in a breath and her thighs trembled.

He followed with warming laps of his tongue, alternately cold then hot, until her moans came fast and her fingertips clawed at his shoulders. "By thunder! *Please, Drake!*"

At last, unable to hold back another moment, he crawled up and covered her, hooking his arms beneath her thighs to tilt her hips and thrust hard inside her, stroking deep, pulling back only to stroke deeper still.

With her throaty groans singing in his ears, he powered into her, faster, harder, tunneling into her moist, welcoming heat, stoking the fire as he pushed her thighs higher. Wet, succulent slaps accompanied the creaking of the mattress beneath them. He leaned over her, pounding harder, careful to breathe to the side as clouds of chilled air gusted from him.

When she shouted, her pussy clamped around his cock and a trembling, pulsing throb caressed the length of his shaft.

Drake roared, slamming into her cunt, milking the gentle convulsions shimmying around his cock then letting his release spill into her womb. He couldn't stop, didn't want to halt the rocking motions that soothed the rage inside his soul.

Her hands caressed his shoulders and his back while her soft, cooing brought him down. When at last he stopped moving against her, he shuddered and nestled his forehead against her neck.

He slipped his arms from beneath her thighs and helped her lower them to the bed. "I'll move in a minute" was all he managed to bite out.

"No hurry," she whispered. "I like this too." Her hands stroked his hair, feathering it back in a restful, lulling motion.

"I love you," he whispered, waiting for the answer to his unasked question.

A soft rasp of breath followed, then "I love you, Drake. Every part of you."

He relaxed, letting her love him with her soft hands and gentle soothing sounds.

Drifting toward sleep, wrapped in the comfort of Larikke's embrace, he made a solemn vow. For her, he'd learn to wield a sword, teach himself to maneuver in the politics of this realm, and become the master of his dragon.

Scorpion King

MARIANNE LaCROIX

PROLOGUE

The year is 2307. Earth's population increased over the centuries until alternative locations became crucial for human existence. Some turned to space while others turned to the oceans.

Aquatic humans evolved, adapting to their new oceanic environment. With the help of genetic engineering, the speed of their evolution increased with the generations.

There seemed to be nothing humankind couldn't adapt to their needs. Underwater cities developed and flourished with advanced atomic power and environmental control. The possibilities were limitless.

However, not everything was so easily manipulated or controlled . . .

ONE

"**Y**OUR MAJESTY, THE ENTIRE city is at risk. The instability of the ocean floor poses a threat to everyone—not just the citizens of Pacifica, but the Land-walkers too," one of the Council representatives called out from his seat. Anger and frustration edged his voice.

Queen Naiya Pisces rubbed her temples, which were pounding a beat so loud she couldn't concentrate. She'd been hearing nonstop complaints and proposals regarding the possible reasons for the latest streak of quakes that rocked her kingdom.

"I propose we investigate the ocean floor outside the city to better understand the dangers to Pacifica," Brendon Aquarius, the spokesman for the Pacifica Council, announced to the roomful of fellow representatives.

"While I agree with this conclusion, I fear this may be seen as a ploy by the Council to seek funds," another member offered. "The citizens are sure to see this as an attempt to levy new taxes. There has been civil unrest throughout the kingdom since the election of the new Council. Rumors of ballot tampering have made the people leery."

"Would the people rather wake up to another quake—one that could crack the force field and destroy the city?" Brendon asked.

Naiya's headache couldn't take many more arguments. Ever since taking the throne several months ago, she'd heard disagreements and debates over everything from minor civil disputes to this newest quake situation.

Just that morning, the entire population had been rocked from its beds as a quake shook the foundation of Pacifica. It was the latest and strongest quake yet. Naiya wished she could just order an investigation, but her Council demanded a debate. To her mind the discussion was a waste of precious time, but she had little choice.

Genetics had made her queen. She was the only offspring remaining of the original Aquatics bloodline, a genetically engineered species of humans designed to live beneath the ocean. Within the city, Aquatics existed alongside Land-walkers—or air-breathing humans. While the Aquatic people could both breathe air and process oxygen through their gills, a crack in the force field that protected the non-Aquatics could kill thousands, like a tidal wave crashing into a seaside city.

Then Naiya got an idea.

"Time wasted here discussing the quakes will do little good without a complete report on what we are up against," she started. "Due to civil unrest, I suggest a joint venture with the Land-walkers to investigate the ocean floor. Both the Aquatic *and* ocean-side Land-walker cities are at grave risk of death and destruction."

Silence fell over the floor of the Council. Naiya was of royal blood, but she was still new in her position as queen. It was a figurehead leadership, as the Council members were the real lawmakers in the kingdom. Much like the ancient American democracy, Pacifica's political hierarchy was such that the queen was more a spokesperson communicating with the people. It was she who set in motion certain political changes and initiatives once decided upon by the Council.

She had a certain power, but her ascension to the throne brought with it whispers of anxiety. Blood ties to the former queens of Pacifica were undeniable, but because Naiya was now the last of her lineage, the people were waiting nervously for something more.

They waited for a prophecy to be fulfilled, waited for a man destined to become king—the Scorpion King.

On the day of Naiya's birth, an oracle foretold of a union between Pisces and Scorpio—a joining of signs and souls that would bring about great change through adversity for the kingdom of Pacifica. Naiya—a Pisces due not only to her birth date, but also as a descendant of the royal Pisces family—would join with a specific man marked by a scorpion tattoo, the symbol of both his sign and his prophesied destiny. Only he could rule alongside the queen. Under their rule, the kingdom of Pacifica would rise to greatness and strength through intelligence, understanding and the harmonious blending of the zodiac symbols that predetermined their future.

At the questioning glances from the Council, Naiya said, "I have sat quietly and heard endless discussions over the ocean floor's instability and its impact on our kingdom. The time for talking is over. We need the facts to determine our next course of action. I will not risk the lives of my people for the benefit of argument."

Brendon stood from his seat at the long table. "Queen Pisces is right. We need more information to know if there is indeed a danger."

The sound of agreement filled the room.

Naiya sighed in relief. Perhaps the Council members were more scared than they let on.

"YOUR MAJESTY, I FEEL this may be a tricky situation, especially when involving the Land-walkers," Brendon said as they walked the halls to her chambers.

"We have no choice. If we send our own scientific team to study the tremors it could spark complaints of unfair investigation, especially if the conclusion is what I fear," she replied, stepping softly by his side. She wondered about Brendon's insistence on escorting her to her rooms. Lately, he seemed to be paying special attention to her. She suspected his interest was more an attraction to the power of the throne than to her as a woman. She was sure the thought of becoming her husband, and therefore the king of Pacifica, had crossed his mind more than once.

"In your opinion, is there a real danger to the city?" he asked.

"Just the fact that the tremors have increased in strength and frequency leads me to believe the situation is extremely critical. The sooner we find out the extent of the danger, the faster we can take action to make sure no one gets hurt."

"Do you think the entire city will have to be abandoned?" It was the question they all feared to ask.

"If the foundation is unstable and the force field is at risk, we may have no choice." She hated the thought of leaving Pacifica.

Her entire family had lived here, as had many other families. For Naiya, leaving would be similar to abandoning a piece of paradise.

"I can tell you, the Council will fight leaving even if the reports indicate danger."

She stopped in the hall and turned to him. "They'd rather die?"

He placed his hands upon her shoulders. It was a simple gesture of comfort, yet it failed in its desired effect. "They are stubborn and rooted here. No matter who tries to reason with them, even if you bring in the Land-walkers, the Council will fight to stay."

"I can't believe they'd take such a serious risk with their lives, along with the lives of their families."

He leaned closer. "I'd help you convince them if only you'd do something for me."

"Blackmail, Bren?"

He chuckled. "Hardly. But you'd have more power in the Council if you had a king by your side."

"Bren, I—"

He cut her off, moving closer, his lips a breath away from hers. "I've wanted to make love to you again for so long, Naiya. You've let me into your heart once before and neither of us has found another." Then he added in a low voice, "Let me love you. . . become your husband."

He kissed her and she leaned into his warmth. She enjoyed the kiss, this gentle mingling of lips, yet it stirred little within her heart. His quest for power cooled her passion.

She'd met Brendon when she was eighteen. He was young, handsome and a fine example of teenage virility. He'd romanced her and she gave him her innocence. For several weeks, she was in heaven as he took her to his bed. But the affair was short-lived and he'd moved on to his next conquest. Having been so young, Naiya was left with a broken heart and had cried for weeks afterward. Her mother had offered a shoulder to cry on. It was also her mother who had cautioned her against giving her heart to just any man.

"You are the royal heir to the throne. Men will be attracted to the idea of becoming king and will try to seduce you into giving over your power. Brendon did you a favor in leaving now. If you had been queen, he may have succeeded in his seduction—all the way to the throne. You have discovered his true nature now, before it was too late."

It had been true. She had seen his true nature—that of a player. Now, ten years later, he hadn't changed.

And he wanted a second chance. But his touch left her cold. She was burned by his betrayal of a young girl experiencing love for the first time. Things were different now. She'd never let him, or any man, find a place in her heart. There was no room for love of a man in a queen's heart. The only love that lived there was for her kingdom, her people.

She ended the kiss and backed away from his touch. With a sigh, she smiled.

"Think it over, Naiya," he said, apparently mistaking her reaction.

"Bren, you hurt me once. I overcame that pain and you've become my friend. I don't want to ruin that. We're better friends than lovers."

He straightened. "You'll need a husband to convince the Council."

"I don't need a man to do my job. If my kingdom is in danger, I will act to protect it—and everyone who lives here."

With that, she turned and strode down the hall to her chamber door.

"You're sadly mistaken," he called after her.

She paused with her hand on the doorknob and shot back at him, "No, it is you and the entire Council who are mistaken. You all underestimate me."

"DRAKE, I WANT YOU to head up the research mission in Pacifica," Admiral Theo Simmons announced.

Captain Drake Scopillo cocked a brow. "Pacifica?"

"We've been getting reports of ocean floor activity that may lead to a full-blown earthquake. Queen Pisces has contacted us, asking for a joint effort in studying the foundation of Pacifica."

Queen Pisces! "I'm not one who cares for ocean work, Admiral," Drake stalled.

Admiral Simmons nodded. "I understand that. Not many of us like being at the mercy of a force field to breathe, especially when it is miles beneath the ocean. But your team is the best, and when a queen asks for help, I think the best we have to offer is appropriate." He paused to examine a large-screen digital map of the globe. Fiber-optic sensors placed around the world—both on the surface and below the waters—read the constant activity of the earth's crust. It was the system the United Global Nations set into place as an advance warning against natural disasters like earthquakes and tsunamis. "We have been reading tremors in that area for some time now, but for the past few months they have increased in strength and frequency. It's time we go in and take a closer look."

The woman I dream of every night. "I don't really like the water, Admiral."

"It's important that you go. Millions of lives are at stake—above and below the ocean surface," the admiral said, turning to him. Within the darkened room, by the blue-green light of the numerous computer terminals reading the crust activity, he looked like a man with the fate of the world on his shoulders. "There is civil unrest in Pacifica. The queen feels our investigative assistance would allow any critical discovery to be taken with less resistance by the people of her kingdom," he continued.

She's in danger and needs my help.

Drake was a man of duty, dedicating his life to the welfare of the planet. He was a geophysicist and an engineer for the UGN Navy, specializing in seismology—the study of earthquakes and the movement of seismic waves through the earth. If the Aquatic queen needed his expertise, he'd go.

"Drake, the study is important. I suspect this is going to be a dangerous situation."

"When do you want us to leave?"

The admiral quirked a small smile. "Immediately."

"Got a team of experts ready for me?"

"Four of the best. They're on their way to report to the *Zodiac*. I asked Captain Sparro to take you to Pacifica and assist in any way he can in setting up the ocean lab. Supplies should be onboard the *Zodiac*. If you need anything else, let us know. Oh yes, and here are the reports we've gotten from the sensors in the area. There's lots of activity going on down there. I wouldn't be a bit surprised if there is some sort of volcanic birth in the making."

The admiral handed Drake a small disc. Although Drake was the leader of this expedition, he was apparently the last member to be informed. He assumed it was because of his distaste for ocean work. The admiral hadn't taken the chance of letting him think too long on the mission before he had to leave.

"I'll report back in a few days with our progress."

As Drake turned to leave, the admiral called after him. "Queen Pisces is new to the throne, and hasn't established her power yet with the Council. You may find your presence isn't wanted or welcome among the Council."

"Great," he muttered. "Political nonsense amid impending danger. The world never changes."

An hour later Drake was at the ship preparing to leave with his assigned research team. Together, the five scientists were experts in six fields—seismology, geological oceanography, physical oceanography, marine biology, marine chemistry and geochemistry. All their combined skills were needed to fully study the ocean floor's activity, test the chemical balance of the water, the pressure of any shifts of the tectonic plates and the development of hydrothermal vents or volcanoes.

"I can't believe you accepted a mission underwater," Captain Jay Sparro commented as he sat in the control room of the *Zodiac*, an AT-2006 all-terrain ship that could travel in or out of the Earth's atmosphere. The *Zodiac* had been used on missions in air and water, on land and in space.

"It wasn't as if I was given much of a choice. Admiral Simmons ordered me to go." Drake took a seat and inserted the disc with the latest readings from the ocean floor surrounding Pacifica. "He wanted the best to go and investigate, so I'm going. I still hate working in the water. I could *never* live in one of those underwater cities."

"I've never been to one of the Aquatic cities. This will be a first for me."

Drake sniffed in contempt. "I try to stay away from those underwater wonderlands. I hate the idea of all that water just outside my window, and all that separates me from drowning is a force field."

"The force fields are the latest in Aquatic technology. I took a class that detailed their scientific advances, and it's pretty amazing how the Aquatics are able to adapt to anything."

"Yeah, they're intelligent, but a bit prejudiced. They don't like us Land-walkers much."

Jay frowned. "I don't know about *that*. I saw a video of the new queen a few months ago on the PlaNET inviting the Land-walkers to visit Pacifica for their next vacation. I think they're trying for tourist appeal." He paused then chuckled. "She got my attention, that's for sure."

"Why do you say that?"

"Man, she's fucking hot."

"Never saw her before." *Liar,* he thought to himself.

"Well, she's pretty damn gorgeous. She has a blue-green shimmer to her skin and her hair is white as snow. One look at her and I got a hard-on."

Drake knew exactly what looking at Naiya Pisces did to *himself.*

He'd seen the reports online of the new queen as well—and saved her image to his private files. He'd been transfixed by her exotic beauty but hated to admit it. She was part fish in his mind, but it did little to cool the fire in his groin. He'd taken to looking at her before he went to bed, imagining her iridescent skin against his during a hot sexual encounter. It never took long to come when he envisioned her sweet mouth about his cock, tasting him as he found release.

And now he was about to come face-to-face with the woman whose image he had masturbated to for the past three months, on a mission so crucial to millions of people—Aquatics and Land-walkers alike. Drake had to push down his desires and concentrate on his job. He was a man on a mission. This was no time to start an affair with the Aquatic queen.

As if she'd see him as anything more than an air-breather, the mere boss of a crew of scientists.

"Best get settled in, Drake. We'll be leaving for Pacifica in about thirty minutes. Should take us about an hour to get there," Jay said, switching into business mode as he continued to tap at his console.

A half hour later, they launched from the UGN command base in Hawaii and were flying out over the open ocean. The Pacific Ocean had changed over the centuries due to global warming and other reactions to the presence of man, but through the UGN's guidance and global peace efforts, most of the toxins destroying the Earth had dissipated and cleaner, more Earth-friendly methods of energy had been implemented.

The planet's main problem was the population boom. It drove people to search for alternate places to live. Some chose space exploration, setting up colonies on other planets and moons. Others turned to Earth's waters.

It was the latter who spawned the Aquatics. Those humans

altered their DNA to enable them to adapt more quickly to their underwater lifestyle. Scales and gills allowed the Aquatics to exist in their water world. They built cities on the ocean floor, using pure, safe and stable atomic energy created with salt water to power a force field that defied the millions of tons of water pressure.

From a scientific standpoint, the feat was amazing. But using atomic energy could prove dangerous if the water's chemical balance was changed by a possible hydrothermal vent spewing out heated hydrogen sulfide, methane and a variety of metals, like gold, silver and iron. They'd be investigating *that* possibility in addition to the tremors.

"Okay, hold on, we're about to go seafaring," Jay chuckled as the *Zodiac* descended toward the ocean surface. The ship jolted as it touched down on the water.

"Tell me you've submerged this thing before," Drake begged, clutching the arms of his chair.

"Of course I have," Jake retorted as the ship began to nose under the water.

"Oh good." Drake sighed. He attempted to relax.

"In simulation," Jay added as they plunged into the depths below.

"Fucking cowboy," Drake muttered. His heart thudded against his chest wall as he prayed to live long enough to start his research of the ocean floor . . . and to meet Queen Pisces.

Two

N AIYA STOOD AT THE docking bay where the Land-walkers were about to park their ship. The dock was a flat metal landing pad just inside the force field, and the ship would pass through an entry portal before actually entering the city. This was the way in and out of the force field, which was itself a credit to Aquatic technology—a wonder to behold, just as much as the beauty of the ocean it held at bay.

The entire surface of the docking bay shimmered with rippling currents that reflected the city lights within the force field, throwing them back into the water. Fish of all varieties—sea bass, hawkfish, snappers, angelfish—dotted the ocean with their brilliant colors of yellow, purple and blue. It was a living rainbow moving through the water, and Naiya sighed at the calm tranquility just beyond her city. It had been too long since she'd taken time for a leisurely swim just to enjoy the beauty of the ocean.

"You didn't have to come and meet them. You could await them in the throne room and I can escort them to you." Brendon arrived, obviously disliking the idea of the queen greeting new-comers at the docking bay.

"No, I want to make sure they feel welcome."

Brendon's response was a grunt.

"It would be wise to show your appreciation to them while they are here."

"I'll welcome them, but that doesn't mean I have to *like* them being here," he retorted. "Pacifica is already overrun with Land-walkers."

Just then the ship emerged from one of the round portals that allowed vehicles to pass through the force field without disturb-ing the energy flow. The ship was tubular in shape, completely seamless on the surface. It appeared to be equally efficient in air or water, adapting to each with ease.

When it approached the landing pad, the underside of the ship's smooth surface opened to allow the landing gear to lower. The ship settled down with a low groan of metal and steam, and within a moment, the gangway opened. More steam flew into the air as Naiya got her first glimpse of the research team.

Her breath caught at the sight of the man who led the way before four others. Tall and lightly tanned, the man leading the small party stepped from the gangway. His hair, black and straight, fell about his shoulders and down his back. He was dressed in a sleeveless, synthetic leather jumper. It allowed her a perfect view of his well-toned arms and the muscular expanse of his chest. At his wrists he wore leather bracers.

"Is this guy a scientist or some space cowboy?" Brendon whis-pered at her side.

Indeed, he looked the part of a warrior rather than a man of science.

"Your Majesty," the hulk in leather said, approaching her with a bow. "I'm Captain Drake Scopillo. Honored to meet you."

His voice washed over her, exciting her with its faint Australian accent.

"Welcome, Captain Scopillo. I'm Queen Naiya Pisces, and I welcome you and your team to Pacifica." She offered her hand and the captain gently touched it, lifting it to his lips. A warm surge raced through her veins at the simple touch of his lips against the back of her hand. Electricity seemed to spark at the contact and it led straight to the apex of her thighs.

She smiled up into his face and recognized a glimmer of sexual interest in his eyes. Or was it just something she hoped to see? Unsure about her own reactions to the newcomer, she reluctantly pulled her hand away and stepped back.

Brendon stepped forward. "I'm Councilman Brendon Aquarius. If you should need anything during your stay in our city, please feel free to let *me* know."

His message was subtle, but clear—Naiya was off-limits.

Drake bowed slightly. "Thank you, Councilman. If you would like to introduce us to your team, we can go ahead and begin setting up our ocean lab and get started."

Brendon turned and waved to the awaiting science team behind Naiya. "These are our best Aquatic scientists. They've been studying the quakes extensively and I'm sure you will find they are experts, the best in the world," he stated in an unmistakably arrogant tone.

Drake looked from Brendon to Naiya. He took a step toward the queen, closing the distance between them once again. "Your Majesty, both our worlds have much to lose if seismic activity is on the horizon. It could set off a chain reaction that would not only destroy your city, but hundreds of cities on land—killing millions of people. We're here to help determine the danger, not get involved in some sort of political debate or a struggle of scientific knowledge."

Angered by Brendon's attempt to dishonor the captain, Naiya nodded and said, "Agreed, Captain. Your expertise is exactly why you are here and why we called for assistance from the UGN. A mutual cooperation between our people is the only way to be sure the best evaluation is made." Noting Brendon's irritation, Naiya added, "And you, Captain, may report *directly to me* your findings. I wish to know the progress of your team daily."

"Thank you, Your Majesty." His lips curled into a small smile.

Brendon huffed at her side.

"After you get your initial look at the site and set up your lab," she continued, "I wish for you to join me here for dinner so we may discuss your first impressions."

"With pleasure, Your Majesty."

Humor edged his words as he glanced at Brendon, who obviously disliked the idea, and that made the captain's eyes sparkle with mischief.

Her heart leapt in her chest. He was the most handsome man she'd ever encountered—a rogue. He seemed to ooze sexual appeal from every pore, and she was transfixed.

When the captain turned to introduce his team, she nodded greetings to the members. Drake bowed to her once more then strode back to his ship with an air of confidence and male arrogance.

"You're out of his league, Naiya," Brendon said, breaking the silence as they began to walk back inside.

"I don't know what you mean," she denied.

"You know very well what I mean. That invitation to dinner was much more than just a meal. I saw the way you looked at him—with lust in your eyes. And the dog knew it."

"You're imagining things."

"Am I? I know an invitation for sex when I hear one."

"Yes, you do. You're well-versed in that field, Bren."

"I'm just trying to—"

She turned on him. "Trying to manipulate me and my position as queen! Know this—*no* man will rule me. I refuse to give the throne to a man simply because he excites my body. We may have been lovers once, but don't think that gives you the right to be jealous or tell me what to do. I will spend my time as I wish, with *whom* I wish."

"I'm just saying I don't like that . . . Captain Scopillo."

"You can rest assured that whatever happens, Captain Scopillo will leave once his study is complete."

"OKAY, ROMEO, TRYING TO romance the Aquatic queen while you're here?" Jay asked, having witnessed the show from the ship.

Drake sat in his chair in the control room of the *Zodiac*. "I wasn't entirely honest with you earlier."

"Uh-huh. Go on."

"I'd seen her before on PlaNET."

Jay laughed. "You thought she was hot, too."

"Yeah, but I never thought I'd actually meet her," he replied as the com-link came to life, announcing that the Aquatic ship was ready to launch.

Queen Pisces was even more beautiful in person and Drake already found himself drawn to her. If not for that stiff-necked politician by her side, Drake was sure his flirtation with the queen could have gone further. As it was, she'd invited him to visit her tonight for dinner.

Or was that invitation for something else? Judging by her reaction to him, she seemed to want more than a dinner companion.

Just the thought made him hard—as if he wasn't already after meeting her.

"So, what are you going to do?" Jay asked, breaking into his thoughts.

Drake sighed. "I honestly don't know."

As much as he would like to, starting an affair during a research mission wasn't the best of timing. He wanted her, wanted to taste her flesh and bury himself deep within her body. But he had to stay focused.

After they passed through the portal and back out to the water, they followed the Aquatic team to an outlying ocean ridge. A few sharks and fish meandered through the water as the number of rocks and ridges increased.

"The water temperature is increasing," their geochemist, Dr. Natalie Tucker, commented through the internal com-link.

"Not a good sign," Drake commented, tapping his console to access the data being gathered just outside the hull.

"Oh fuck," Jay said in awe.

"What?" Drake glanced up and saw the video relay that played inside the control room.

There, between two ridges, was a hydrothermal vent.

It was unlikely the city would have been built near a known vent. This one had to be fairly new.

Drake activated the com-link to the Aquatic ship. "How long has that vent been there?"

"For about fifty years. It's nothing new," came the tinny reply.

As the heated gases poured from the vent, pushed to the surface by bubbling magma below, Drake was sure this was an advance warning Pacifica should have heeded fifty years ago. It was the possible beginning of a larger problem.

There was no way he could even think about sex when such dangers lay only a few hundred feet from the city.

"Looks like we've got work to do, and fast," Drake started. "No time for playing."

Drake pushed forward, giving the mission his undivided attention as he began barking orders via the internal com-link to set up the ocean lab near the vent, but not close enough to let the heat affect their readings.

He was all business. The lives of millions were in his hands.

"WHAT ARE YOU DOING here?" Brendon demanded as he entered his study, spotting his brother Leo. His home, located just outside the palace, was close enough to enable him to keep tabs on Naiya and the Council, while allowing enough distance to unsuspectingly dedicate time to his own agenda.

Leo smirked as he flicked on the lamp sitting atop the end table next to him. "Checking on how things are going with those Land-walkers nosing around the vent."

"Naiya has taken an interest in the leader of the Land-walker science team."

Leo cocked a brow as he watched Brendon begin to pace the

study floor. "I thought you had the queen's heart under your control?"

"That space cowboy geek, Captain Scopillo, waltzed off
his ship and she was wet and ready to spread her legs with one
glance."

"You know they're going to find the vent unstable."

"I know it," Brendon snapped. He stopped pacing and turned
to his brother, who sat comfortably in his favorite chair, one
leg up over an armrest. "Once they deliver their report, I will
be sure to argue the results with the Council to buy us some
time."

"Maybe you should concentrate on continuing your pursuit of
the queen instead. If they eventually discover you've been embez-
zling money, they'll have little power against you if you've already
become king," Leo suggested.

"Naiya is not likely to agree to marriage. She's using that ridic-
ulous Scorpion King prophecy to keep her power to herself. I
doubt she even believes in that nonsense. It's infuriating."

"Well then, maybe she needs a bit of stimulation to change
her mind. If she gets suspicious and starts checking the use of
those tax dollars you've been diverting into bogus programs,
particularly the disaster relocation program, we're both going
to jail—you for embezzlement and me for helping you set up
the fake accounts." Leo swung his leg off the armrest and sat
forward in the chair. "If your attempts to persuade her don't
work out, we may have to take matters out of her hands—by
force if need be."

Brendon stepped closer to his brother. "And what sort of 'force'
are you suggesting?"

Leo stood and closed the distance between them. "Whatever it takes to protect us and place you on the throne."

NAIYA ORDERED A MEAL to be served in her chambers. The royal dining room contained only a single dining table that spanned thirty feet for formal dinner parties. Naiya opted to entertain in the sitting room of her chambers. It was more intimate and less intimidating.

She carefully planned the dinner to offer the best in Pacifica cuisine. Grilled shrimp, steamed clams, boiled lobster with butter sauce and sautéed sea cucumbers were all part of the evening menu.

Glancing in the mirror, she smoothed her white hair. Light reflecting off the tendrils gave it a silvery shine, and the mass hung loose about her shoulders and down her back. Her blue-tinted skin had a pearlescent luster and her aqua eyes shone like polished gems. Hers was considered an exotic beauty—she just hoped the Land-walker captain would think so as well.

A knock at her chamber door startled her. He had arrived. As a servant who had been setting up the dining table answered the door, Naiya's stomach lurched in anticipation. She couldn't wait to see the handsome captain again.

"Your Majesty, Captain Scopillo is here," the servant announced at Naiya's bedroom door, which separated the sitting area from her bedchamber.

Drake's mouth was drawn in a grim line as he stood examining the exquisite dining table. Silver and white was the theme for the evening, casting a magical hue to the entire room. Candles on the table and votives spread along the nearby shelves cast a soft light within the room.

"I'm pleased you could join me, Captain," she said, drawing his attention.

His eyes immediately softened when he looked up at her. "I'm not sure I deserve such an elaborate evening," he said.

"Nonsense. How often do you dine with a queen?"

He smiled. "Certainly not on a daily basis."

His warm smile struck a chord within her and a jolt of awareness shot through her body.

"But really, Your Majesty, this is probably not a good time to entertain." He straightened, his manner cooling as he spoke. "You have a potentially serious problem just outside the city."

She took a seat at the table. "What did you see?"

"A hydrothermal vent."

"There are thousands of vents all over the ocean floor."

He nodded. "But this one is between two ocean ridges. It indicates there is a break in the earth's crust."

She took a moment to absorb the news. The city had been built several generations before the vent appeared. Minor quakes and vents were normal occurrences for many underwater cities. Engineers and scientists had declared Pacifica safe from danger. Perhaps they were wrong.

Or maybe they were persuaded by a Council to report otherwise.

"But the vent has been there for so long," she reasoned. "It never posed a problem before."

"I think it has been building up over the years. As the crust weakens, molten lava and gases push upward causing seaquakes."

Her eyes searched his face for any sign of hope. There was none. "How long do you think it will take you to back all this up with evidence so I may present it to the Council?"

"Just a few days."

She sighed in sadness. "Very well, then." If what he said was true, there was much to be done to save her people—and to convince the Council.

"Now if you don't mind, Your Majesty, I will go back to the lab."

"Oh." She stood quickly and stepped toward him. His manner was cool, businesslike. He reminded her of the scorpion—calm and calculating, poised to strike if cornered. She had to be cautious not to become the target of his sting. "Please, Captain, stay for dinner at least. I had a wonderful meal planned and it is just waiting to be eaten. It's some of the best Aquatic cuisine."

His gaze roamed her body and a shiver scurried down her spine. Her pussy hummed beneath his heated examination and her juices began to flow between her legs.

"Please stay and eat with me. It would be a shame to waste all this food."

His eyes softened. "I really should get back to the lab and my crew," he started. "I only came because you asked for a report. I mainly wanted to tell you my first-impression hypothesis."

She stepped closer to him, drawn to the warmth of his skin. "And I am asking you to stay and eat with me, Captain." She laid a hand upon his forearm.

So close to him now, she felt energy radiate from his body, wrapping about them in an embrace. Their attraction was mutual and it crackled in the air like twigs popping in a fire.

"What does your councilman think about you inviting me here tonight?" he asked.

"He disapproves."

"And it doesn't bother you that one of your Council members doesn't like this arrangement?"

"I am queen here. I don't need Council approval of whom I see privately."

He cocked a brow and moved in closer. "You're a beautiful woman. If this were another place, another time, perhaps we could explore this . . . attraction. But now . . . "

She watched a muscle at his jaw twitch as he struggled for control.

Taking a step back, she let her hand drop away from his arm. "Perhaps, Captain." She turned and stepped back to her seat at the table. "Come. Let us at least enjoy a meal together this evening."

He smiled and bowed slightly. "Yes, Your Majesty."

"You may call me Naiya when we meet casually like this."

He took his seat opposite her. "And you can call me Drake— *Naiya*."

Her name was like a term of endearment from his lips. She shuddered in her seat.

She pushed a button to summon the start of the meal service. Then, lifting a glass of wine already poured, she said, "So, tell me about yourself, Drake. How did you come to study earth science?"

"When I was a teenager fresh out of high school, I went to the UGN Naval Academy. Once I graduated, I went to work for the Navy studying volcanoes in Hawaii. Over the next ten years I became an expert in the field of seismology and tectonics."

The servants began to bring in their meal of lobster and shrimp.

Naiya said, "I've never gone there to see the volcanoes, just to see the humpback whales. Hawaii is a lovely spot from which to watch the whales breed in the winter."

"It's hard to believe they were on the brink of extinction back in the late twentieth century," he offered.

As they ate, Naiya continued to ask Drake questions of his past and of other missions. She began to feel at ease talking with him, but an edge of tension remained within the room, floating between them. Every once in a while a fire lit his eyes when he grew silent. But then the glint of desire would flee with the blink of an eye.

Then the conversation turned to the stars as Drake mentioned a former mission on the planet Mars.

"How long has it been since you've seen the stars in the sky?" he asked.

"I've not seen the night sky in a long time," she said sadly. She hadn't given it much thought over the years.

"Perhaps I can take you to the surface and reacquaint you with the stars sometime." His voice was husky, unmistakably seductive.

Their gazes met as she reached across the table to lay a hand upon his. "I would like that very much . . . Drake."

"I will show you Pisces in the stars."

"I've never seen my sign in the stars," she admitted.

He wrapped his fingers about her hand and she felt the contact throughout her entire body.

"Well then, I'll show you Pisces and my sign, Scorpio."

"You're a Scorpio?" She chuckled.

"Yes. I've been told the scorpion is my spirit guide, whatever that means. On the day of my birth, an oracle arrived in our village. He said I was to be led by the scorpion to my destiny. I was tattooed that very day with the mark of the scorpion upon my back."

She nodded. *Could this be possible?* Could the man she'd been waiting for truly be a Land-walker? "I should have known," she murmured.

"What?"

Trying not to alarm him, she said, "Scorpios are determined and powerful, but then they are passionate and magnetic."

His lips curled into a small smile. "You think I'm magnetic?"

"Definitely magnetic."

"What about passionate?"

She pulled the hand that held hers toward her mouth. Without a word, she bent her head and nibbled his thumb.

He inhaled sharply.

"I think you may be passionate," she said, flicking her tongue over the pad of his thumb. Then she looked up into his face. "I want to experience your power and passion, Drake."

He sat transfixed as she then took his thumb into her mouth and suckled gently. She swirled her tongue, tasting his skin, wishing for more. She needed to taste more of him, experience much more . . .

He pulled his hand away almost reluctantly. Then he stood. "I thank you for dinner, Your Majesty, but I must be going. There's much to do in the morning."

Hurt by his cool rejection, she also took note of his sudden use of her title. "I'm sorry, Drake," she said, sitting back in her seat.

He bowed slightly then turned, stepping to the door. As she watched him leave, Naiya felt completely abandoned.

He'd rejected her.

Bastard.

The challenge was on.

She got up from the table, storming from the room and into her bedchamber. Pacing in front of her vanity, she let her frustrations bubble to the surface. Tugging at the gown she wore, she peeled off the scratchy material and tossed it to the floor.

Her body buzzed with need—need that Drake had ignited with his mere presence.

Naked, Naiya continued to pace as she heard the servants clear away the table. Her body tingled with the awareness of sexual excitement. She could easily dip her fingers into her cunt and relieve the pent-up need for orgasm, but the sensation would be empty. She'd only find temporary relief in masturbating to the thought of Drake touching her.

She had sensed his arousal, but he was so determined to focus on work. She should be just as single-minded, concentrating on the danger to her city and people—and normally she would be. But since meeting the handsome scientist, her thoughts trailed to heated nights of sex.

Turning to the mirror, she gazed at herself. She was so unlike the Land-walker women with her blue-green shimmer and icy white hair. She touched her body, feeling the softness of her skin. Cupping her breasts, she tested their weight. They filled her hands with their firmness. She rubbed her nipples to a point, succeeding in not only puckering the skin but exciting herself further.

Yes, it would be so easy to cup her sex and send herself into a shattering climax. But she wanted more than her fingers strumming her clit.

If only there was some way for her to keep the captain from returning to the lab tonight. Maybe a direct invitation to her bed would bring him back.

The com-link chimed.

Naiya approached it and pressed a button. "Yes?"

"This is Lieutenant Granger. Your Majesty, Captain Scopillo is having engine troubles with his ship."

She cocked a brow, incredulous. "Engine troubles?"

"Yes, Your Majesty."

"See to it the captain is escorted out to the lab in one of our ships." She wished she could order him to stay, but . . .

"But there is nothing available at this time, Your Majesty. The *Nautilus* is the only ship in port and it is undergoing repairs to the hull."

She smiled to herself at the perfect opportunity. "Then arrange for the captain to be given guest quarters at the palace for the evening. In the meantime, send a maintenance crew to repair his ship."

"Yes, Your Majesty."

She clicked off the com-link and began to formulate her plan to seduce the unsuspecting Drake—the man bearing the scorpion symbol. *He'll have no choice but to succumb to my temptations.* She'd make sure of that.

THREE

*H*ER VOICE ON THE com-link had sent his blood pressure rising. He thought maybe the walk back to the palace would help, but it didn't. He was torn. Nothing seemed to divert his mind, not even the vent just outside the city.

He wanted the queen. He'd rejected her and he felt like a fucking asshole. A fucking *idiot* may be a better description. He must be insane to turn down a chance to have sex with Naiya— the woman he had lusted after for months.

Once at the palace, he was met by a servant who showed him to his room for the night. The room was huge and a massive, double king-size bed sat to one side. It was elaborately made up with pastel green- and coral-colored fabrics that shimmered in the dim lighting. The rest of the room reflected the soft color scheme in the thick rugs and the drapes at the windows. Opposite the bed was a sitting area for a guest to relax in the afternoon. A wide-screen television was surely hidden somewhere behind the bookcases that covered one wall.

Walking over to one of the floor-length windows, he pulled back the curtain to gaze out onto the darkened street below. Sunlight never touched an Aquatic city, but the artificial lighting throughout supplied each with ample illumination. It dimmed in the evening hours and brightened during the day.

A knock at the door drew his attention.

"Come in," he called.

A young Aquatic woman stood in the doorway. Her bluish skin glimmered as the bright hall light cut a silhouette about her lithe figure. She couldn't have been much more than sixteen years old, and already quite attractive and curvaceous.

"Yes?" he asked, wondering why she was there.

"Please, Captain, Queen Pisces has a gift for you this night. If we may bring it in . . . " Her voice trailed off as nervousness surfaced in her shaking voice.

"We?" The curtain slipped from his fingers. "How big could this gift be?"

"May we bring it in?"

"Yes, please."

She pushed the door open wider to reveal two young men carrying a long, rolled-up rug.

"A rug?" He was very confused. What could they possibly be delivering a rug for at this time of night?

The men placed the rug inside the room at the foot of the bed and, without a word, turned to leave.

"Wait. What am I supposed to do with a *rug?*" he asked them, but they refused to lift their eyes to his face. Drake turned to the girl but she just softly ushered the men out.

"Good night, Captain," she said before closing the door.

Cocking his head, he stared at the rug. It was wide and thick. Probably when unrolled it would span the entire length of the room.

Why would she send him this? He didn't understand. If she wanted to give him something, he could think of several things he'd prefer. Like her body.

Unable to take his eyes off the strange gift Naiya had given him, he strode over to the bed and sat down.

He had never really intended to stay the night in the palace. It had been a fluke—or fate—that his ship had engine problems. Well, maybe in his innermost heart he had hoped the queen would invite him to stay—in her bed. She wouldn't now, not after the way he'd acted—rejecting her obvious display of desire. Aroused, he had fought an inner battle, wishing he could act upon his passions but also needing to stay focused on his mission. He had fled from her, and now was damning himself for his stupidity.

He was initially attracted to her exotic beauty, but after meeting her, he sensed a depth to her soul he wished he could have the opportunity to explore. Something was unique about Naiya. She was a strong ruler to her people, much like some of the greatest queens of Earth's history—England's Queen Elizabeth or Cleopatra, the last pharaoh of ancient Egypt. If only Naiya was as determined in her desires as that legendary Egyptian queen— seducing two powerful men to serve her needs politically and sexually. He had no interest in politics, but he was *very* interested in sex.

As if on cue, the rug began to move. It began to unroll before his eyes, revealing a beautiful Aquatic design of coral and colorful fish.

Then he had the shock of his life.

There, hidden inside the rug, was Queen Pisces.

As the rug flopped completely open, she rose and stood regally, completely naked before him.

She smiled and struck a pose of seduction, running her hands over her body from her hips, up her sides, then to her breasts.

His mouth watered as she cupped her perfect mounds and squeezed them gently.

She knew exactly what to do to give him an erection as hard as iron.

"Captain Drake, I believe we have personal business to attend to." Her voice was like silken ties about his determination. And they tightened to the breaking point as she pinched her jewel-toned nipples to achy points.

"Personal business?" he croaked.

She released one of her nipples and let her hand travel down her abdomen to the perfect V of her sex. She dipped a finger lower and he moaned.

"Yes—very personal." She sighed.

"What do you want, Your Majesty?" He felt his blood pressure rise as he watched her slowly massage her sex. He wanted to dip his tongue into that wet heaven. Right then, he envied that finger.

"To have you as my lover."

He stood from the bed and strode across the room to stand before her. He couldn't give in to this. He shouldn't even consider it. "And what if I say no?" He didn't sound convincing.

She giggled as she reached out a hand and cupped his hard cock through his pants. "I don't think you want to say no."

Her hand upon his straining penis drove thoughts of right and wrong from his mind as longing took over.

Without a second thought, he grasped her by the shoulders and kissed her with a bruising passion.

SHE HADN'T BEEN THINKING beyond her physical needs tonight when she'd come up with this scheme. Inspired by an ancient tale of Cleopatra smuggling herself into the chambers of Julius Caesar in a rug, Naiya decided to use the same method. She took a chance that he'd storm out of the room in a rage, but hoped he'd throw her onto the bed and take her—again and again and again.

He kissed her deeply, his tongue swiping along hers in intense longing. She answered his demanding lips, opening her mouth to him.

He held her tightly, one hand behind her head, aiding her in losing her senses within his kiss. His other hand molded her body against him.

It was hard to think clearly as his passion consumed her. She met his demands, his tongue urging for more and his hands pulling her closer. She didn't know where her body began and his ended. They were one—bound by desire, pure sexual desire.

He broke his kiss, his breath labored and his skin slick with sweat. "We shouldn't be doing this," he said breathlessly.

"Why? Because you're a Land-walker?"

He caressed her cheek with his fingertips. "Because you're a *queen.*"

"Yes, but I'm also a *woman.*" She let her hands roam over the smooth muscle and sinew across his chest and down his perfect abdomen. "A living, breathing woman that desires you."

He pressed her tighter to his body. "I shouldn't want you like I do."

"I want you too." She wrapped a leg about one of his, moaning at the glorious sensation of her labia opening. It was one step closer to offering herself to this magnetic man.

"I don't take sex lightly, Naiya."

"Let's not analyze this moment. We're two people wishing for pleasure and companionship tonight. You're not a scientist hoping to save a city, and I'm not a queen waiting on edge to hear her kingdom is about to be destroyed. We're just a man and a woman finding comfort with each other." She rubbed her body along his solid frame, her clit teased further with each movement. Her cream began to ooze from her cunt and down her thigh. "Please, Drake . . . I want you."

It was the plea that broke his restraint. He kissed her again, bruising and possessive. His hand ran along her back and then down to her ass, where he grasped her flesh and held her pelvis securely against him. His other hand cupped her face, guiding her mouth against his, holding her prisoner to his desire.

She answered his demands willingly, wishing his clothes were gone, what little barrier they were between them.

As if reading her mind, he quickly released her and undressed before roughly pulling her back into his arms and kissing her once again, his tongue delving deep into her mouth. She groaned into his kiss as her skin seared against his. Her nipples, hardened and sensitive, rubbed against his chest, and she whimpered as she held on to his shoulders for support. Her legs went weak beneath her but he held her securely as he continued to feast upon her mouth.

His lips and tongue tasted her deeply, and when he broke the kiss they continued their sensual assault upon her senses. He licked and kissed a trail down her neck to her chest, where he began to worship her breasts. He took one nipple into his mouth, his tongue swirling about the tip, driving her to the very edge of control. Her cunt ached for his touch and cream continued to seep from her in anticipation of his invasion of her body.

Drake caressed one breast with his hand while his tongue and lips devoured the other, making Naiya incapable of clear thought. Pure need drove her to succumb to his ministrations. She threaded her fingers through his hair as he sucked upon her breast, guiding him to increase the pressure building within her.

He released her breast from his mouth and she whined in disappointment, only to sigh as he began to lick her other breast. She shuddered as her nipple tightened within the moist heat of his mouth. With one hand he caressed the skin at her hip, his thumb traced small enticing circles upon her flesh, and she was lost. Then he traced a finger over her closely clipped mons. He teased her labia with a gentle pass of his fingers, never delving deeply enough to relieve the ache building in her clit.

She tightened her fists in his hair, a silent plea for him to end the torture. But he was unwilling to obey. He removed his fingers from her folds and released his mouth from her breast.

"There's no turning back, Naiya. I want you with every cell of my body. Tell me that you want me—desire me—to make you mine." His voice was breathless and filled with unspent passion.

"Take me" was all she could say in response. Her body quivered and shook with need. She wanted him to possess her, make love to her, drive himself deep into her, answer every desire she'd ever thought possible—and those she never even imagined in her most erotic fantasies.

Without another word, he lifted her into his arms and carried her to the bed. He rocked her gently as he stood next to the bed and she liked the loving care he took in holding her, delicately, tenderly. Naiya felt like a fragile porcelain doll, carefully handled lest she break in the hands of such a powerful man.

She sank into the welcoming softness of the mattress as he laid her on the bed, as if reclining on a cloud reaching up to embrace her from below.

He paused, looking down at her figure sprawled before him. Her breasts were taut and firm, aching for him to touch them once again.

"You are so beautiful, Naiya."

Her face heated. "Thank you." She paused and met his gaze.

"You feel different than . . . than other women." He reached down and traced the curve of her breast with his fingertips. "Soft and exotic," he whispered as he watched her nipple pucker even more at the slightest hint of his touch.

She sighed and closed her eyes. Her body arched into his touch as she enjoyed the simple ecstasy of his caress.

He pulled his hand away and she whimpered softly at the loss. Small goose bumps rose across her skin as the cool air caressed her sex, exciting her further.

"Bend your knees and open your legs," he commanded in a soft voice.

As she obeyed his request, it was as though the heat from his eyes bore into her body. A flush pinked her skin as he stood silently examining her, his gaze riveted to her thatch.

With a finger, he reached down and passed through her slick folds and across her clit. Naiya cried out as she arched toward his hand to continue the sweet torture.

"You want to clamp down on my cock, don't you?" he asked, his voice strained with desire.

Her answer was a whimper as she lifted her ass off the mattress in a plea for him to delve his fingers deeper into her body.

"Tell me, Naiya. Tell me how much you want me to fuck you right now." He swirled his fingers through her juices, coating his fingertips and massaging the little organ demanding attention. "Come on, honey. Tell me," he repeated.

"I want you to fuck me!" she gasped.

"As you command, Your Majesty."

She felt the bed dip beneath his weight as he climbed upon it. She felt exposed as he crouched between her legs, laid his hands upon her knees and spread them open even wider.

Her labia opened farther before him and he moaned. "Such a sexy sight. If it were up to me, I'd have you on your back just like this all day long so I could see that wet pussy."

"And how would I rule from such a position?" she giggled.

"By com-link."

He adjusted his position on the bed and covered her body with his. She felt vulnerable to his strength, his command over her body as well as her senses. The tip of his cock brushed lightly against the edge of her clit and she groaned.

"You're in a hurry, aren't you?"

"Sorry, I just need—"

He kissed her gently, silencing her explanation. "Don't be sorry. I want you so bad, but I don't want to go too fast, either."

"Please . . . fuck me now. We can go slower later."

With a primal growl, he pushed his cock into her. She cried out as his thick length filled her, stretching her internal muscles. He stilled as she adapted to his size, but she didn't want gentleness now that she had his cock wedged inside her. She thrust up her hips, taking him deeper into her.

"Oh, honey, you're going to kill me with such eagerness," he moaned as he began to move, withdrawing from her then slamming back inside. She squealed as she flexed her hips to meet his thrust.

Naiya saw ecstasy for the first time in her life with his cock pulsing inside her. No one—not even Brendon—had ever made her body come alive with such rapture. She felt every beat of Drake's heart as the blood pumped to his cock nestled within her slick cavern.

She clenched down upon him and wrapped her legs about his waist in an attempt to keep him from pulling out too far. Sweat-slicked skin slid along hers. The sounds of flesh against flesh and heavy breathing filled the room as Naiya succumbed to her inner desires, her intimate needs.

Her climax began at the point of their joining, then radiated up and down her body in a sizzling instant of uncontrolled bliss. The spasms washed over her entire being as her vaginal muscles clamped his cock in rhythmic contractions, and she screamed out at the intensity.

He quickened his pace, matching the rhythm her body set, and joined her in a powerful orgasm of his own. He yelled as his seed pumped again and again deep into her. The heated fluid sprayed within and she was overwhelmed with the joy of taking his essence into her body in their moment of sensual euphoria.

As they began to calm, he rested his body upon hers. She enjoyed the intimate closeness of the moment while they tried to recover their breathing. She felt his heart slam in his chest and the beat matched her own.

Their breaths mingled and she tasted a hint of peppermint upon her lips. And even as his flaccid penis slipped from her wet core, she wanted him again.

Tracing the toned muscles and sinew of his back and shoulders, she brought her face to his and kissed him tenderly.

He returned her kiss as he rolled his body from hers, capturing her in his arms and nestling her body at his side. His hands dipped into the thickness of her hair and she surrendered to the gentle touch.

This wasn't just physical submission. During those moments of ecstasy, Naiya had crossed a line she never dreamed she'd cross—never contemplated.

Naiya had let her heart be touched.

When Naiya awoke in the middle of the night, Drake lay beside her on his belly, sound asleep. With a lift of the sheet, the proof she needed was revealed.

Drake indeed bore the mark of the Scorpion King.

FOUR

*I*N THE MORNING DRAKE slipped from the bed, leaving Naiya still sleeping. He would've stayed behind to hold her until the moment her eyes opened, but he had to get back to the lab. He dressed in silence and before he left, leaned over her and kissed her forehead.

It was hard to walk away from such a sight—Naiya naked in bed, her skin glimmering in the soft lamplight, her silvery hair fanned over the pillow in luscious waves and her breathing even in deep sleep. She looked content . . . and satisfied. A smile curled his lips, happy to have been the man to satisfy her.

As he left the room and closed the door behind him, a determined thought crossed his mind. He didn't want to think of her with any other man. Drake wanted to be the only man to make her squirm in bed with desire, to make her scream in orgasm and then to hold her through the night in contented satisfaction. He had never before had serious feelings toward any woman, to the extent of wanting to claim her as his own.

Upon his arrival at the docking bay, Drake found his ship completely repaired. The night of passion was over and serious work lay ahead. As he cleared the force field, he wondered if they could ever possibly have a future together. A one-night stand with the queen was hardly the basis of a long-term relationship. He wasn't certain there was even a future for the city of Pacifica. The city was in danger. It wasn't the smartest move to start an affair under such perilous circumstances.

Even after tasting the delights of true passion with Naiya, he still felt unsure of the intelligence of his actions. No one on this mission could afford to be bleary-eyed. Sharp attention to the data they were collecting was foremost in importance. He had to remain strong and clear-minded—professional.

Arriving at the lab, Drake was greeted with stares from the team. He said nothing, just strode to his work station and sat down.

"Just getting in, Drake?" Jay asked as he sat down on a nearby chair.

"Yeah. I had some engine troubles last night so I stayed until the Aquatic repair crew could fix the problem."

"Uh-huh."

Drake glanced up at his friend and cocked a brow. "Are you trying to get at something?"

"Engine troubles to prevent you from coming back to the lab after meeting privately with the queen . . . sounds kind of convenient."

"Convenient? I don't like the direction you're going with this conversation."

"Fine, fine," Jay said, rising from his chair. "I'll keep my mouth shut."

Drake sighed. "I'm sorry, Jay. I'm a little touchy this morning."

"Why?" Jay sat back down and rolled his chair closer.

"Because I think I've made a mistake."

"What do you mean?"

"I mean, this is not a good time to start an affair."

"You slept together?"

Drake nodded.

"You know, sometimes you can't predict when things like this will happen," Jay offered.

"But the timing sucks. I should've been here last night reading data rather than spending time with the queen." *And having the best damn sex I've ever had.*

"I wouldn't worry about it. The sensors were quiet last night." Jay paused then asked softly, "Are you worried that she'll read into the night more than you intended?"

"No, no," he insisted. "I'm worried that *I'm* reading more into it than *she* intended."

"Captain Drake," Dr. Tucker interrupted. "The chemical composition of the water near the vent is changing on a continual basis. Liquefied metals—gold, copper and silver—are spewing up into the water and mixing with the natural salts. It is perfect for the formation of new life here in the depths."

"But not so good for a nearby city with a large population of Land-walkers and Aquatics," Drake offered.

Dr. Tucker nodded. "According to my calculations, the density of the ocean waters and its changing chemical makeup may have a dire effect on the force field of Pacifica. Since the field utilizes the salt content of the ocean water, a change in the balance could cause a malfunction."

Drake leaned forward. "You mean the force field could short out and the entire city would be flooded?"

"Precisely. The pressure of the ocean water would destroy the entire city without an earthquake."

"And that is definitely coming," broke in Lieutenant Johnson, the ocean geologist on the team. "We've arrived too late. At the rate the vent is growing, and with the rising temperatures coming from the center, the event may well happen in the next few days."

Drake couldn't believe what he was hearing. An entire city was located near a ticking time bomb. "I need you all to get me status reports by five o'clock so I can present our findings to the queen. She needs to get the city evacuated before the whole thing blows. I'll also need to report to the admiral our findings so the cities in the immediate area above can also be evacuated. I need to know the approximate magnitude of this so we can plan."

"Captain, I fear this is going to rival the biggest natural disasters in Earth's history."

Drake rose from his chair. "Then let's make sure we get our findings to the right people so it won't be the most costly in human casualties."

NAIYA AWOKE TO AN empty bed. Startled at first, she scanned the room. Drake had gone. How long ago, she couldn't say.

She stretched and the soreness of last night settled throughout her body. Her muscles were tender and moving was slightly painful, but she didn't mind. Never was there a more delightful reason to wake up with a bit of stiffness. Drake had satisfied her on so many levels last night, and the price this morning paled compared to the ecstasy she discovered within Drake's arms.

But he left without a word, without waking her to say good-bye. When *did* he leave? She reached for the com-link on the nightstand and called the docking bay.

"Lieutenant Granger here," the voice answered, breaking the silence.

"Yes, Lieutenant. What time did Captain Drake leave this morning?"

"About an hour ago, Your Majesty."

She thanked him and clicked off the com-link.

She proceeded to her own chambers to get ready for the day. After bathing and dressing, she received a message to join Brendon for breakfast in the morning room, where there was a less-formal dining table with a buffet set out for the queen and her palace guests and royal advisers. She often preferred the casual meal, where she could be herself and not a queen expecting to be catered to.

"Good morning, Naiya," Brendon said when she walked into the morning room.

She groaned inwardly. By the look on his face, he surely knew of her night with Drake. Spies were everywhere, and an affair involving the queen was newsworthy.

And Brendon was a jealous man hungry for power.

"Morning, Brendon. I got your message. I didn't think you ever ate breakfast beyond a cup of coffee."

"I don't normally, but today isn't like any other day."

Naiya moved to the buffet and picked up a plate. "Really? And why is today any different than yesterday?"

"Don't act coy. I know what happened last night."

She filled her plate with some eggs and fruit. "I know what happened, too. So at least there is no mystery there."

"How could you, Naiya? You slept with a lowly commoner, a man below your station and rank. You are meant for greatness, and only a man fit to be king should share your bed."

As she took her plate and sat at the table, she refused to let his words pierce her soul. "We've been through this already. I am the best judge of who is fit to share my bed."

"I think you need to reconsider Captain Drake as a lover. He's nothing more than a common soldier in the Land-walker Navy. He's an opportunist searching to elevate his own status through any means possible, including bedding a queen," Brendon spat out, his anger evident. His plate in front of him was filled with eggs that had gone cold.

Drake was more than a lover. He possessed the mark, the sign of the scorpion. He was destined to be Scorpion King, the man to rule by her side as foretold by an oracle upon the day of her birth. The prophecy was widely known, and for years the entire kingdom had searched for the man marked to become king. The search had been to no avail. Naiya had surmised years ago that the oracle was wrong—until last night.

How could she even tell Brendon of the tattoo? He'd claim it was a trick of some sort, Drake's attempt to manipulate the queen and capture the throne and all its power.

Somehow she couldn't see Drake drunk with power, unlike Brendon, who reveled in glory and authority. Many times she'd had to set him straight, putting caution into motion to restrain Brendon and his need for wealth and power. She had already learned of certain taxes and levies Brendon had proposed to the Council before her reign. Money she feared might have been misused—public programs and projects had not increased in proportion to the treasury.

No, she couldn't tell him that Drake bore the mark of the scorpion. It wasn't the right time. He'd never believe it. And she wouldn't doubt an assassination attempt would be made in the form of a convenient accident.

"Are you listening to me?" Brendon asked, breaking into her thoughts.

"What do you want me to say?"

He paused and gazed at her face. She was struck by the anger simmering behind his eyes.

"Don't get involved with him."

She lost her appetite. "Here we are living on the verge of possible destruction, the entire city at stake, and all you care about is that I am fucking another man?"

His hands slammed down on the table. "Damn it, you are mine!" He rose from his seat and charged around the table toward her. "Do you think I will sit by and let some commoner claim my place?"

She got up from her seat and tried to back away as he approached at full speed. He caught her arms and pulled her against him roughly.

"Brendon, don't do this!" She tried to pull away, but he held her with a steel grip.

"No, Naiya! It is past time you see who the true king of Pacifica really is." With that he claimed her mouth roughly. The brutality of his kiss bruised her lips and his hands gripped her arms tightly, without any gentleness. She struggled in his grasp, but it only increased his anger.

When he broke the kiss, his breathing was ragged. She pushed against him, but he held her tighter still.

"Tell me, does your scientist lover kiss you with such passion?" He shoved her back across the table and pinned her down with his rock-hard body before she could regain her balance and escape.

"What will you do? Rape me? Force yourself upon me?" She refused to let weakness waver in her voice.

"If I have to take you by force, I will. Just to wipe away that bastard's face from your memory."

"You forget there is only one man destined to become king!"

Brendon chuckled. "That is nothing more than a bedtime fairy tale. I shall become your king, and I will enjoy having you bow to my desires."

"I will never give myself to you," she spat as he leaned down to nibble her neck. She tried to kick at him, to strike his body as it held her securely to the table, to no avail.

"Does it matter?" he whispered. "When I am king, you will come to me when I call. Whether you enjoy it or not is entirely up to you." He pressed his groin against her and nausea swept over her as his hard cock pressed against her mound. She stilled when he chuckled, as her movements simply drove him closer to her center.

He kissed her again with violent force as he held her wrists against the smooth tabletop. He ground his cock against her painfully. If their clothes hadn't been a barrier, he'd surely have been inside her already.

He broke the kiss then released her wrists. He pushed off her and backed away from the table. Straightening his clothes, he smirked. "You say you don't want me, but your body reacts to mine like a bitch in heat. Yes, I think you will enjoy pleasuring my every whim."

"You're a bastard!"

He just laughed as he ran his fingers through his blond hair. "My blood is pure royalty. My family should have been rulers of Pacifica. And now, I will see the Aquarius family upon the throne at last." His smile faded as hate poured from his eyes, boring into her painfully. "You will announce to the Council that you will marry me and make me your king."

"I won't!"

Without a word, he stepped forward and tugged on her arm roughly. With his other hand, he smacked her across the face. "You will, bitch! I *will* be king, and unless you don't want to see your precious scientist live beyond today, you will do as I say."

He released her, spun on his heel and marched out of the room.

Her cheek stung where he had struck her. Her wrists were reddened where he'd held her down with his superior physical strength.

"Brendon," she said quietly to the now empty room, "you may be able to overpower my body, but you'll *never* overpower my will. You will *never* command me or the people of Pacifica."

She made her way to a chair and sat. Still shaking, she activated the com-link.

"Lieutenant Granger here."

She breathed deeply, trying to calm her nerves. "Arrest Councilman Brendon Aquarius for treason and attempted rape."

"DRAKE, APPARENTLY ONE OF the Council members was arrested this morning for trying to rape the queen," Jay told him quietly, as he sat at his workstation poring over the data that his team was collecting.

"Rape?" He threw the papers onto his desk. He knew exactly who without thinking on it. "Councilman Aquarius."

"Yeah, you guessed it."

"Bastard." He rose from his seat and, as he rushed out to the transport shuttle, turned and asked, "Is Naiya okay?"

"Not sure. I only heard about the arrest, not much else." Drake turned to leave, but Jay caught him by the arm. "Dude, there's something you need to know about the queen of Pacifica."

"What?"

Jay hesitated. "You know that tattoo on your back, the big scorpion?"

"Yeah, what of it?"

"Do you remember anything about how you got it?"

Drake cocked his head. "What does *that* have to do with any-thing?" he asked impatiently.

"It has to do with *everything*." When Drake stood silent, Jay continued. "Did your parents ever tell you why you have that mark on your back?"

Drake paused at the door. "Jay, I don't have time for this! I have to go to Naiya."

"The mark has to do with your destiny—and hers. Just wait."

Jay took a deep breath and asked, "What do you know about that tattoo?"

"My father told me that an oracle visited the day I was born and I was marked with the symbol of my zodiac sign, Scorpio—the scorpion. The man told my father that the scorpion was the guide to my destiny," Drake explained impatiently. "I never understood why my parents tattooed me on the word of some stranger that showed up on their doorstep." He looked at Jay's troubled face, the lines of his forehead deep with concern. "Everyone called me Scorpio throughout my childhood. Where are you going with this? I'm kinda pressed for time here."

Jay sighed. "Did you know there's a prophecy regarding the queen of Pacifica and the man bearing the mark of the scorpion?"

"No, what do you mean?"

"The Scorpion King. Dude, I think *you're* the man destined to become the Scorpion King—the man who's supposed to marry Queen Pisces."

"Huh?"

"There's a prophecy from Naiya's birth, as well. An oracle proclaimed only the man bearing the mark of the scorpion could marry Naiya and rule Pacifica by her side."

Drake shook his head. "No, I can't be. I mean . . . no. It's just a dumb tattoo."

"Sorry dude, but that's the story."

"How did *you* hear about it?"

"I heard a mention of the Scorpion King while listening to some Pacifica Council transmissions." Jay shrugged. "I got curious and looked it up."

Drake stared at him, dumbfounded. "I don't even know what to think right now. All I want to do is see if Naiya is all right."

"Go on, Drake. Go and see her."

The Scorpion King? It had to be a coincidence. The whole thing was preposterous. Drake simply had a tattoo on his back. It was the result of his parents listening to a senile old man who claimed he had second sight, nothing more. For years Drake had tried to find meaning in the mark on his back, searching for reason and purpose. None ever seemed to present itself. And now, thirty-two years later, he finds out that he's to become a king of an underwater kingdom?

He didn't even like the water!

Unbelievable.

It didn't matter now. He just had to get to Naiya. He pushed the Scorpion King legend from his mind, dismissing it as nonsense and hearsay. He was a man of science, and not prone to believing some idiotic tale of destiny and magic. Only the facts as he saw them mattered. He had to think like a scientist, not some love-struck schoolboy.

Drake didn't waste time in getting to the shuttle. A thousand thoughts crossed his mind. He wanted to get his hands on that bastard Brendon and strangle him, to sweep Naiya into his arms and swear never to let anything like that happen again. He was torn between wanting to commit murder—justifiable homicide, in his mind—and loving the queen into forgetting her pain.

This was not what he needed during this mission, yet here he was, rushing off to his lover's side. He had to see her just to be sure she wasn't hurt. By God, if Brendon so much as bruised her skin, Drake would break him in two.

Within minutes, he was passing through the Pacifica force field. He was primed and ready to attack as his vessel set down in the docking bay.

Storming through the city to the palace, Drake tried to understand the urges driving him. Which did he want more—to kill Brendon or make sure Naiya was okay?

To see Naiya.

But why?

She was queen of a genetically enhanced human race, and he was nothing more than a regular air-breathing human scientist. He worked his way through the military to gain the knowledge he needed to make a living. He had very little money to speak of, earning a modest income that he hardly had time to even spend. Compared to a queen, Drake was a man without rank, a commoner. What could he offer her other than his devotion and love?

He slid to a stop. The realization hit him with the strength of exploding magma. He had fallen in love with Naiya.

No woman had touched his heart like her. In fact, women were not often a part of his life. He chose to submerge himself in his studies, to become the best in his field, forgoing the roller coaster of love. He'd obtained his dream of becoming the foremost seismologist on Earth, but loneliness became the price of a stellar career.

He began to run toward the palace. He'd never felt so alive, and it was all because of Naiya.

Drake was in love for the first time in his life and he was not going to let anything stand in his way of winning the woman of his dreams.

FIVE

AIYA PACED HER BEDROOM, wringing her hands. Drake had arrived moments ago in the docking bay and was on his way to see her. How could she face him? He'd left her sleeping that morning and so much had happened since. Brendon had tried to force her into sexual submission in an attempt to place himself on the throne! He'd been captured, and when the Council heard she had charged him with treason along with attempted rape, they had been skeptical. Their lack of support troubled her beyond the situation with Brendon. What would they do if both scientific teams determined the city unsafe? Would the Council believe the facts presented or would they claim disbelief?

They were less than enthusiastic over the news of her affair with Drake. Brendon's disapproval echoed through the Council chamber. She held her tongue as to the mark of the scorpion Drake bore, wanting their approval on his merit as opposed to a tattoo.

As they berated Drake and his common origins, Naiya realized her heart had quickly betrayed her. She'd fallen in love. Tears burned her eyes when she had stood before her Council earlier, as they proposed an investigation into the treason and rape accusations. They didn't believe her. Her Council had turned against her. She needed Drake—not only to strengthen the power of the throne for the benefit of her people, but to stand by her as her one true love.

Could Drake ever love anything other than his work?

What worried her more was the tattoo—the mark of the Scorpion King. Would he accept the prophecy and marry her to lead their people into a promising future, or would he dismiss it all as coincidence?

Did she truly want him to marry her for a throne?

She loathed Brendon for his ambitions, but how could she know Drake wasn't capable of becoming drunk with the idea of power over an entire kingdom?

No, that wasn't Drake. He was a man of intelligence, a self-made man who had worked his way to his current status as captain. He was the head of a science team sent to pass sentence on an entire society. The Land-walkers wouldn't send anyone but their best man to oversee such a mission. He was a man to be trusted.

And she trusted him immensely.

She hadn't known him long, but trusting him seemed completely natural for her. It was an odd realization considering her proclamations to never trust a man with her heart again. When Drake had strutted off his ship, Naiya instantly recognized confidence and a genuine, sincere willingness to help her and her people. All she had ever seen in Brendon's gait was arrogance and dark secrecy.

Perhaps the secrets Brendon held from her were the very reasons she found a need to trust Drake. She wasn't sure if it was in
her best interest to lay her trust with the captain, but she couldn't
help herself. It was as though something inside of her *knew* him to
be a good man, a true gentleman.

A servant knocked on her door, breaking into her thoughts.

"Your Majesty," the girl stammered nervously, bowing slightly.
"The Captain—"

Drake pushed past the girl and into the room. "I heard what
happened." He strode to Naiya and pulled her into his arms. "I
had to make sure you were all right."

Within the circle of his embrace, Naiya relaxed. "I'll be okay."

"Bastard! I ought to go and break one of his legs for touching
you."

"No. It isn't necessary." She gulped down her pride. "Brendon
trying to force himself on me is nothing new."

He took a step back and held her at the shoulders. "You mean
to tell me he's tried this before?" Anger rang in his every word.
His body shook as he fought to control his building fury.

"Well, this was the first time he ever acted out like that."

"First and *last*. He better not cross my path any time soon or
he will most certainly regret it." He paused. "Are you sure you're
okay?"

She stretched her hand up to his face and traced his jaw with
her fingertips. "I'm better now that you are here."

For a moment, he hesitated. It was only a split second of internal struggle that reflected within his eyes before he captured her
lips in a sudden kiss.

The tender meeting of lips quickly flamed to a hungry passion as they began to pull at each other's clothes. Fabric ripped away from heated flesh then Naiya was naked and free to feel him against her. He was the only man she wanted in her bed. Never had a man excited her so quickly, so completely.

Doubts fled her mind and heart as his hands held her firmly to his body, and she sank into ecstasy as his hands molded her, studied her—consumed her.

She threaded her fingers through his hair, deepening their kiss, and a moan escaped his throat, low and primal. His tongue dove into her mouth, sliding along hers in a mating dance that was ancient and entirely instinctual. Her breasts pressing against his hard chest ached as his skin rubbed against her nipples. They hardened into ripe berries, throbbing for him to hold them in his hands and suckle their tight tips.

Suddenly he picked her up, his hands under her buttocks, and he backed them to a nearby wall. Her back against the cool surface was in stark contrast to the hot man pressing into her.

He kissed her hard, possessive and controlling. She liked it—and wanted more.

And then he lowered her over his cock, sliding up inside her in one thrust. She yelped as she took in his massive size deeply. She held on to his shoulders as he moved in and out, her back rocking against the wall for support. She wrapped her legs about him and he continued to guide her ride over his cock.

With each push into her channel the world swayed before her eyes. Colors seemed to mix together in a kaleidoscope across her vision. She entered a surreal place where there was no concept of anything but the joining of her body to Drake's. There was nothing beyond the two of them.

His hands held her steady against the wall as his rhythm increased in tempo. His cock grew in size within her sheath and she moaned at the perfection of their fit. Her juices flowed and the sound of his cock diving through her wetness accompanied the slap of their skin with each push, with every plunge into her depths.

He broke the kiss and nestled his face against the crook of her neck. Like a vampire searching for his lover's nourishment, he bit down as his climax overtook him.

The pain of his love bite was nothing compared to the glory of the orgasm that swept over her senses. Her vagina clenched his penis within her, and she screamed in delight as the hot spray of his cum shot against her cervix.

Her nether muscles tightened about him in rhythmic spasms as she rode out her first climax and straight into a second. This time, she felt every inch of his cock stab into her with every beat of her heart.

She closed her eyes and gave herself over to the ecstasy and she panted and cried with each wave of delight.

As their orgasms began to fade, he whispered incoherent words. She didn't need to hear them clearly to know their meaning. He cherished her, adored her. This was much more than a physical fling of the flesh.

Easing her legs from around his waist, she reached for the floor with her toes and he let her slide from his hold using the wall for balance. She held on to his shoulders for support, her legs weak with exhaustion.

Gently he guided her to the bed where she reclined, welcoming the softness beneath her. He left her side, but only for a moment. When he returned, he held a wet cloth within his hand. He went about cleansing her thighs and the evidence of their spontaneous lovemaking. His touch was oddly gentle for such a powerful man. He spread her legs open and a shiver of anticipation traveled through her veins. As he spread her labia to better wipe away his seed seeping from her body, a renewed desire built within her. When he passed the cloth over her clit, she gasped at its heightened sensitivity.

He was tender and loving as he cared for her. And once she was clean, he leaned in to her mound and lightly kissed her nether lips. The delicate pressure of his lips nibbling and the soft kisses quickly drove her out of her mind. Never did he touch the aching bud hidden within her fold. And it was sending her higher into ecstasy. Her mind clouded once again under the power of pure rapture as he tantalized her sex into a frenzied need.

Then he spread her labia wide and slowly licked her clit. He used the tip of his tongue in a torturous touch across the surface, tormenting her body with his relaxed speed.

Just a little quicker. Oh please, lick me harder. Drake . . . Drake, my love, yes, lick me!

And as though he heard her innermost wishes, he took her sweet clit between his teeth and licked ferociously. He sucked and licked her pleasure point, driving her to the edge. And when she thought the pleasure was too much to bear, he dipped two fingers into her hole and massaged the spot within that drove her into a climactic hurricane of bodily convulsions.

Her pussy clamped around his fingers as they danced within her and he continued to worship her clit. The climax was unlike anything she'd ever experienced. And he did it without thought to his own needs, his own desires. This was entirely for her pleasure.

She sank back into the pillows as fatigue washed over her, contentment easing her body and mind. She was comforted by the knowledge that her greatest lover was her destiny.

But one question still troubled her dreamy mind.

Would Drake accept his fate as her husband and king?

DRAKE LAY BY NAIYA after she'd fallen asleep. He stayed awake worrying over whether he had risked too much in succumbing to the queen's desires—and his own. Part of him held regrets, fears that he'd overstepped his place in society.

But love knew no boundaries. Or was it that love *broke* all boundaries? He wasn't sure.

He wanted to tell Naiya his feelings, but he was unsure how. Does one blurt it out in a moment of passion, or should he wait for a quiet, romantic moment to proclaim his love?

Damn, this love thing was more complicated and difficult than memorizing the entire periodic chart and each element's density, boiling point, atomic number and ionization potential. At least the elements remained constant and predictable.

Women were many things, but never predictable.

However, Drake's main worry wasn't about guessing Naiya's innermost emotions. Her actions spoke loud and clear, even if she hadn't voiced them. No, it was the prophecy of the Scorpion King that bothered him.

Could it be possible that he was here for a greater purpose than a scientific mission? Had fate stepped into play and placed him here to meet Naiya? And was it possible that he was the fated Scorpion King?

His father had often spoke of the old oracle who had appeared in the village the day Drake was born. The man had claimed he'd followed images within a dream—a scorpion leading his unconscious mind onward.

The oracle had been Aquatic, and he claimed his vision brought him to the Land-walkers in search of the one destined for greatness as written in the stars. The man insisted Drake be tattooed with the mark of the Scorpio, so his destiny would be realized without fail. What that destiny would bring had been a mystery . . . until now.

He glanced down upon Naiya's sleeping form and realized she'd known since their first night together. He refused to believe her attentions continued because of a prophecy. No, this was much more than a fulfilled destiny.

He was about to shake her shoulder to awaken her—when the bed began to shake beneath him.

"Seaquake," he whispered as Naiya's eyes shot open when the tremors increased in force.

"Oh my God!" She clutched him as the walls about them shook and the floor moved with the quaking earth.

Items on shelves fell to the floor, paintings on the walls crashed down and books stacked on nearby tables shuddered and skidded across their surfaces.

The shaking continued for a few minutes and cries rose from the city outside as men and women dodged falling debris from buildings and other structures.

"They've never lasted this long before," she said in a shaky voice.

"I think we may have run out of time," Drake replied.

Six

THE SEAQUAKE BEGAN TO die down slightly in intensity, but several pictures lay shattered on the floor, statues and other glass objects joining them as the tremors continued. Her room was a mess but she didn't care. What was the rest of the city suffering after this last tremor?

A com-link chimed.

Drake jumped from the bed, uninhibited by his nakedness, and ran for his com-link. "Captain Scopillo here. Report," he ordered with the flick of a button on his wrist communicator that had been tossed aside the night before.

"Drake, the vent is growing right before our eyes. Lieutenant Johnson reports that there is building pressure just below the surface and according to his calculations, it is intensifying quickly," Jay said over the link, his voice shaking slightly.

Drake turned to Naiya and their gazes locked, and without looking away, he spoke to the communicator. "And what is the chemical balance? Can the force field hold up while the city prepares to evacuate?"

There was silence on the link as Jay retrieved the report. Drake didn't speak, but no words were necessary. She read his apprehension in each tense muscle as he began to dress.

The building's shaking decreased further, but Naiya's fear was the exact opposite. How was she going to convince the Council that they were all in danger? Perhaps they would accept the reports now that another, more violent quake had hit the city. Brendon, a longtime member now serving his third term in office, had poisoned them, claiming her affair with Drake was irresponsible, painting her as someone of loose character before the Council. They had seemed too quick to disbelieve the charges against him, and she realized he had most likely been nurturing a distrust in her ability to rule since she'd ascended to the throne. They could possibly dismiss any claims Drake made of the seriousness of the situation, now knowing that he was the queen's lover.

But he wasn't just any man she'd taken to her bed. If she were to reveal the tattoo to the Council, they may shrink back in disbelief. The Council was made up of superstitious men and women, and they would not dispute the evidence of the mark—partly out of fear, but mostly out of awe.

How would Drake take the news that he was to become not only her husband but a king foretold by an ancient oracle years ago?

The com-link crackled back to life as Jay finally began to speak again. "Drake . . . the Lieutenant says her calculations give the force field another day or two, according to the current figures. With another tremor like the last, she said the time could be even less."

"Okay, Jay. Tell the team to beam their reports to the admiral. I'm going to talk to him about our findings and have him order the evacuation of the villages and cities on the surface. When the vent blows and the ridges collapse, the seismic tidal wave above could wipe out millions of people."

Drake paced the bedroom as Naiya listened intently to the conversation.

"What will you tell the queen?"

Drake stopped and looked at her. A shiver ran down her spine as he said, "She knows already." He flipped off his com-link and took a step toward her. "You heard everything." He didn't ask, but she still nodded. "You have to evacuate immediately."

"Yes, I know." She pulled on a long blue robe. "I am just wondering how the Council will react to the news."

"I suggest you bypass the Council, Naiya. Your people don't have time for politics. You have to act and give the order." He paused. "Is there a city that can take in refugees?"

She nodded. "Yes. That won't be a problem. I'd already contacted Laurentia before your team arrived. I asked them to be prepared just in case."

"Good." He strode to her and held her by the shoulders, squeezing them gently. "You are the strongest woman I've ever known. A true queen. It's time your people see that. Make the order."

DRAKE STOOD OFF-CAMERA AS Naiya used the PlaNET to order the evacuation. She opted to make the announcement in her private quarters. Her servants were already bustling to pack her things but paused as the queen broadcasted live the order for all Pacifica citizens to leave in the next twenty hours or less.

"Due to a hydrothermal vent located dangerously close to our city, we have been plagued by numerous tremors over the years. As you know, their intensity has increased dramatically. Now, according to a group of scientists, both Aquatic and Land-walker, they have determined the situation can no longer be ignored.

"I order all citizens to leave our city within the next twenty hours. The city of Laurentia has offered haven for all, with added assistance in transporting all citizens to safety.

"Please, *do not* ignore this order. Leave the city now. Save your families. I will be with you in Laurentia. It is too dangerous for any of us to remain here."

At the end of her broadcast, Drake saw the tension in her body. He immediately went to her and took her in his arms. She fell into his embrace, leaning on him for strength to endure.

As the servants went about finishing the packing, Drake continued to hold Naiya. It was a natural place for him to be. He wanted to tell her his feelings, the emotions that had struck him like lightning. In his heart he suspected Naiya felt the same, but was unable to bring herself to admit her feelings. She was a woman who inherited power, but it was hard for her to support all that power upon her shoulders.

"I'll stay with you, Naiya," he whispered. "As long as you want me by your side, I will be here for you."

She nestled further into his embrace. "Thank you," she breathed softly.

A surge of sensual awareness pumped through him and his cock hardened at her slight movements.

"I spoke to the admiral and they have started evacuations on the surface. They are also sending us ships to help transport everyone to Laurentia."

A servant, the same girl who delivered the rug to him a couple nights ago, cleared her throat.

"Yes, Crystal?" Naiya asked as she inched away from him.

"We are receiving numerous calls from Council members. They seem . . . upset."

Naiya nodded. "I knew that would happen. And they will have their answers once we settle in Laurentia."

Crystal stood shaking slightly, her eyes darting from Naiya to Drake.

"What is it? Is there something else?" Naiya turned in his arms, her back to his chest. He laid his hands upon her shoulders to offer his strength.

"They are gathering in the Council chambers already. And . . . Brendon was ordered to be there as well."

"How *dare* they question my orders? We don't have time to debate!"

Drake lightly squeezed her shoulders. "We'll go meet with them now."

She closed her eyes and took a deep breath. "Tell them we will meet with them in fifteen minutes."

Crystal bowed and ran off with the message.

Naiya leaned back against him. "Brendon will do everything in his power to cause trouble."

"He wants the throne, the power . . . and you. It drives him insane that he can have none of it."

"How did you know?"

"Because for a man like him, power and wealth are his only passions. He will stop at nothing to obtain them, including the rape of the queen."

MINUTES LATER DRAKE AND Naiya arrived before the Council. As they entered the Council chambers, the entire room buzzed with arguments. Drake squeezed Naiya's hand as she strode through the men and women loudly discussing the surprise evacuation order. She held her head high and was unwavering as she took her seat at the head of the table. Drake stood behind her, offering his support.

"How could you issue an evacuation order without consulting the Council?" a member sitting by a brooding Brendon asked above the others in the room.

Drake leaned forward and whispered to Naiya, "Who is that?"

"That is Leo Aquarius, Brendon's brother," she whispered in response.

Drake straightened as he glared at the dark-haired man at Brendon's side. Drake could see a family resemblance in the men's faces and builds. Brendon's blond hair was lighter and his skin fairer than his brother's.

"The Council was not consulted for the evacuation. I demand this act be canceled until we are able to examine the evidence," Leo insisted, slamming his hand on the table for emphasis. His face was turning redder by the minute.

"I saw no reason to consult the Council during an emergency. Precious minutes of debate are better spent getting everyone out before disaster hits." Naiya stood firm on her decision. Her hands grasped the armrests of her chair tightly. There was no mistaking the evidence that she fought her anger in order to appear calm.

"You're new to the position of queen, very young and inexperienced to make such a rash decision," Leo spat. He paused to quickly glance at Brendon, who nodded his approval. Leo stood from his chair and pointed at her, his richly embroidered robe sleeve dripping from his arm in vain wealth. "I hereby request the Council take to a vote regarding the removal of Queen Naiya Pisces from the throne of Pacifica."

Gasps and sounds of agreement echoed through the room.

Naiya scanned the room, watching her Council debate her fate as ruler.

The only member not vocalizing his call for her removal sat and glared at her, an evil, knowing smirk curling his lips. Drake wanted nothing more than to punch that bastard's smile clear off.

Naiya raised her hand and the entire room fell silent. "If you were to remove me as queen, who will take my place as ruler?"

Leo smiled and with an exaggerated swipe of his arm in the direction of his brother, he announced, "Brendon Aquarius shall be our king!"

"But what of the Scorpion King?" another Council member asked. "The oracle swore to us the Scorpion King would come to Pacifica in our time of need."

Some murmurs of agreement followed—and it was then that Drake realized his destiny.

It was fate that brought him here. His love for Naiya would see them through. He couldn't sit by and let that twit Brendon become king and cancel the evacuation, costing hundreds of thousands of lives. They would surely all die when the vent became a full-fledged volcano.

"There is no such person as the Scorpion King," Brendon announced over the roomful of noise. His voice silenced the crowd. "The Scorpion King prophecy is a dream made up by an old senile man. No miracle leader will present himself to us. It is time to face facts and place me on the throne as your king. My family's lineage is unquestionable, and it is I who am destined to rule Pacifica!"

"No, you are wrong," Naiya called out commandingly. "The Scorpion King exists."

Brendon's triumphant smile began to fade as Drake stepped forward.

In a clear, authoritative voice, he declared, "I have arrived."

Naiya watched in awe as Drake pulled his shirt over his head, revealing the mark of the Scorpion King.

He knew.

She was in as much awe as the entire Council as Drake swept his hair aside and displayed a large, black scorpion tattoo upon his back, near his right shoulder. Every detail and line imprinted upon his skin elegantly.

For a moment, she wished they were back in her chambers. He had the back of a god. There was nothing like a strong pair of shoulders and flexing muscles to get her hot and needy—especially if those shoulders belonged to Drake.

"It's impossible!" Brendon shouted, rising from his seat. "How did you get that?"

Drake turned to face the room of awestruck faces. "The day I was born, I was tattooed by order of an oracle who visited my village. He said the scorpion would lead me to my destiny." He turned his head and looked Naiya in the eye. "I didn't know what it meant until yesterday."

He knew, but not before he had arrived in Pacifica. Somehow it relieved her to know that his driving force to come had not been influenced by a throne.

"I don't believe this!" Leo exclaimed. "How can you stand here and let this . . . this . . . *person* claim he's the future king? An Aquatic should be the next ruler, not some Land-walker!" Leo passed his flabbergasted brother and strode around the table to stand before Drake.

"The prophecy didn't mention the nationality of the king," Drake pointed out, his voice dry and void of emotion. He clenched his fists and the muscles in his arms flexed as he fought to control his growing anger.

"I will not sit by and let you take what rightly belongs to my brother," Leo spat.

"The mark means nothing unless Naiya agrees to take me as her husband."

Silence fell over the room as all eyes turned to the queen.

Drake turned and kneeled before her, taking one of her hands in his. "Will you take me as your husband, Naiya? Will you marry me and be my wife?"

Tears filled her eyes—then a glint behind Drake caught her eye.

"Drake, look out!"

In a heartbeat, Leo had pulled a knife while Drake's back was turned. Leo lunged, but Naiya's warning gave Drake the split-second advantage to miss the assassin's blade.

Drake dove to the side, avoiding the strike, and flipped out his own blade that had been hidden in his boot. He expertly threw the weapon at Leo.

The Councilman was no warrior, his battle reflexes nonexist-ent. The knife hit him in the chest, plunging straight through his heart. He gasped and looked down at the protruding blade. Stunned, Leo absently pulled it from his body and the blade fell to the floor with a loud clank.

"No!" Brendon yelled from across the room. He ran to his brother as Leo dropped to the floor, blood gushing from the wound.

"No, no! This is not how it was supposed to end. Leo, my brother! You can't die!"

"Bren . . . " Leo gargled on his own words as blood began to ooze from his mouth.

"Leo, wait! You have to give me the pass codes to the accounts. What are the codes? I need that money!" Brendon began to shake his dying brother. "Damn it, don't you die now!"

When Leo's strength left his body and his breath was gone, Brendon cried a torturous scream.

In the moments of silence that followed, Brendon's grief and incredulity subsided only slightly—but enough for him to realize where he was, and what he had said. His deceit had been revealed before the entire Council.

Naiya motioned to a guard by the door. "See that Councilman Aquarius is taken into custody and transported to Laurentia, where we will further examine his crimes after the evacuation. He has much to answer for." The guard nodded and went to gather the weeping Brendon.

Brendon fought against the guard and broke away. Punching the guard in the jaw, he dropped the man and turned to Drake to deal out his next blow.

Drake was too quick and ducked away. Brendon's fist just missed his cheek.

The two men began to exchange blows within the Council chambers. Equally matched in strength and training, neither was easy to strike. Brendon swung a left and hit Drake in the abdomen, then struck him in the jaw with his right. Drake stumbled, but only for a moment before he pulled back and hit Brendon in the jaw, knocking him to the ground.

"Enough!" Naiya yelled. "Take Brendon away! This is no time for fighting! We are in a state of emergency."

Brendon was recaptured by the guard with the help of two others. A trickle of blood ran from his lip.

"We'll go to Laurentia then deal with this. It is better to be safe there than wait here in danger," one of the other Council members announced to the room. He was answered with their agreement.

"And we will look into the authenticity of his claims to the throne," added another.

"Captain Scopillo is our Scorpion King. He will be my husband, and as such, there will be no question to his position of king."

Drake rubbed a hand over his sore jaw, and heedless of the pain in his abdomen, knelt once again before Naiya. "You honor me, my queen."

"There is no need to kneel before me. From this day forward, you may stand beside me as we rule together."

SEVEN

HAT NIGHT NAIYA LAY within her bed in the Laurentia royal palace. The day had been stressful and tiresome, and her strength was all but gone when Drake slipped in between the sheets next to her. He gathered her in his arms and held her close. She welcomed his warm embrace. It only took moments for him to fall asleep and she relaxed as his breathing deepened.

He was amazing. After the meeting with the Council, Drake had headed up the immense evacuation efforts. Outside at the docking bay he commanded the empty transports, helping people board before directing the ships to depart. He had called his friends on the surface and hundreds of Land-walkers arrived with cargo containers to help store and transport people's most precious belongings to Laurentia.

Drake had brought order to a potentially chaotic situation, and his cool command and keen intelligence made him easy to follow. Many of the people boarding the transports had been in obvious awe of his natural strength at this time of city-wide danger. With one glance at his bared back and the black scorpion tattoo, the people were also filled with hope.

Naiya herself had assisted many of the elderly out of their homes, knocking on doors alongside her massive contingent of guards to make sure everyone got to the necessary ships. She swore no one would be left behind, and gave no thought to her status as she went door to door making sure her people were safe.

When the city had finally emptied and she and Drake had boarded their ship to leave Pacifica, Naiya's eyes had welled with tears. It had been hard to leave her home . . . the only one she'd ever known.

After their transport passed through the force field, she had watched her city fade into the distance.

Now, hours later, she lay awake wondering. Where would she go from here? What kind of future could she give to her people?

What worried her more was Drake. She'd only known him for a few short days, yet she felt like she'd known him all her life. Love struck quickly, but was it forever? Could she place all her hopes and dreams, and those of her people, on his shoulders? Would he be able to bear the responsibility and demands of being king?

Drake's hold on her loosened and she slipped from his arms. Tired but not sleepy, she got out of bed and padded across the hard marble floor to the window seat. Pulling back the curtain, she looked out upon Laurentia.

It was another underwater city but more modern in its design. Built only a year ago, it was a new settlement twice the size of Pacifica that had not even been close to its population capacity.

Until now. She was thankful such a convenient place could take in an entire city of refugees.

Outside her window was a private garden filled with tropical plants brought from the surface. Palm trees, brightly colored hibiscus and orchids, and tantalizing papaya and breadfruit trees heavy with fruit grew within the mini-oasis. It was made for those who longed to forget their troubles, and it would be easy to do so within the garden's lush flowers and sweet-smelling fruits.

Unable to resist, she picked up her robe and left her room quietly. She had to explore that little garden up close, if only to find a few moments of peace when her heart and mind were so weighted down with worry. The day had been beyond stressful, and as difficult as it was, the troubles had only just begun.

She found her way outside to the garden and breathed in the fresh air. Above she could see the ocean swirling just outside the force field. Sharks and colorful fish passed by, looking like specks of color against the massive black ocean.

Nearby on the surface were the Hawaiian Islands. The area surrounding the islands was carefully preserved with reef life. She wished she had a moment to truly escape her duties and take a swim in the beckoning ocean waters. Her skin rippled in anticipation of touching the cool, salty water.

But pleasure would have to wait. She couldn't just leave the city when so much needed to be done. A new plan for Pacifica needed to be put into motion. Where would an entire population go to resettle?

She walked deeper into the tropical foliage and found a stone bench along a grassy pathway. She sat and yelped as the cold surface touched her scantily clad bottom.

Sighing, she thought of Brendon and Leo. Leo's death had revealed the depths of betrayal against her and the entire Council. She'd have to launch an investigation into the accounts Brendon mentioned. How much money was involved in their scheme? She imagined it was a king's ransom.

Or a king's bribe to the throne.

The entire discovery made her sick to her stomach. How could she have trusted Brendon? Hadn't she been wary of him for years? And how could she have believed his evil streak was focused on her alone? She could only imagine how many people were affected by Brendon's and Leo's greed.

"There you are," Drake said as he walked out into the garden. "I missed you in bed."

"Couldn't sleep," she said absently.

He sat next to her. "Thinking about the meeting?"

"Yes."

"I *had* to kill Brendon's brother. It was either him or me."

She turned her body toward him. "Oh no, it isn't that. That was self-defense."

"Brendon, then?"

She nodded. "It hurts to know that he would go so far to try to take the throne. But it isn't just that. It is everything. I love my city . . . the only place I've ever known as home."

"I'm sorry." He wrapped an arm around her shoulders. "I wish there was something I could do to make you feel better."

"Well, now that you mention it . . . " She pulled her body from his embrace, looked up into his face and smiled. "There is something I would love to do."

"Oh yeah, and does it have anything to do with getting naked?"
he asked with a devilish tone.

She laughed. "As a matter of fact, it does." She got up and
pulled on his arm to follow her. "Come on."

"OKAY, WHEN I SAID 'getting naked' I meant something more sexual
than swimming." Drake was not happy about Naiya wanting him
to follow her to explore a nearby reef. The sun was rising on
the surface and the darkness began to lift, but seeing was not his
greatest fear. "I hate to tell you this, Naiya, but I have a confession
to make."

"Here is a re-breather. Just put this little device in your mouth
and breathe. It will equalize the water pressure and allow you to
stay underwater safely for as long as you wish," she said.

She wasn't listening to him.

"Naiya . . . honey . . . stop for a second."

She began to engage the water pressure room to fill with seawater. "What?" she asked distractedly. As the water began to fill
the small room, her skin changed to a deeper hue and her scales
became more prominent.

"I don't like the water." There, he admitted his greatest fear.

"Why?" Her hands mutated before his eyes, thin membranes
growing between her fingers at inhuman speed.

"Because I don't want to drown." His voice sounded panicky,
even to him.

She just smirked. "Big warrior. Put the re-breather in your
mouth. Now!"

He slammed the small tube in his mouth and began to breathe as the water climbed to his chin. Within moments he was completely submerged and Naiya opened the diving portal to the outside.

Okay, I definitely don't like this.

And since when did Aquatics mutate into some sort of merperson?

Naiya took his hand and pulled him outside the city into the ocean. He used all his strength to breathe as normal as possible while kicking with all his might to keep from sinking.

He needn't have worried. Naiya was in her true element. Her gills, previously hidden, were now prominent upon her neck. She took to the water like a true fish born of the sea—a Pisces. Even her feet had transformed into . . . finlike appendages! It was amazing.

Her strength intensified within the water and she was able to hold on to his hand and swim quickly. Soon they were on the edge of a massive coral reef abounding with marine life. Orange tube coral and antler coral grew along rocks and what looked like an old sunken plane from the twentieth century. Metal had rusted and broken away in areas, and the sea had taken over the form. Along with the coral, algae and sea grasses grew along the surface. The reef seemed to spread on for miles.

Never had Drake experienced such beauty. Red- and orange-striped squirrelfish, bright yellow longnose butterfly fish, silvery trumpet fish and others swam in schools all around them, picking at the coral for food. Some swam right up to Drake's hand looking for a snack.

It was an awakening for him. He felt amazingly free within the ocean depths as he glided through the water by Naiya's side. For the first time in years Drake experienced an emotional breaking of bonds, escaping the constraints of life just to live and enjoy the wonders about him.

And the greatest treasure to cherish was Naiya.

He looked at her, jolted by her beauty as a woman—an Aquatic woman. Her skin glowed with a pearlescent vibrancy and her hair flowed about her head and shoulders in a slow motion, hypnotizing and alluring.

The realization hit him like a blow—he was about to marry the woman he loved, the woman of his dreams.

Life was truly a miracle. And as the fish darted about his arms as he pushed through the water, Drake was humbled by his strong and beautiful wife-to-be. It didn't matter that they were of different backgrounds. They were destined to be together. This bond was much deeper and stronger than a prophecy told through the years. The prophecy was merely a guide for them to find each other. In the face of danger and impending destruction, they had fallen in love.

Drake smiled to himself at the thought that it took no less than the queen of his heart to persuade him into swimming the blue waters of the Pacific.

She caught his look of happiness and raised a brow. Drake pulled upon her arm lightly, bringing her into his embrace. She fit perfectly, molding her body to his.

I will love you forever, my love, he thought. He brought her closer and nuzzled her neck. *Thank you. Thank you for bringing me here.*

They swam for a while longer before Naiya began to lead him back to the city.

Once they returned to the pressure chamber and the water began to drain out, Naiya transformed once again, back to her former self.

"I can't believe it! It was so . . . *otherworldly* out there." Drake was elated and he swooped in to hug Naiya. "Thank you. Thank you for showing me your world."

"I thought you might like it. Scorpio is truly a water sign, and the scorpion has several species that can live on land *or* in water."

He stroked her wet hair away from her face as he held her close. Emotions flooded him strong and hard. She was an angel. She hardly realized that she'd made him face one of his greatest fears. With Naiya, anything was possible. And he had to tell her.

"I love you, Naiya," he said quietly. "And I hope that you can find it in your heart to come to love me."

She tilted her head and for a moment, he was unsure how she'd react. Did she want a man to be a true husband, not just a co-ruler?

"Drake . . . I've loved you since our first night together."

"I was worried that you were being forced into marrying me."

"Why would you think such a thing?"

"Well, you know . . . " He shrugged, a little embarrassed at his admission of vulnerability. "You had a prophecy to fulfill. You needed to marry me to appease the Council's concerns. I don't like the idea of you being forced into a union just to make your government officials happy. I want you to want *me*—not the mark on my back, but the man."

She cupped his face between her hands. "No one forces me to do anything I don't want. And I *want* to marry you. Now, take me back to our room and make love to me."

He scooped her up into his arms and replied, "Yes, Your Majesty."

MINUTES LATER HE PLACED her naked form upon their bed.

He wanted to pleasure her, thank her for opening his eyes to the beauty and wonders of the ocean.

Naiya had other ideas. She rolled them over in the bed and laughed. "No, I want to take my fill of you."

"Sounds dangerous," he said with a laugh.

She moved down between his legs, tucking her own beneath her and laying her hands on his muscular thighs.

At her touch he felt a surge of desire course through his veins, and his cock hardened before her.

"Mmm. I'd say someone is happy to see me."

"Woman, you are driving me nuts."

"I just want to get a good look at my king."

The sound of her voice, husky and seductive, made him want to push his hands through her hair and guide her mouth over his length.

He closed his eyes and gave himself over to her touch as she began to caress his thighs lightly. She barely brushed the coarse hair along his inner thigh and his cock jumped at the contact.

She laughed low and sultry, and he groaned, grabbing a handful of the sheet beneath him as he held back his urge to fuck her immediately. His body was fighting against his control as her fingertips glided over the surface of his sac. His balls tightened and she increased the pressure.

"Relax, my king," she said as she repositioned her body and

took his cock between her breasts. Their full size cushioned his length as she leaned over his abdomen and began to kiss his skin. Her tongue flicked out, tasting him as she passed her luscious lips over his flesh.

He released the sheets and plunged his fingers into her hair. He pulled her up his body and captured her lips in a lustful kiss. She tasted of fine wine and promises of love and happiness. Her scent of salty seawater from their swim only added to her natural allure, and drove him deeper into an ocean of need and longing.

Her lips tantalized his as he urged on their mating of mouths and tongues. He couldn't get enough of her. He was a man in desperate need of fulfillment, and only Naiya had the lips to quench his thirst for passion.

She broke the kiss, but his disappointment was short-lived when she left a trail of kisses across his jaw, down his neck and across his chest to a hardened nipple. He gasped as she gingerly sampled his puckered skin. Her tongue tasted the tip and he groaned at the feel of her sweet wet flesh against him.

She suckled one nipple and then the next, keeping him in a state of arousal.

She continued to map his body with her lips and tongue until he thought he would shatter from the pure need for release.

When she finally grasped his cock in her hand, he moaned.

"My king, I wish to taste you." Her voice was sweet, but her request was sweeter.

"Please," he croaked.

Her tongue was warm and soft, her mouth hot when she took in the head of his cock. His hands guided her over him.

Slow, my love. Take me slow.

Up and down she moved her mouth over his length. She took him deep into her throat and sucked then retreated to lick away the fluid seeping from the tip.

Slow and relaxed, she pleasured him with her mouth while massaging his sac, caressing the hidden treasures within.

Every time he thought he couldn't take any more she released him, his cock, wet with her saliva, cooling in the air before she kissed the underside to keep him on edge.

When she grazed her teeth over the bulbous head of his penis, he cried out and reached for her. With a laugh she slid over his body and, with his hands upon her hips, she slammed down over his length.

"Oh, dear God," he moaned as her tight cunt surrounded him with slick heat.

She waited a moment, holding him deep within her body then began to move her hips. She bent one leg, balancing on one knee and one foot, gaining more control over her thrusts as she moved.

Slam! Her channel encased his cock before she pulled back, only to slam into his body once again. The sounds of sex—wet flesh joining and heavy breathing—echoed through the room.

He was so close to the edge. He reached between her legs and ran his fingertips over her clit. It was the button that needed to be pushed, and she climaxed loudly.

As her muscles tightened about his cock and the sounds of her release filled his ears, Drake came. He screamed out her name while he spilled into her body, wishing the moment would never end.

His climax shook his entire being as he joined with Naiya in orgasm. He reached up to her breasts and pinched her taut nipples. She cried out as she tumbled over into another climax.

Colors seemed to brighten about him as he continued to fill her channel with his essence. His body reveled and his spirit escalated as she gripped him deeper still.

"Naiya, I love you," he panted, his breathing ragged and labored.

"Love . . . you . . . oh *yes!*"

She was in ecstasy, and as his body began to calm, he was content that he'd be the man to satisfy her each and every night for the rest of his life.

Wherever that might be.

EIGHT

*N*AIYA SAT AT THE head of the Laurentia Council chambers. She met not only with Pacifica representatives but Laurentia members as well. Queen Áine had invited the Pacifica Council to join with hers while the two groups of people resided within one city.

Queen Áine sat by Naiya's side looking pale and weak. The older woman seemed tired and sick.

"Please, Your Majesty. Go back to your bed. You look so tired," Naiya pleaded with the woman quietly.

"Yes, perhaps it is best." When she tried to rise from her seat, she fell back exhausted.

Drake rose from his seat and assisted the queen to her feet. From there, one of her aides escorted her out of the chambers.

"Now," Naiya began, "we must deal with old business. Bring in Brendon Aquarius."

Silence fell over the room and her Council members glanced nervously at each other.

"What is it? Where is Brendon?"

"He never made it to Laurentia," a member said aloud to the entire room. "Neither he nor the escorts charged in bringing him ever arrived."

"Brendon never made it to Laurentia?" Naiya was astounded. She activated her com-link. "Find Brendon Aquarius. Send a search team to Pacifica and bring him here. Make sure the team is armed. Consider Councilman Aquarius extremely dangerous."

She clicked off her communicator and glared about the room at the faces of her advisors before turning her attention to those of Laurentia. "I thank this great city for taking in our people on such a short notice. But we need to discuss the future of our people. Where do we go from here?"

"Shouldn't we see if the danger passes first? Wait to see if Pacifica truly falls?"

"It is still untouched," another Council member responded. "We evacuated and nothing has happened. If devastation was to occur, wouldn't it have done so by now?"

"No," Drake cut in. "The data is unmistakable. We left sensors by the mouth of the vent and the reports show continuous tremors that are growing in intensity by the minute. The city has proved strong but we were lucky to get out unharmed. Going back is out of the question."

"But where will we all go?"

"We can rebuild." Drake sat forward in his chair. "We will rebuild Pacifica in a new location."

NAIYA AGAIN SAT WITHIN the lovely tropical garden at the palace. She'd come to love the place.

Was it only a few days ago that they had arrived here? She'd been so busy with the Council and their endless debates over building a new city that time seemed to flash by her. Only at night, when Drake took her into his arms and rocked her to sleep after bringing her to a shattering climax, did she find time to breathe.

"I knew I'd find you here." Queen's Áine's voice cut through the calming silence.

"I just needed a few minutes of peace. If I hear another argument from the Council, I think I may go insane."

Áine sat next to her on the bench. "I'm afraid I have some news to tell you, and I thought this would be the best place."

Naiya turned to the aging queen. "What is it?"

"Pacifica has been destroyed, as predicted."

"Destroyed . . . " She began to cry quietly. "I can't believe it finally came true. It doesn't feel real. When did it happen?"

Áine's face was very pale as she sighed. "It happened a few hours ago. We had tremors even here while most of us were asleep. The seaquake was huge. The . . . the city was consumed. It was as devastating on the surface, as well. A tsunami rolled across the Pacific and caused a lot of damage. However, because of the advance warnings, lives were saved." She smiled sadly and added, "Your scientist saved countless people."

Naiya did take comfort that many were spared. Rebuilding cities was minor compared to the loss of life.

"I like him. He reminds me of my son, Evan."

"I've never met your son."

The woman's eyes filled with tears. "I lost my only son last month in a shark attack. He was too bold all his life, too confident. He paid for his arrogance with his life, and now the city has no heir to rule after my death."

Naiya sat in stunned silence. "I didn't know. I'm so sorry."

The older Aquatic patted Naiya's hand. "You had so much to worry about."

"Yes." She sighed. "And I'm afraid I don't even know if I will ever again be queen of anything now."

"You are the queen of your man's heart. That is all you need."

Naiya smiled through her tears. "True. Drake has become so important to me. I love him very much."

"And he loves you." The queen paused then grasped Naiya's hand. "Be good to him."

"You really *do* like him."

"He's so much like Evan. Maybe that is why I have been considering something . . . " The old queen's voice trailed off.

"What is it?" Naiya prompted.

"You have no city to rule, and I have no heir. Instead of rebuilding Pacifica, I would like you and Drake to remain here and rule Laurentia."

"Rule Laurentia!?"

The woman brought Naiya's hand to her heart. "You have a bright future ahead. This city is still new and ripe for a new pair of rulers—a queen and king."

"But Drake and I haven't set the date of our marriage. With the loss of Pacifica, perhaps we should delay further."

"I think you should marry immediately. Don't wait. Give the people hope and let your love radiate out to them in this desperate time. Give them cause to celebrate."

"Maybe you're right."

"I am. Love like you two share is to be celebrated. Tell me that you will become my heirs—you and your Scorpion King. I know I can trust you both. I see how much you care for your people and each other. I can't think of better hands in which to leave Laurentia."

NAIYA SOUGHT OUT DRAKE and found him sitting alone in the royal dining room, where an entire wall was a glorious living ocean scene. He sat in silent wonder, watching the sharks and fish swim by in silence.

"Beautiful, isn't it?" she asked as she sat down next to him at the table.

Stacks of papers were spread before him on the table—reports from his mission. "I thought I would find a little quiet time in here to organize these reports and add my own written assessment for the admiral before I officially resign from the UGN Navy."

"But you were sidetracked."

He nodded. "I can't believe all these years I refused to even go near the ocean, only to end up living in an underwater city." His voice was light despite the devastating news earlier in the day.

"You don't have to try to amuse me. I'll be okay."

"It was your home and it isn't easy to accept the knowledge that it's gone."

She reached over and took his hand in hers. "It was hard to hear the news, but I am glad we were here when it happened. If it wasn't for you, the entire kingdom would have still been there. I don't even want to think of all the people we would've lost if we had remained."

He glanced at her face, apprehensive. "There's a report I haven't told you yet."

A jolt of fear rushed through her body. "What is it?"

"Brendon escaped the day we evacuated, taking refuge somewhere within Pacifica. The guards charged with bringing him here were found dead just before the quake."

"Is Brendon . . . do you think he's dead?" Her voice stumbled over the possibility. As much trouble as Brendon had caused, she still didn't wish him dead.

"I had the search team do a sweep of the city after the guards were found." Drake paused. "They found Brendon's body in the throne room at the palace. Naiya . . . he'd stabbed himself."

She gasped in horror as tears began to burn her eyes.

He brought her hand to his heart. "I'm sorry, Naiya," he said tenderly and full of sympathy. "I would have told you sooner, but the quake began shortly after they found the body."

She nodded and drew closer to him, finding comfort within his embrace. "The Brendon I knew as a child had died long ago. I just can't believe he's truly gone."

They sat there in peace, holding each other, trying to find solace after all the devastation.

"Once I get done with these reports and resign, then I can concentrate more on our plans to rebuild Pacifica." He moved from her arms and thumbed a pile of papers.

"We won't have to."

He turned to her. "What do you mean?"

"Queen Áine has asked us to rule Laurentia and rebuild our society here."

"What? Why would she do that?"

"She has no heir, and you remind her of her late son. I think she believes you would be a good king in his place."

He reached over and gently touched her face. "A good king needs his queen by his side. I wouldn't be able to do anything without you."

"I think that maybe we should become husband and wife first, though."

He took her into his arms, lifting her from her seat and onto his lap, and she laughed aloud at his playfulness. "I do believe we should rectify that situation right away, don't you agree?" he murmured.

She stroked the hair at the back of his neck and giggled. "Yes. The sooner the better."

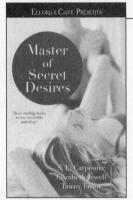

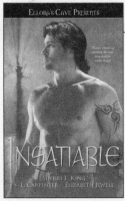
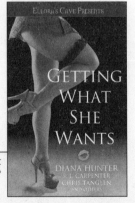

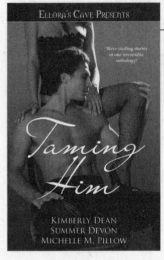
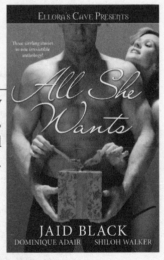